Hope, Faith
&
a Corpse

Also available by Laura Jensen Walker

Bookish Baker Mysteries
Murder Most Sweet

Phoebe Grant Series
Dreaming in Black and White
Dreaming in Technicolor

Getaway Girls
Daring Chloe
Turning the Paige
Becca by the Book

Other Novels
Miss Invisible
Reconstructing Natalie

Hope, Faith & a Corpse

A FAITH CHAPEL MYSTERY

Laura Jensen Walker

CROOKED
LANE

NEW YORK

Copyright © 2021 by Laura Jensen Walker

Published in the United States by Crooked Lane Books, an imprint of The Quick Brown Fox & Company LLC.

Crooked Lane Books and its logo are trademarks of The Quick Brown Fox & Company LLC.

Library of Congress Catalog-in-Publication data available upon request.

ISBN (hardcover): 978-1-64385-504-2
ISBN (ePub): 978-1-64385-505-9

Cover illustration by Tsukushi

Printed in the United States.

www.crookedlanebooks.com

Crooked Lane Books
34 West 27th St., 10th Floor
New York, NY 10001

First Edition: January 2021

10 9 8 7 6 5 4 3 2 1

For Edie Decker, the sweet, lovely, and oh-so-stylish inspiration for Dorothy. You are missed. And for my dear friend and beloved sister-in-law Sheri Jameson. We miss you.

Chapter One

It's not every day you find yourself walking down the sidewalk on a pleasant day in Northern California and hear someone shout the name of the King of Rock and Roll, but that's what happened to me.

"Elvis!" the voice cried. "How many times do I have to tell you? Don't be cruel."

I hesitated, wondering what I would find beyond the tall hedge I was approaching. As far as I knew, there hadn't been any sightings this far north, but you never know . . . I rounded the curve and smacked straight into the King. "Ow." My hand flew to my forehead, where I could feel a goose egg forming.

"Oh darlin', I'm so sorry. Are you all right?"

I looked through splayed fingers and saw stars.

Gold stars on a white Vegas jumpsuit open to the waist . . . of a garden gnome. An Elvis garden gnome held in the age-spotted hands of a beehived woman oozing Shalimar. I shook my head to clear it. Big mistake. A wave of dizziness rolled over me, and I clutched at the nearby picket fence to steady myself.

Beehive woman set Elvis down and grabbed my arm. "Honey, you need to sit down." She guided me over to a bistro set in the front yard. The woman—whose bouffant hair matched her canary-yellow, above-the-crepey-knee dress—patted my hand. "You poor thing. I feel terrible. Elvis has been naughty, but he's usually such a gentleman. That's the first time I've seen him treat a lady that way. Now you wait right here while I go get you some ice."

I stared after her retreating go-go boots as she wound her way through a maze of gnomes, fairies, and assorted woodland creatures scattered across the yard. I felt caught in a mash-up of *Grimms' Fairy Tales* and *The Twilight Zone*. Gingerly, I touched the goose egg.

Beehive woman returned with an aged man trailing in her perfumed wake. He sent me a shy glance as he deposited a glass of orange liquid and a plate bearing a baggie of ice and a Twinkie on the table. Beehive batted her crooked false eyelashes. "There you go, darlin'. I find a little Tang and a Twinkie always makes everything better."

A Ding Dong might be more appropriate. (And isn't Tang what the astronauts drank back in the sixties?) "Thank you." I applied the ice to my throbbing head.

Beehive linked her arm with the man next to her, a man clad head to toe in beige—slacks, shirt, cardigan, loafers. The sole relief from the sea of beigeness was his pale-blue eyes and a tuft of white hair in the center of his otherwise bald head. "Sugar," she said, "this here's the poor darlin' Elvis ran into. I declare, he's been actin' up all mornin' causing trouble between Buddy and Bobby, but when he was fixin' to get into it with Frank, I knew I had to separate them. Elvis may be the King, but Frank's the Chairman of the Board."

Not sure whether to laugh or call the Rat Pack, I glanced at Beige Man, but he had eyes only for his beloved.

Beehive babbled on. "I'd taken Elvis out to the sidewalk so he could choose where he wanted to be, and he was havin' a look-see around when this poor girl came round the curve and bam!" She narrowed her eyes at the offensive gnome, causing one of her false eyelashes to dangle. "I have a mind to put him in the backyard. I don't care how much he complains."

I wolfed down the Twinkie and chased it with the Tang, wincing inwardly at the artificial taste of the powdered orange drink but hiding my distaste from the kindly odd couple. "Thank you so much," I said with an appreciative smile. "That really hit the spot." Then I took my leave, regretfully explaining that I had an important appointment.

*   *   *

The theme from *The Twilight Zone* played in a recurring loop in my head as I power-walked across town. I couldn't afford to be late for my very important date—my first day of work at my new job. A big step for me, an exciting step, but also a little scary. In an attempt to settle my first-day jitters, I made a mental note to ask my new boss for the scoop on Beehive woman and to let me know if there were any more like her in town. I hadn't lived in a small town since I was a kid in Wisconsin, but even that was an urban metropolis next to this sleepy little place: Apple Springs, California. After the noise, congestion, and traffic of the Bay Area where I had lived and worked for the past two decades, this tranquil town an hour east of Sacramento was a welcome respite. My new beginning. A beginning I was at last ready for—and looking forward to—after the pain and loss of the past couple of years.

I stopped in front of the 160-year-old wooden building to catch my breath and dug out my compact. Yes! The goose egg had receded. I twitched my brown bangs around, covering it, but by tomorrow I'd look like Sylvester Stallone in one of the *Rocky* movies. Not quite the professional, dignified impression I'd hoped to make.

I glanced at my watch. Eight thirty. Right on time. Pushing open the side door of Faith Chapel Episcopal Church, I stepped inside and removed my light jacket and scarf to reveal my clerical collar. "Hello?" An empty reception area with worn green carpet, an ancient plaid love seat, and an Army surplus desk holding teetering stacks of paper and a vase of tired silk flowers greeted me. Beyond the vacant desk stood a closed door with the faded word *Rector* in the center.

"Father Christopher?" Hesitantly, I knocked on the door. No answer. I checked my phone. No messages or missed calls.

I knocked again. Harder. "Christopher?" I called out. "It's Hope." Nada. I turned the doorknob and poked my head in. Another silent and empty office. Except this one was chaos— papers everywhere. Desk. Chair. Filing cabinet. Even the floor. It looked as if a tornado had swirled through, leaving a swath of office-supply destruction in its wake. As I entered, however, I noticed pathways among the myriad piles and realized it was organized chaos. Somewhat. Christopher Weaver, my new boss, had warned me he was a "bit of a pack rat" and had become "somewhat disorganized" since losing his secretary a few months ago.

4

He hoped I could help bring order to the office, and my inner neatnik itched to jump in and start tidying up right then—the by-product of a clean-freak mother. She had instilled within me the mantra "A place for everything and everything in its place" at an early age, and it had stuck. Unlike most of her other maxims, such as "Never wear white after Labor Day," "Let your husband wear the pants in the family," and "Always, always be a lady."

This lady wondered where her boss might be. I thought of texting him, but then remembered he was old-school and didn't text. He had a cell, but mainly for emergencies, and had confessed, embarrassed, that he often forgot to turn it on. We had agreed to meet at the church at eight thirty so he could give me a complete tour of the buildings and grounds, including the small chapel and columbarium (wall crypt) behind the main church.

Doh. Think. I rapped my knuckles on my forehead, then winced as the goose egg reminded me of its presence. My boss was probably waiting for me at the chapel annex around back.

Pretty pink camellias bloomed on either side of the shade-dappled stone walkway, nestled between clumps of colorful prim-roses and budding azaleas, which would be glorious in another week or two. Thankfully, I didn't see any garden gnomes. Spring is my favorite time of year, and I looked forward to seeing the parish garden in full bloom. Humming "In the Garden," I pushed open the wooden chapel door.

"Father Christopher?"

Silence. I entered the shadowy small chapel and sniffed. The place reeked of alcohol. *Has someone spilled communion wine?* I took another step and almost tripped over something. A man, passed out on the floor. *So that's the source of the smell. Drunk in this holy place.* I knelt down to shake him awake, but my knees landed on something hard, which rolled beneath me and almost threw me off-balance.

I steadied myself and picked up the hard object—a heavy burial urn.

My eyes adjusted to the dim light filtering in through the stained-glass windows. That's when I saw the blood and the tweed cap. My stomach clenched, and I murmured a prayer as I leaned forward to check for a pulse.

A scream rent the air.

Whirling around, still clutching the urn, I saw two blue-haired women, their arms filled with altar cloths and their eyes filled with horror, standing in the now wide-open doorway, the morning sunlight flooding the small chapel.

My missing boss, Father Christopher, appeared behind them. "What's going on here?"

"Stanley's dead, and she killed him!" one of the women shrieked, pointing a trembling finger at me.

Worst first day ever.

Chapter Two

I t went downhill from there.

As a priest, I had seen my share of death—it comes with the territory. I had prayed with and comforted the dying and had been granted the sacred privilege of being there when some of them, including my beloved David, took their last breath. However, I'd never stumbled upon a dead body before, and definitely not a murder victim. This was clearly murder. It was possible the drunken man had fallen and hit his head on the altar or something, but then why was there blood on the bottom of the burial urn and none on the altar? No, it looked obvious, at least to my inner Trixie Belden, that the container of ashes had been used to hit Stanley King over the head and kill him.

And at the moment, it looked like I was the prime suspect.

After the rector and the altar guild ladies discovered me with the dead Stanley, Father Christopher called the police, then herded the two shaking women and me into the rectory adjacent to the church. I was shaking too, but in times of tragedy or crisis, a priest needs to maintain composure and offer pastoral comfort.

Except the woman who had accused me of murder wasn't accepting any comfort from me, and her timid friend followed her lead.

Minutes after Father Christopher's call, police chief Harold Beacham and his wife Patricia, the elected head of the parish council (or as Episcopalians call it, the *vestry*) arrived. They were followed soon after by the county medical examiner, Stu Black, who was now doing a preliminary exam of the body in the columbarium chapel. Chief Beacham, a slim, distinguished-looking man with mocha skin and close-cropped steel-gray hair, sat across from me in the rectory study. He flipped open his notebook. "Now, Pastor, tell me what happened."

I explained how I'd arrived at the church to meet Father Christopher and how, when I found the office empty, I'd gone in search of him but found the dead Stanley in the columbarium instead. As opposed to Professor Plum in the library with the candlestick.

"Did you see anyone on your way to the chapel annex?"

"Not a soul." *Why was that, anyway? Where the heck was Father Christopher? He couldn't have had anything to do with this, could he?* As soon as that disloyal thought entered my brain, I dismissed it. Not Christopher. He was a kind, sweet septuagenarian and a priest to boot. A good priest with a good heart. Incapable of murder. *For from within, out of the heart of men, proceed evil thoughts, adulteries . . . murders . . .* Unbidden, the scripture popped into my head. I popped it right back out and returned my attention to the police chief.

He scratched a note. "Did you notice anything unusual when you entered the chapel?"

You mean besides the dead guy on the ground? I didn't say that aloud, however. As the new associate pastor and first woman priest in Faith Chapel's history, it was best to keep my inner snark silent. At least for now. Once I had gotten to know everyone, proven myself, and been cleared of murder suspicions, I could let my freak flag fly.

"Pastor Hope?"

"Sorry. What did you say?"

"Did you notice anything unusual when you entered the chapel?"

"Yes. The smell. There was a strong smell of alcohol."

The chief scratched another note. "Anything else?"

"Then I saw the man on the floor. I thought he was drunk until I saw the blood."

"Okay, a couple more questions." Harold Beacham fixed me with a penetrating stare. "Why were you leaning over him with the bloody urn in your hand, and how did you get the nasty bump on your head?"

"Courtesy of Elvis—thank you very much," I said, parroting the King. Although Elvis hadn't been part of my growing-up years, both my husband, David, and his older sister, Virginia, were big fans of his music. They introduced me to the King of Rock and Roll, and I too became a fan. We danced the first dance at our wedding to "I Can't Help Falling in Love With You."

The police chief lifted a salt-and-pepper eyebrow, but before he could reply, a knock at the door interrupted us. Patricia Beacham, Harold's elegant wife and senior warden of the vestry, poked her head in. "Sorry to disturb, Hal, but Stu said he needs you in the chapel."

"Thanks." Chief Beacham stood up. "Thank you for your time, Pastor. Please stick around, though. I may have more questions."

"I promise not to make a run for the border."

Did I say that aloud? Smart move, Sherlock.

Harold frowned, but his wife, whom I had met and bonded with during a recent vestry meeting, linked her arm with mine. "Shall we rejoin the others, Hope?"

"Good idea." I gave the chief a weak parting smile before Patricia and I returned to the dining room, where Father Christopher and the two blue-haired women waited. As we entered the room, my accuser, Marjorie Chamberlain, sent me a look that was equal parts suspicious and self-congratulatory. I had gotten off to a bad start with Marjorie when we met at a gathering of the other vestry members and Father Christopher during their pastoral search. My potential new boss had warned me that Marjorie was not a fan of women in the pulpit, so I knew I had my work cut out for me if I wanted the vestry (the committee elected by the congregation to manage the affairs of the church) to recommend me for the associate pastor position.

During drinks and hors d'oeuvres at that meeting, Father Christopher had ushered over a sturdy blue-haired woman in an unflattering purple pantsuit who wore a skeptical expression on her lined face. "Hope, I'd like you to meet a longtime member of Faith Chapel. Marjorie Chamberlain. Marjorie's head of the altar guild."

"Nice to meet you, Marjorie. How long have you been at the church?"

"Eighty-two years," she said proudly. "I'm a cradle Episcopalian. My great-grandfather Richard Chamberlain was a founding member."

"Ooh, I loved him in *The Thorn Birds*. He made my tweenage heart go pitty-pat."

Marjorie gave me a blank stare.

"The eighties miniseries with the hot Father Ralph?" The one I'd had to sneak out to watch over at my best friend Cindy's house. Until my vigilant TV-and-movie-monitoring father found out. That was the end of both *The Thorn Birds* and my friendship with Cindy.

"I have no idea what you're talking about." The blank stare turned icy. "My grandfather wasn't a priest, hot or otherwise. He wasn't even alive in the eighties."

Nice job, Pastor Open-Mouth-Insert-Foot.

Now, as we sat around the dining table drinking the hot tea Patricia Beacham had made (Lipton, unfortunately), Marjorie's altar guild shadow, Lottie Wilson, kept clasping and unclasping her arthritic hands. Father Christopher tried to soothe Lottie with Fig Newtons as Marjorie glared at me over her delicate English china teacup and saucer.

Marjorie set the cup down and blotted her mouth with a napkin. Then she zeroed in on me. "We all heard Stanley say it would be over his dead body before you preached at Faith Chapel. Well you sure took care of that, didn't you, *Pastor?*" Her blotchy face threatened to grow as burgundy as today's pantsuit.

Seriously?

"Now Marjorie, calm down. I know you're upset," Father Christopher said. "We all are. Stanley's death—may he rest in peace—is a huge shock. Especially seeing him like that. However, we don't know what happened. That's up to the police to determine, so let's let them do their job and not jump to conclusions or make wild accusations."

Preach.

"Marjorie, I'm sorry we got off on the wrong foot," I said, "but if I killed everyone who doesn't like women priests, there'd be a trail of dead bodies from here to the Bay Area." And beyond. Including a small town in Wisconsin.

Lottie tittered, and Patricia barked out a laugh.

Marjorie harrumphed.

The timid Lottie spoke up. "Ethel and Stanley butted heads all the time. There was no love lost between them. Ethel said many times how much she'd like to 'murder that man.' And if you think about it"—Lottie released a nervous giggle—"now she has."

Patricia barked out another laugh, Father Christopher's mouth twitched, and I coughed to cover an un-pastor-like snort, which I knew left unchecked could morph into the out-of-control I-love-to-laugh scene from *Mary Poppins*.

"Lottie, show some respect for the dead."

"I'm sorry, Marjorie. I didn't mean to disrespect Stanley."

"I'm not talking about Stanley." Marjorie made a face. "I'm talking about Ethel. I don't think our dear friend would appreciate her beautiful burial urn being used as a murder weapon."

Ethel Brown had been a beloved member of the parish for years, as well as Father Christopher's longtime secretary. She had passed away a few months ago, and Christopher had told me the church honored her with a memorial service—one her lone surviving relative, a distant niece, was unable to attend. The niece, however, would be in California next month, and had asked to delay the official inurnment of her aunt's cremains until then. While waiting for that private service to occur, the urn containing Ethel Brown's ashes stood on a small table beside the chapel altar. At least it had until recently.

"Actually," Patricia said, a mischievous smile tugging at the corners of her mouth, "knowing Ethel and how she always liked to get in the last word with Stanley, I think she'd get a kick out of it."

The room was silent for a moment. A slow grin stole over Marjorie's face. "You know what? I think you're right." Then the most extraordinary thing happened. Marjorie Chamberlain giggled. Lottie joined in, and soon all three women were giggling nonstop. It took everything I had not to join the gigglethon, but a priest needs to be circumspect and dignified after a death. I stole a sideways glance at Father Christopher and noticed his mouth twitching beneath his bowed head.

"Glad to see you've recovered from the shock," said Harold Beacham, lifting an eyebrow as he rejoined us.

The giggling came to an abrupt halt.

"Well?" Marjorie asked.

"Well what?"

"What happened to Stanley? Did someone kill him?"

"I can't comment on an ongoing police investigation." The police chief turned to his wife. "Can you stay here while I go notify the next of kin?"

"Of course."

Todd and Samantha King. Stanley's children. I grabbed my jacket.

"Where do you think you're going?" Marjorie demanded.

"To do my job." I turned to Harold. "If that's all right with you?"

"I don't see any problem, since we're both going to the same place."

Was it my imagination, or did the police chief look at me with less suspicion? *Why? Far too early to be cleared by the medical examiner's findings.* Maybe he had his mind on other things. Like grilling me again, since I was in his custody. More or less.

"But—" my nemesis sputtered.

"Marjorie, Hope is in charge of pastoral care," Father Christopher said. "That includes offering prayer and comfort to the bereaved."

Lottie's forehead wrinkled. "But you've always been the one to do that, Father."

"Yes, and I'll continue to do so, but it's now Hope's main ministry." He picked up his keys. "I'll come along too, Hal, since I've known Todd and Samantha all their lives. Hope, are you ready?"

On our drive over to the King residence, I thought of the first—and only—time I'd met the dead man. The Faith Chapel leadership had been looking me over during one of their vestry meetings a few months back to see if I'd be a good pastoral fit for their church when an imposing older man in an expensive sport coat and gray tweed cap burst into the rectory, followed close behind by a redheaded young couple.

"Where is she?" bellowed Tweed Cap, swiveling his head around the room and swaying on his feet.

One of the vestry members leaned over and whispered, "That's Stanley King, former senior warden, and his children, Samantha and Todd." She heaved a sigh. "Poor kids. Stanley is a tyrant. Not a nice man on the best of days, but even worse when he's had too much to drink."

I glanced over and saw the King family in a heated discussion with Father Christopher, who was trying to keep the peace. Stanley King mopped his forehead and yelled at his son, "You're nothing but a useless good-for-nothing."

Several vestry members looked away in embarrassment, except for cradle-Episcopalian Marjorie, who seemed riveted by the family feud. Todd King threw up his hands, shrugged at his sister, and left. Samantha King laid her hand on her father's arm, but he shook it off and muttered something that made her pale face flush. She left also.

Then Christopher moved in closer to Stanley and said something.

"You've got some nerve," Tweed Cap said. "How dare you talk to me that way?" He stabbed his finger into the old priest's chest, causing Father Christopher to stumble. "I've had it with your holier-than-thou crap."

As I hurried to rescue my possible new boss, Patricia and Harold Beacham joined me. Stanley King's bloodshot eyes zeroed in on us, his mouth twisting in an ugly sneer. "Here comes the diversity cavalry, but where's Fu Manchu? And Speedy Gonzales?"

"That's enough, Stan," Father Christopher said.

As the former vestry member removed his cap and mopped his sweating forehead again, Harold Beacham said, "Why don't we go outside and cool off?"

"Good idea," I said. "How about if we all take a nice deep breath and relax?"

"No woman's going to tell me what to do," Stanley said, his potent whiskey breath causing me to take a step back. "And do *not* think you'll be preaching at Faith Chapel anytime soon, missy. Over my dead body."

All at once, my father's mottled face yelling at me, my sister, and my mother filled my head—a memory I'd thought I had exorcised years ago. Dad never drank; he was a teetotaler due to his religious convictions. Yet other than that, he could have been a twin to the enraged Neanderthal in front of me. Now, unlike the cowed child I had been, I knew how to cope with men like him. Reminding myself not to cast pearls before swine, I took a deep breath, expelled it, and relaxed.

Stanley King shot me a look of disgust, then barreled past, slamming the door behind him.

Now the man was dead.

"What can you tell me about Stanley?" I asked Christopher as he drove us to the King family home in his old Ford Taurus.

"Well, I'd like to say your introduction to him was an anomaly, but it was classic Stanley." The rector gave a helpless shrug. "Stan is—*was*—a lawyer and member of Faith Chapel for decades. Unfortunately, the church did not have much of an impact on him—something I had hoped and prayed for over the years. I think Faith Chapel was a tax break for Stanley and simply another way for him to display his wealth and success. He was the church's largest benefactor, and he made sure everyone knew it."

"Not a big believer in the whole giving-in-secret admonition?"

"I'm afraid Stanley wasn't a big believer in anything except Stanley. And I'm sure he had quite a few secrets, but donating money wasn't one of them."

I wondered what kinds of secrets Stanley King had hidden. Any that might have gotten him killed? I glanced at my boss, but he appeared lost in thought, his eyes fixed on the road in front of him. *Could Stanley have confessed any of those secrets to his priest?*

Moments later, we pulled in behind Harold Beacham's police cruiser parked in front of a creamy historic Italianate mansion with green trim, bracketed eaves, and a striking square cupola. Chief

Beacham opened his car door and got out, squaring his shoulders and removing his hat for the painful task ahead. I offered up a silent prayer for him as Christopher and I joined Harold on the trek to the front door. Then I focused all my prayers and thoughts on Stanley King's children.

Harold Beacham rang the doorbell. Moments later, the door swung open to reveal Todd King in a Grateful Dead T-shirt, board shorts, and flip-flops.

"Whoa!" the freckled twentysomething said. "Two priests *and* the police chief. I must really be in trouble." Todd grinned and held up his hands in mock surrender. "I promise, Father, I did not steal from the collection plate."

Chief Beacham inclined his head. "May we come in?"

"Sorry. Forgot my manners." Stanley King's son ushered us inside.

"Todd?" a female voice called. "Who is it?" Samantha King, the other half of the redheaded sibling duo that I'd seen at the infamous vestry meeting with the drunken Stanley, rounded the corner. Her pale skin grew even more pale when she saw us. "What's wrong?" she asked in a tremulous voice, drawing near to her brother, who put his arm around her protectively.

"Why don't we all go sit down," Harold said, gesturing to a room off the foyer.

Father Christopher gently held on to Samantha's hand as he escorted the King children into a sumptuous living room, followed by Harold. I brought up the rear.

When the two were informed of their father's death, Samantha wept. Father Christopher patted her back comfortingly as her tears wet his vestments. Her younger brother, however, remained dry-eyed and stoic. Over the years, I have learned that everyone responds differently to death and that grief takes different forms. I thought back to when my David lost his battle with brain cancer. We'd had only a dozen years together, and when he died, I wanted to die right along with him. Even though I'd known the day was coming and thought I was prepared—especially since I was a priest—nothing prepares you for such a deep, profound loss.

I wondered how Stanley's friends and fellow church members would respond to his loss. And would their response cause me—their new priest—to lose my job? I already had one strike against me with the traditionalist old guard because of my sex. Add in the dead Stanley and my hand holding the bloody urn? Strike two. It was clear I needed to learn more about Stanley King so I could figure out who might have wanted him dead.

Otherwise, it was strike three and I'm out.

Chapter Three

The choir finished its opening hymn with a booming—and flat—bass drowning out the three altos, two sopranos, and lone tenor. (The other bass, who doubled as a baritone, had defected to the Baptists last year, I later learned.)

"Thank you, choir," said Father Christopher. "God said, 'Make a joyful noise,' and we're grateful each week to our beloved choir for doing so."

A silver-haired woman in the pew in front of me leaned over to her friend and said in a stage whisper, "I doubt God meant *that*." Her friend hid a giggle behind an age-spotted hand.

Light streamed in through the trio of diamond-paned stained-glass windows above the altar. Looking up, I admired the vaulted wooden ceiling in the small A-frame church, which bespoke a time past of proud artisanship and detail. When I looked back down, I caught a few suspicious glances directed my way. The rumor mill must have gone into overdrive about the new girl in town. Especially when that new girl had been found kneeling over a dead church member holding the probable murder weapon. I steeled myself and repeated my internal mantra, which always saw me through difficult times: *If God is for you, who can be against you?* Then I focused my full attention on my new boss and rector.

"Good morning, and welcome to Faith Chapel," Father Christopher said. "I'm sure most of you have heard about the unexpected passing of our longtime member Stanley King two days ago. Stanley contributed a great deal to Faith Chapel over the years, including funding the remodel of the chapel annex and columbarium as well as the landscaping of our beautiful court-yard, for which we are grateful. Please keep Todd and Samantha King in your prayers. We'll let you know the funeral plans once they're settled."

Good job, Christopher. Short, sweet, and diplomatic. No croco-dile tears or false sentiments. I made a mental note for the future.

"And now, in happier news, I'm delighted to share that the bishop has sent us a wonderful new associate pastor." Father Christopher sent me a warm smile. "A few years ago when I was guest teaching at seminary, a student came up and peppered me with questions—some I couldn't answer." He paused. "I know you're shocked your priest doesn't have all the answers." The congregation tittered. "Anyway, since then I've been following that young student's—well, young to me—journey to ordination and beyond. Please join me in giving a big Faith Chapel welcome to Pastor Hope Taylor."

Uncertain applause broke out along with scattered murmur-ings. A woman priest? And possible murderer? With a black eye, no less? (I had tried applying makeup to cover up my Elvis goose egg, which had morphed into a shiner, but the amount necessary to cover the bruising on my Scandinavian skin had left me look-ing like a lady of the evening. I'd settled for the shiner.)

"Well, it's about time." A snowy-haired woman in red, who bore the familiar widow's hump of osteoporosis, stood up and applauded.

"Hear, hear," said the middle-aged man next to her, who also got to his feet, along with Patricia Beacham, a young couple in the first pew, two altos, and the lone tenor. Several of the old-timers exchanged looks that ranged from dismayed to disgruntled, while two teen girls at the back of the church stood and raised their fists in solidarity. "Women rock!"

"Thank you, everyone, for your enthusiastic response," Father Christopher said. "Please be seated. Hope, please come up and tell us a bit about yourself."

I shed my light jacket and scarf, feeling like Scarlett O'Hara in that red dress Rhett made her wear to Ashley's birthday party. Thankfully, my black clergy vest and priest's collar were a lot less provocative. "Good morning, everyone. Thank you for the nice welcome." I sent what I hoped was a reassuring smile to the mostly blue- and gray-haired congregation. Patricia gave me an encouraging nod. "As Father Christopher said, when we met, I bombarded the poor man with questions. I had *so* many questions. Up until then I'd been a teacher—which I loved—but about six years ago, God called me to become a priest, and I heeded that call."

Joan of Arc heeded the call too, and look what happened to her. Ingrid Bergman's luminous face at the stake flashed before me, but I banished her to *Casablanca.*

"Bah," a wrinkled man in the front pew said. He stood up and glared at me, then stalked out of the church as fast as he could move his tennis-ball-bottomed walker. The metal walker made an angry clacking on the thin carpet with every step.

I love the smell of sexism in the morning. Outwardly I maintained my spiritual serenity, while inwardly I wanted to deck the guy. Not the most pastoral response. I returned to my pew and turned the other cheek—something I had done a lot since my ordination. As the congregation joined the choir in singing, "It is Well With My Soul," I breathed out, closed my eyes, and sang my favorite hymn from memory, the words filling me with peace.

The peace was short-lived. At the parish hall after the service, a few dozen people stood around sipping coffee, munching on pastries, and chatting.

"I hate you!" shouted a magenta-haired teenage girl to a blonde middle-aged woman by the coffee urn. The woman put her hand on the teen's arm, but she shook it off and rushed past us, a river of mascara coursing down her face. Another teen, clad all in black except for a vivid sleeve tattoo of hearts, flowers, and dragonflies, gave me an apologetic smile as she followed her friend.

"I should go make sure she's okay," I said to Christopher.

"Best to leave them alone. When Megan gets like that, the only one who can get through to her is her best friend Riley. It would be good for you to meet her mother, though." We approached the attractive woman, who had two red spots staining her cheeks.

"Sorry, Father," she said, twisting and untwisting her pearls. "These raging hormones are going to be the death of me."

"It's okay, Bonnie."

"My stepdaughter and I had our share of knock-down, drag-outs during her teen years," I said, "but now we're good friends."

"You mean there's hope?"

"I should say so," said Father Christopher. "Bonnie Cunningham, may I present Pastor Hope?"

She giggled.

"Prettiest priest I've ever seen." A man in a charcoal-gray trench coat with thick glasses and wispy hair on his brown-speckled head appeared next to Bonnie. He gave me an appreciative once-over. "If you preach as good as you look, we're in for a real treat."

"Dad!"

"Oh, don't 'Dad' me. I'm too old to be politically correct. Don't know what the world's coming to when a man can't give a pretty girl a compliment without getting in trouble."

I smiled at my admirer, who reminded me of Henry Fonda in *On Golden Pond*. "Thank you for the—"

"Eh? You'll have to speak up. I'm deaf in one ear."

"Thank you for the kind words," I said louder. "I like your London Fog, by the way—my husband had one just like it."

"He has good taste." He gave a bow. "Albert Drummond, at your service. Anything you need, you let me know. I've been here a long time, and I know where all the bodies are buried."

"Good to know. I'll keep that in mind."

He peered beyond me. "Where's your husband? I'd like to meet him. Didn't he come with you today?"

"I'm afraid not." My heart stopped for a moment, as it always did when I was asked about David. Then it started up again, another thing it always did. "My husband passed away a couple years ago. Cancer."

"I'm sorry to hear that. I lost my wife to that awful disease." Albert's eyes filled. "It's been fifteen years, and I still miss her."

"I know the feeling."

"Dad, would you like some of Patricia's carrot cake?" Bonnie asked.

"Is the Pope Catholic?" He tugged out a handkerchief and wiped at his eyes, then blew his nose.

Father Christopher gave his shoulder a comforting squeeze. "If you'll excuse us, Al, Bonnie, I'd like to introduce Hope to some more folks."

"Go right on ahead. Happy to have you at Faith Chapel, Pastor."

"Thanks. I'm very happy to be here."

As we moved away, I heard Albert say, "That is one good-lookin' priest. I like a woman with a little meat on her bones."

"Dad!"

"I'd say you have a fan," Christopher murmured.

"I'll take as many as I can get."

The next few parishioners Father Christopher introduced me to were not as welcoming. They shook my hand but regarded me with wary looks, lingering on my black eye and responding to my attempts at conversation with only brief replies. Some excused themselves on the pretext of an urgent need to talk to someone or other about what they needed to bring to Wednesday's potluck.

Just kill me now.

"Father Christopher? Over here." A familiar humpbacked, white-haired woman in red waved us over with her cane.

"Why Dorothy, don't you look as pretty as a picture," the rector said. "Hope, I'd like you to meet Dorothy Thompson, the sweetheart of Faith Chapel."

"Oh, Father." Her creased cheeks pinked with pleasure.

"Thank you for leading my cheering section this morning, Dorothy."

24

"Happy to do so, Pastor. My goodness, it is the twenty-first century, after all." She shot a look at the wrinkled man who had stalked out during my introduction and was now holding court in the far corner with a few other old-timers. "Some people need to get their heads out of their you-know-whats and realize we left the fifties a long time ago."

"Preach it, Dorothy." Todd King pushed his floppy ginger hair out of his eyes as he joined us.

"Todd." Dorothy's eyes widened. "What are you doing here?"

"Welcoming our new priest."

"But . . . I . . . we didn't expect to see you so soon after—" The sweetheart of Faith Chapel stopped herself and hugged the young man. "I'm so sorry about your father. How is Samantha?"

A shadow crossed Todd's face. "Not great, but she'll be okay. Thanks." He turned his attention to me, obviously eager to change the subject. "So, Pastor, what do you think of our church? She's a beauty, isn't she? Especially that gorgeous old tongue-and-groove ceiling."

"Yes, I was admiring it earlier."

"Todd's an artist," Dorothy said. "A wonderful one."

"Oh? What medium do you work in?"

"Fused glass, mostly, but also some acrylics and watercolors."

"I'd love to see some of your work. Do you have a studio here in town?"

"Not anymore." He scowled.

"I'm the proud owner of several art pieces from this talented young man," Father Christopher said. "I'll show them to you, Hope. Maybe after service tonight? You can join me for dinner, if you don't mind leftover chili."

Nearby, my nemesis Marjorie Chamberlain, who had been listening to our conversation, spoke up, "Why, Father, don't you remember you're having dinner with Lottie and I tonight?"

"I'm so sorry, Marjorie. Please forgive me. I'd forget my head if it wasn't attached. See, this is why I need Hope."

Marjorie gave me a fake smile and passed by me to enfold the skinny Todd King in a crushing hug. "You poor boy. I'm so sorry for your loss. You and Samantha must be devastated. I remember how I felt when I lost my beloved papa." She sniffled. "Now you both come for dinner tonight too. Your church family will take good care of you."

"Uh, thanks, Marjorie." Todd managed to extricate himself from her grip. His eyes took on a trapped look, however, when he saw Chief Beacham, Patricia, and a line of church ladies ready to offer their sympathy. "Let me check with Sami, and I'll let you know. Gotta go." He sprinted for the door.

Now that's what I call a quick getaway. Was it the church ladies who scared him off? Or the police chief? I made a mental note to find out more about artist Todd and his relationship with his father.

* * *

The lunch rush had ended at the retro diner on Main Street, leaving only a few families remaining at the Formica-topped tables. I'd chosen to nestle into one of the vintage booths, where I removed a PG Tips tea bag from the plastic-sandwich-bag stash I always kept in my purse and plopped it in the cup in front of me. After pouring boiling hot—never tepid—water into the cup, I stirred twice, then removed the pyramid-shaped tea bag and set it on the saucer.

Adding milk and sugar, I stirred again, lifted the cup to my lips, and took a long, greedy drink. "Ahh. I needed that."

The middle-aged server, who had been watching my entire ritual with a bemused expression, shook her head. "Now that's a first. I've never seen anyone carry on so much over a cup of tea."

"I went to England on my honeymoon and came back a tea lover." I took another sip. "Nectar of the gods."

The server, whose name tag read *Susan*, lifted an eyebrow. "Gods? As in plural?" She glanced at my clerical collar. "You Episcopalians sure are mixing it up over at Faith Chapel."

"It's good to mix it up every now and then. I take it you're not an Episcopalian?"

She shook her head. "Nor Presbyterian. Catholic. Methodist. Baptist. Or any of those other *ists*."

"Not a church fan?"

"I'm good with God. It's his people I'm not too crazy about. Nothing personal."

"I understand. I feel the same way myself sometimes." When I accepted the position at this small rural church that had never had a woman pastor in its entire 160-year history, I had known I would encounter some resistance, so I was prepared for it.

I wasn't prepared for murder.

"So, you're the new preacher they're saying knocked off Stanley King, huh?"

I choked on my tea. Before I could formulate a pastorally correct response, Server Susan grabbed my hand and shook it. "You did everyone a favor. The guy was the biggest jerk in town. Actually, jerk's way too nice a word, but there are children present." She lowered her voice. "Stanley King was a lousy, miserable excuse

27

for a human being. And you'll find there won't be many, if any, in Apple Springs shedding tears for him."

"Really? Why?" As a rule, I don't like to take part in gossip. Not a very priestly attribute. In addition, there's that pesky ninth commandment about not bearing false witness against your neighbor, but desperate times call for desperate measures.

Susan pushed her thick dark hair with its Bonnie Raitt streak of gray behind her ear. "You got all day? Because that's how long it'll take to catalog the man's sins."

"Can you give me the *Reader's Digest* version?"

The families left, leaving the diner empty except for a young guy at the counter intent on his phone. Susan slipped into the red vinyl booth across from me to dish the dirt. "First of all, Stanley is—correction, *was*—an arrogant SOB who thought because he was rich his shit didn't stink and the whole town should bow down to him. The guy was a cheat, liar, and total user who treated everyone like crap, including his own children."

She lifted her hand and began ticking off the man's sins on her fingers. "Stanley was a real player, dating and dumping a host of women—married, unmarried, didn't matter. He thought he was God's gift and his wealth entitled him to hit on every woman around. Some who were barely legal."

Hmm. Maybe an angry husband or father killed him.

Susan raised a second finger. "He cheated his former law partner out of the business and left the poor guy bankrupt and divorced."

Or business associate.

She lifted her middle finger. "He owned several properties in town—including this one—and kept raising the rents sky-high, which caused many longtime mom-and-pop businesses to fold."

Tenant?

Ring finger. "When Todd moved out of the King mansion in an effort to break away from his father's control, Stanley kicked him out of the art studio he'd been leasing from dear old dad. From then on, the jerk never missed an opportunity to put down his son in public. Putting people down was one of Stanley King's favorite indoor sports."

His son? Could it be patricide?

Susan extended her pinkie. "His constant verbal abuse and manipulation drove his daughter Samantha to drink and gamble, until she became so deep in debt that daddy had to bail her out, thus ensuring she'd never break free from his clutches. Unlike his young wife, whom he drove to suicide years ago."

My stomach turned. "And that's the *Reader's Digest* version?"

"Yep. Kind of leaves a bad taste in the mouth, doesn't it?" Susan stood up and stretched. "What you need is a nice piece of pie. I've got apple, chocolate, and today's special, coconut cream."

"Before lunch?"

"You can have lunch afterwards. Life is short. Eat dessert first."

"But I didn't even have breakfast."

"Then you need some fruit. How about a nice piece of my hot apple pie with cheese on top? That way you get your protein too."

"You make the pies?" I glanced out the window at the neon diner sign. "Wait. You're the owner. Suzie?"

"Yes and no." She puffed out a sigh. "Yes, I'm the owner—half owner—and no, I'm not Suzie. *Never* Suzie. The sign was already there when we bought the place. Mike, my husband, insisted we keep it. 'It's a landmark,' he said." She scowled. "It may be a landmark, but I hate it when people call me Suzie. No one calls him Mikey."

"I can call him Mikey if you like. *Mikey likes it.*"

"Works for me, but you may not like how your food turns out." She jerked her head over her shoulder in the direction of the kitchen. "Mike's the cook."

My inner movie geek did a mental fist pump. For the first time, I noticed the classic movie posters hanging on the walls above the black-and-white-checkerboard floor: *North by Northwest, True Grit, Butch Cassidy and the Sundance Kid, The Great Escape,* and *Casablanca.* I've always had a thing for old movies. While my high school classmates were laughing at *Dumb and Dumber* and *Ace Ventura: Pet Detective,* I was soaking up Bogie and Bacall, both Hepburns, and Cary Grant. Always Cary Grant. Be still my heart. "Which one's your favorite?"

Susan tilted her head and examined the posters. "It's a toss-up between *North by Northwest* and *Butch Cassidy,* but if I had to pick just one, I'd go with Butch and Sundance. I mean, Paul Newman and Robert Redford? What more could you ask for?"

"Katharine Ross," yelled a male voice from the kitchen.

"Simmer down, big boy, we weren't talking to you," Susan yelled back. "Mike's had a crush on Katharine Ross since he snuck into *The Graduate* in junior high," she explained.

"Understandable." My stomach growled. "Guess I'd better order."

"As long as you start with pie."

I chose the apple with cheese and a tuna melt. Fifteen minutes later when Susan returned and sat down again on a coffee break, only crumbs remained. "That's the best apple pie I've ever had," I

said. "Even better than my sister-in-law's—but don't tell her I said
so. Virginia's a great baker and cook, while I, on the other hand,
cannot cook to save my life. Except for my killer scrambled eggs,
thanks to my secret ingredient."

"Which is . . . ?"

"If I told you, I'd have to kill you."

Susan looked around and behind her. "But there's no burial
urn here."

"Susan, I think this is the beginning of a beautiful friendship."

She clinked her coffee cup against my teacup. "Here's looking
at you, kid."

The bell over the front door jangled, and in walked Beehive
woman and Beige man. Minus Elvis, thankfully. Today Beehive
wore head-to-toe pink, while her sweetheart was again clad in his
ubiquitous beige—broken up by a navy tie. They slipped into the
front booth, where they held hands across the table and had eyes
only for each other.

My hand involuntarily moved to my forehead. "Who's that?"

Susan leaned forward and said quietly, "Bethann and Wendell Jackson. She headlined a girl group called Bethann and the
Blondelles back in the day. She's a bit eccentric. Not sure if it's a
side effect from all those drugs in the sixties or what. Bethann
is harmless, though, and a total sweetheart. Her husband adores
her."

Susan got up and walked over to their booth. "Hey, Bethann.
Dell. How's it going? You want your usual?"

"Yep," he said, "but skip the milk. We're going to have a chocolate malt today with our pie."

"Whoa. Living large. What's the occasion?"

"We're celebratin'," Beehive Bethann said. "Finally after all those years of tormentin' us, our awful neighbor got his just desserts." Then she noticed me and my dog collar. Her eyes widened. "Oh my goodness, darlin', look. It's that woman Elvis gave the shiner to!" She crossed herself and hurried over to my table, her husband on her heels. "*You're* the lady priest everyone's been talkin' about?"

"Guilty as charged."

Bethann's false-eyelashes-ringed eyes widened even more. "Well, don't you worry, honey. We know a good lawyer." She turned to her husband. "Dell, sweetheart, do you have Don Forrester's card for the reverend so he can defend her for horrible Stanley's murder?"

"What?" I looked from Beehive woman to Beige man.

Wendell put his arm around his wife's waist. "Sugar, that's a figure of speech."

"But she said she was guilty."

"Of being the woman priest the whole town's talking about," I said. "We weren't properly introduced the other day. Hi, I'm Hope Taylor, and you are Bethann and Wendell. Did I hear you say Stanley King was your neighbor?"

Bethann's heavily made-up face flushed as pink as her crocheted jumpsuit. "Yes. He lives—lived—behind us. What a mean, nasty man. He was always complaining about our yard. Said it was an eyesore. Called us poor white trash. Even tried to drive us out of our home using his legal mumbo jumbo." Her lips quivered, and her eyes glistened with tears. "The only real home I've ever had."

Wendell squeezed Bethann's waist. "Don't get yourself all upset, sweetie. Our home is safe, and Stanley can't say or do any

32

more awful things to us. Or anyone." He kissed her cheek. "Forget about him. Remember, we're here to celebrate."

"You're right, darlin'." Bethann blinked back her tears and gave him a dazzling smile. "I'm lookin' forward to some delicious coconut cream pie, and a yummy malt. Now, Susan, don't forget to bring two straws."

"You got it."

Bethann sped back to their booth and Wendell followed, mumbling a hasty good-bye. She said over her shoulder, "And don't you worry, Reverend honey, I gave Elvis a time-out, and he's in Jailhouse Rock right now."

And I am back in The Twilight Zone. As I watched the couple tuck into their pie, I thought of how Bethann right away had assumed I killed Stanley. Did everyone believe that? It made no sense. *I'm a priest, for goodness' sake. My job is to help people, not hurt them.* That's why I'd been so eager to come here—to help Father Christopher, and to minister to the people of Faith Chapel. And yes, to begin again. *Why would I murder the man? I didn't even know him. I had nothing to gain by killing him, and everything to lose.*

My thought train stopped in its tracks. *Gain.* That was the key. Who'd had something to gain from Stanley's death? I looked over at Bethann and Wendell again, now sharing their chocolate malt. Hadn't she said Stanley had tried to drive them out of their house? Was Bethann really as harmless as Susan thought? After all, she had bonked me in the head with an Elvis gnome. What might she do with an urn?

"Do you want another cup of tea?" Susan appeared beside me with more hot water.

"Yes, please." I fished out my PG Tips and dropped a fresh tea bag into my cup.

The bell over the front door jangled again. I looked up to see Todd King guiding his chalk-faced sister to a back booth.

"Uh-oh," Susan murmured. "Is daddy dearest still plaguing that sweet girl from beyond the grave? Between you and me, I'm glad someone whacked him before Samantha wound up like her poor mama. There have been plenty of times Mike wanted to take a two-by-four up the side of Stanley's head himself, and he's not the only one." She poured hot water into my cup, then left to wait on the King children.

I pulled out my smartphone and thumbed in a Google search to see if I could find any background on Todd and Samantha's mother. It didn't take long. The newspaper story was a familiar one: a young woman with a history of drug and alcohol abuse had died of an accidental overdose twenty years ago. What was not so familiar was that this young woman, Lily, had been married to the wealthy, powerful, and much-older Stanley King. Rumors at the time said her death was a suicide, but Stanley squelched those rumors and called the loss of his "beautiful, beloved wife" a "tragic accident" instead. Lily left behind a six-year-old daughter and four-year-old son.

Those poor kids. I thought of my stepdaughter Emily, remembering how devastated she had been to lose her dad. David had been a kind, loving, and engaged father. Thankfully, he had been there for Emily's major adult milestones, for which I was eternally grateful. He had seen his daughter graduate from college, walked her down the aisle, and wept when his first grandchild was born. Lily King had missed all that, and her children had missed a mother's love and guidance. Now they had lost their father as well.

Time to pay a pastoral visit.

* * *

The siblings were sitting on the same side of the booth, their backs to me, and didn't notice my approach. "What are we going to do? I don't know what to do. What if someone finds out?" Samantha stifled a sob.

"It's okay, Red. It's going to be okay. Don't worry."

"Excuse me—"

They both jumped. Samantha stared at me, wild-eyed and trembling.

"I'm sorry. I didn't mean to startle you. I wanted to let you know that if you ever need to talk, I'm happy to listen. Anytime. Just give me a call."

Samantha continued to stare at me.

"Are you all right? Is there anything I can do?"

"It's okay, Pastor." Todd gave a forced chuckle. "We, uh, saw a big old rat outside, and it freaked Sam out. She's always been afraid of rats."

His sister nodded agreement.

Uh-huh. It wasn't a rat—unless it was the two-legged variety. I kept those thoughts to myself. My ecclesiastical training had taught me that there is a time for silence and a time to speak— a lesson I am still learning, considering my natural tendency to blurt out whatever pops into my head. After my prior two years as a deacon and pastor in the Bay Area, however, I had gotten much better at buttoning up my blurts.

Oh? What about your "hot Father Ralph" comment to Marjorie? I stifled my pesky inner I'm-not-a-perfect-priest reminder and reached into my pocket. "Here's my card with my cell and office number. Call me anytime."

As I walked back to my table, I thought of my own family upbringing. My father was a stern authoritarian, like the guy played by Robert Duvall in *The Great Santini*, and my mother was a doormat whom the women's movement had passed by. Talk about a Stepford wife. The time-warp church we attended growing up taught that women should not work outside the home and must submit to men and serve their every need. Mom bought into that master-slave scenario completely and expected my older sister, Rachel, and me to do the same. Rachel escaped by joining the Air Force after high school and shipping out overseas, while I fled across the country to a West Coast college at eighteen.

I wondered if Samantha had ever tried to flee. Then I wondered what she had meant by "What if someone finds out?" Could it be she had finally had enough of her father's controlling ways and verbal abuse, snapped, and killed him in the columbarium? And if I was wondering that, were the police?

Chapter Four

As I opened the door to my house, seventy-five pounds of black fur hit me. Tail-wagging, face-licking, paws-on-my-shoulders fur. "Hi, Bogie-boy, did you miss me?" I returned my black Lab's hug, knowing as I did that my clergy vest would need a thorough going-over with the lint roller. At least his hairs matched the vest.

I'd met my dog six years ago with David at a Lab rescue place and instantly fallen in love with the tiny black pup. And he fell in love with my husband. When David died, Bogie and I mourned him together.

"Does someone want to go outside?" Bogie raced me to the kitchen, his tail helicoptering all over the place and his nails clickety-clicking on the linoleum. I opened the back door, and he zoomed out to do his business and then race to the tennis ball in the far corner of the yard. The large fenced-in backyard of the 1940s bungalow was the main reason I had bought this house. Bogie needed room to run. The original hardwood floors (every-where but the kitchen) and classic details didn't hurt either. For houses, like everything else in my life—movies, music, men—I prefer vintage. Granted, some of the vintage wasn't exactly my style, like the glittery gold linoleum on the kitchen floor and the avocado-and-gold floral wallpaper that screamed sixties, but I planned to do improvements.

In the bedroom, I exchanged my clergy clothes for my *Keep Calm and Ring Carson for Tea* T-shirt and favorite jeans. Then I returned to the kitchen, expecting Bogie to be waiting at the back door, tennis ball in mouth, which was his norm—at least at our old house—but he wasn't there. I went out onto the back patio and scanned the yard. No Bogie. My heart dropped. *Please oh please, let me not have lost my dog, my best friend.* "Bogie?" I whistled.

Woof! Woof! A reassuring bark met my ears, and a delighted giggle from next door pierced the air. "Funny doggy."

I hurried over to the side fence, where I noticed an opening between a few loose wooden slats I hadn't seen before. Likely because the opening was recently made by my curious dog. I sucked in my stomach, wishing I had already lost those extra fifteen pounds. Then I spread the slats and squeezed through into my neighbor's yard. There I found my dog licking the legs of a laughing, curly-headed child.

"That tickles!" The little girl giggled. "Do it again!"

But Bogie had spotted me. *Woof!* He bounded over and lay on his back in front of me, raising all four legs in the air as he did his "Beam me up, Scotty" routine.

I knelt and scratched his tummy. He wagged his tail and released a contented noise, which sounded remarkably like a purr.

"I wanna do that too." The dark-haired child plopped down beside me and stretched out her hand toward Bogie.

"Okay, but be gentle."

She patted his belly. "So soft." Then she looked up at me with striking cobalt-blue eyes framed by the longest lashes I had ever seen. "What's his name?"

"Bogie."

"Hi, Bogie." She stroked his fur. "My name is Maddie." Then she looked up at me. "What's your name?"

"I'm Hope. Nice to meet you."

"Do you wanna be my friend?"

"I would love to." As I looked down at the adorable child enraptured with Bogie, I got the distinct feeling I would be a second-string friend to my dog, and not for the first time.

"You live in Harry's house. Harry was my friend too, but he's in heaven now." She waved up at the sky. "Hi, Harry."

Before I could respond, a slim, striking young woman in yoga pants and a tank top with hair the same dark Belgian chocolate as Maddie's strode across the grass to us, smiling.

"Mommy, see the pretty dog?"

The mother dropped to the ground beside her daughter and joined her in stroking Bogie's belly, which sent him into further ecstasy. "What a sweet boy." She looked across at me and smiled. "I'm Nikki McNeal. Welcome to the neighborhood."

I introduced myself to the hard-bodied twentysomething across from me, all at once conscious of my middle-aged muffin top poking over the top of my jeans. Especially since the same ultra-fit young woman was now staring hard at my T-shirt. Casually I plucked the fabric away from my midriff pooch.

"I *love* Carson," Nikki said, her sapphire eyes sparkling. "He and Mrs. Hughes are my favorite couple from *Downton Abbey*."

"Mine too. It used to be Mary and Matthew until he went and got himself killed to go make movies. But I have to admit, he made a good Beast in *Beauty and the Beast*."

"I know, right?"

"I like *Beauty and the Beast*," piped up Maddie. "Belle reads books."

"That's why she's my favorite Disney character. Like Belle, I love to read." I recited, "'In an old house in Paris that was covered in vines, lived twelve little girls in two straight lines.'"

"That's from *Madeline*!" Maddie beamed at me.

"I loved the Madeline books when I was your age. Is that who you're named after?"

She nodded and puffed out her chest. "Madeline Clare McNeal." She held up four fingers. "I'm almost four."

Bogie interrupted our literary love fest by batting at my leg with his paw and giving me a beseeching look.

"What? Does someone need a walk?"

He wagged his tail at the w-word, which quickly morphed into an excited tail thumping. I stood up and brushed off my jeans. "I'd better take this big boy for some exercise."

"C'n I help?" Maddie scrambled to her feet.

"You haven't had lunch yet, young lady," Nikki said. "And it's not polite to invite yourself."

"How about if you help me walk Bogie tomorrow, Maddie? Maybe once I'm settled in, you and your mom could come over for a tea party. Would you like that?"

Her cobalt eyes shone. "With sparkly cookies?"

"I think we can manage that."

We said our good-byes, and while Maddie was busy hugging Bogie, Nikki took me aside and said, "Don't let the haters get you

40

down. Believe me, there's plenty of people in town with actual motive to knock off Stan-the-jerk-man."

"Thanks. I appreciate that."

Back home, I clipped on Bogie's leash and grabbed a zip-up hoodie from the coatrack. "C'mon, boy, let's go check out our new town." We strolled through the leafy neighborhood, which was a mixture of cottages, bungalows, Craftsmen-style homes, and the occasional Victorian. No cookie-cutter urban sprawl here. Crab apple trees and wisteria bloomed on both sides of the street, leaving a heady fragrance in their wake. I basked in the peaceful stillness of the morning, enjoying the quiet of my new small-town neighborhood. Life in the Bay Area had been anything but quiet, especially these past few years with David regularly in and out of the hospital in San Francisco.

"Yoo-hoo!"

A woman in an aqua housecoat interrupted my reverie. She click-clacked down the driveway of her Victorian in mules with fluffy turquoise puffs. Puffs that shed with every step she took. As she drew near, her carroty hair, tomato-red lipstick, and blush that looked like a mound of Cheetos plopped onto her pancaked cheeks blinded me. The heavy makeup creased in the crow's feet on the sides of her stonewashed denim eyes. "Beauty School Dropout" from *Grease* popped into my head. Thankfully, it did not come out my mouth.

"Why hello there!" Aqua woman came to a breathless stop in front of me. "Ah wanted to welcome you to the neighborhood." She extended a freckled, age-spotted hand. "I'm Liliane Turner. Delighted to meet you."

I shook the scarlet-nailed hand. "And you. I'm—"

"Oh, I know who you are." She released a tinkling laugh. "Everyone does. You're Hope Taylor, the new Episcopal priest who is living in Harry Guthrie's old house. Ah hope you'll be happy in our sleepy little Apple Springs. We're not as sophisticated and exciting as San Francisco and the Bay Area."

"I don't need exciting. Small and sleepy suits me fine."

Bogie nosed at her housecoat, and Liliane took a hesitant step back. "My, what a big dog."

"Don't worry. He's harmless. Aren't you, sweet boy?" I knelt down and hugged him, which elicited a doggy kiss on my neck in return. "The only danger you're in is of being licked to death." I grinned and looked up at the fluttery Liliane in time to catch a glimpse of a grimace on her pancaked face.

She quickly replaced her distaste with an expression of concern. "Ah can't even begin to imagine what it must have been like to find Stanley dead in the chapel. How awful." Liliane fanned herself with her hand. "I'd have probably fainted plumb away."

Another southern belle in Apple Springs? What are the odds? "It wasn't one of my favorite things. Certainly not how I hoped to start my first day on the job."

"You poor dear." She patted my arm. "Such a terrible thing. I hear poor Ethel's burial urn had blood all over it. How could you even bear to pick it up? I know I never could." Liliane's blue eyes were bright with curiosity. "Why did you pick it up anyway?"

Nice try, but no cigar. "By chance is Bethann your sister?"

"Bethann Jackson?" Liliane shot me an incredulous look. "I should say not," she huffed. "Crazy doesn't run in my family."

"I'm sorry. You both have southern accents, so I assumed you were related. It's unusual to have two southern belles in the same small California town."

Liliane preened, releasing another tinkling laugh. Her accent, which I now noticed seemed to come and go, increased exponentially. "Ah can see how you might make that assumption, bein' new in town and all. And ah do thank you for the southern belle compliment, but I'm a hometown girl born and raised right here in Apple Springs." She placed her hand on her chest and released a dramatic sigh. "My heart, howevah, belongs to the South. Why, I wouldn't be surprised if in a past life I lived in Charleston or Savannah." Liliane looked down demurely. "I have, however, played Miss Scarlett O'Hara on occasion and Clairee from *Steel Magnolias*. To great acclaim, I might add."

"Ah, that explains it." I glanced at her painted face and smiled.

"Explains what?"

"You're an actor. What play are you doing? Are you on your way to rehearsal?"

"Ah happen to be between plays at the moment," she said in a glacial tone.

Oops. Backpedal. Backpedal. "Well, you're clearly a good actress. You had me convinced you were a southern girl."

"Why thank you." Her frost melted like butter in a skillet at the word *girl*. Liliane squinted at the writing on my T-shirt. She put on a pair of tortoiseshell glasses hanging from her neck on a beaded chain. "Oh my goodness! You're a *Downton Abbey* fan too? You simply *must* join our Downton Divas. We hated to see that delicious show end, so a few of us girls get together once a month to drink tea and watch the DVDs."

After promising to connect with her later to get all the Downton details, I resumed my walk with Bogie. He pulled at his leash. "You ready to run now?" His tail wagged. "Okay, let's go." We jogged together down the sidewalk heading toward the town center, enjoying the slight breeze rustling through the trees.

Two blocks later, a white ball of fur hurtled itself at us, barking furiously. Bogie stopped and did his best Scooby-Doo impression. *Aarug?* Looking down at the petite Westie standing her ground in front of my large Lab reminded me of the Jack Palance line in *City Slickers*—"I crap bigger than you."

Bogie sidled behind me as the white dog continued barking.

"Nessa, stop that!" A man clad in basketball shorts and a T-shirt, who reminded me of George Clooney with his gray-flecked hair, sprinted down the driveway of a Craftsman house. "Sorry about that." He scooped the white fur ball into his arms. "She's a big dog in a little dog's body."

"I can see that. Is she named after the Loch Ness monster?"

"No, that's Nessie. This is Ness*a*."

"And this is Bogie." At the sound of his name, Bogie's ears perked up and his tail began to thump.

The Clooney-resembler extended the back of his hand, which Bogie sniffed happily and licked, making the Westie bark again. "Now don't get jealous, Nessa. Be nice." She looked up at her person adoringly and licked his face. "Good girl. Now go make friends with Bogie." He ruffled the back of his dog's head and set her down. Nessa took a cautious step over to Bogie, sniffing madly and circling him. Bogie sniffed back and did his happy dance.

"Since Ebony and Ivory are getting acquainted, maybe we should too. I'm James."

"Hope."

"*Pastor* Hope?"

"The one and only."

"I thought priests always had to wear those dog collars?"

"They let us off the leash every now and then."

He zeroed in on my black eye. "Looks like the leash snapped back."

"No, that was Elvis."

His eyebrows lifted.

"Long story."

"I'd like to hear it sometime. Meanwhile, I wanted to thank you for your kindness to my niece and nephew. Samantha said how much she appreciated your visit Friday."

"Samantha King's your niece? Are you Stanley's brother?" *Because you sure do not look like him. Or act like him.*

"Brother-in-law. My sister Lily was his wife." A shadow crossed his Clooneyesque features.

"I'm sorry about your sister."

"Me too. More than you know. Luckily, Stanley can no longer destroy Todd and Samantha's lives like he did Lily's. Rumor has it I may have you to thank for that." He sent me a lopsided grin.

"I simply found the man. I didn't kill him, contrary to popular opinion."

"Shame. Although"—he cocked his head at me, checking me out—"I suppose if you did, you'd wind up in prison, and that would be an even bigger shame."

Is he flirting with me? I don't do flirting. I left those days behind when I met David. Since becoming a priest, however, I had discovered that, unlike a nun's habit, my clerical garb was not

45

a deterrent. Instead, it seemed to be like catnip to some men—particularly the elderly ones, of which there are many, since the Episcopal Church tends to run older. I'd had more than my share of too-long full-frontal hugs from several old men in my previous congregation, so I'd learned to become the master of the one-armed side hug. I'd also learned to counter any unwelcome advances by assuming my motherly confessor role instead. Priests are spiritual leaders, teachers, confessors, psychologists, and mothers and fathers all rolled into one.

Although James was light-years away from the old-men category, and I wasn't cloaked in my clerical garb, I still donned my mother-confessor hat. "I understand why you had issues with Stanley. From what I've heard, he wasn't a very nice man—"

He snorted. "That's rich. That SOB drove my sister to drugs and eventual suicide and began repeating the same scenario with Samantha. The poor kid had two stints in rehab before she was twenty. Happily, she's been clean for five years now, no thanks to her father." His face darkened. "Unfortunately, daddy dearest made sure he introduced her to another addiction. But why am I telling you this?" He glanced at my neckline. "It must be the invisible collar. Besides, you've probably already heard this. In a small town, everyone's lives are an open book."

"As long as it's not *Fifty Shades of Grey*."

"Why Pastor, you read mommy porn?"

"No." I could feel my cheeks reddening. "But since several of the young women in my last parish were reading and talking about what was at the time a huge pop-culture phenomenon, I thought I should at least be aware of it."

"So, you did read it."

"Only the first chapter, plus a few paragraphs in later chapters to see if the writing improved."

"I already know that answer." He grinned. "To quote my English-major niece, 'What dreck.'"

Eager to steer the conversation away from the embarrassing rabbit trail we had gone down, I told James I would be happy to help Samantha and Todd any way I could and asked him to tell them that.

Bogie nosed my hand. "I think someone's trying to tell me something. We'd better get going."

"See you around." James scooped up Nessa and jogged back up the driveway. Halfway to the backyard he stopped and turned. "Welcome to Apple Springs, by the way."

I lifted my hand in a wave, and as Bogie and I continued our walk through town, I added James-the-uncle to my list of possible suspects. He clearly hated Stanley and blamed him for his sister's death. Who knew what he might do to avenge her?

Avenge? This isn't The Princess Bride: "My name is James Montoya. You killed my sister. Prepare to die."

Too late, I realized I should have asked James more questions. Like, maybe, where had he been the day of the murder? Trixie Belden would be ashamed. Then I prayed that James would not turn out to be the guilty party, for Todd's and Samantha's sakes. They had already lost a mother and father. They didn't need to lose an uncle too.

Chapter Five

As we turned the corner onto Main Street, the breeze that was formerly cool and welcoming now turned into a brisk wind. I stopped in front of a closed barbershop and pulled on my hoodie. Bogie and I passed several brick-and-wooden storefronts: Bonnie's Blooms, The Mane Event, Apple Springs Market, Sonnets and Stuff Bookstore, and Margheritaville, a compact pizzeria wafting heavenly aromas. If I hadn't had lunch an hour ago, I'd have gone in and had a slice.

"Pastor Hope. Hello! Who's this gorgeous creature?" Dorothy Thompson, Faith Chapel's sweetheart, clad in a lavender velour tracksuit and wearing purple-pansy earrings, held out her hand to my dog, who licked it eagerly.

"Bogie, that's not polite."

"That's okay. I was eating some peanut butter pretzels, and I know how much dogs love peanut butter. Isn't that right?" she cooed, petting his black head. "Are you named after Humphrey Bogart?"

Bogie woofed.

"Humphrey Bogart was my husband's favorite actor. David especially loved his movies with Lauren Bacall." I adopted the actress's trademark sultry tone. "'You know how to whistle, don't you, Steve? You just put your lips together and blow.'"

"Good job." Dorothy giggled. "Although I can't say I've ever heard a priest recite that famous line before."

"Maybe we should keep that between us."

"My lips are sealed." She made a zipper motion across her mouth. "Did you know Bogie and Bacall met and fell in love while making *To Have and Have Not*? So sad they only had a dozen years together before he died."

My heart clenched. "Yes. He was the love of her life."

Bogie snuffled Dorothy's hand, searching for food. "I'm sorry, boy," she said. "I don't have anything for you."

"Don't be a beggar, Bogie. You'll get treats when we get home." His tail helicoptered at the word *treats*. As I glanced down at my dog, I noticed Dorothy leaning heavily on her cane. "Would you mind if we sat down? I need a rest. Bogie's tuckered me out."

"You read my mind." Dorothy lowered herself gratefully onto one of the wooden benches ringing the camellia-dotted town square. She kissed her fingertips and touched them to a bronze plaque on the back of the bench.

I leaned in to read the inscription. *You know that place between sleep and awake; that place where you can still remember dreaming? That's where I will always love you. That's where I will be waiting. —Peter Pan. In loving memory of Randall Thompson.*

"Your husband?"

She nodded. "My Randy." Her eyes glistened. "When he passed, I didn't think I could go on. I didn't want to. Sometimes I still don't. I miss him every day."

I squeezed her hand as I felt the prick of tears in my own eyes. "After my husband died, I could barely get out of bed, much less function. I went to the bishop ready to tender my pastoral resignation, but he wisely suggested I take a sabbatical instead, so I fled to England."

"England?" Her wet eyes widened. "My favorite place in the world. We were stationed there, years ago, when Randy was in the Air Force. We loved it and always wanted to return but never got the chance before he passed. Instead, I went on a tour of Great Britain with my sister and fell in love with it all over again. When were you in England?"

"Two and a half years ago."

"Not that long ago." She offered an understanding widow-to-widow look. "What did you do on your sabbatical?"

"Stayed in a Devonshire monastery where I cried myself to sleep each night. During the day I slept or aimlessly wandered the grounds, unable to even pray, meditate, or attend vespers."

"Thank you for telling me that, Pastor, rather than spouting scripture or trite platitudes about such a devastating loss." A tear escaped and slid down her cheek. "When Randy died, I heard a lot of that. We weren't at Faith Chapel yet, and for some reason people felt it was their spiritual duty to bombard me with sayings or scriptures like, 'He's in a better place.' 'God needed a new angel.' 'And we know that all things work together for good to them that love God . . .'"

"People don't know what to say when someone dies. They often blurt out thoughtless things." *It was God's plan. You're young—you'll get married again.*

"They should learn to take a page from the 'Silence is golden' book." Dorothy shook her head and then collected herself. "But tell me more about your sabbatical. Did you stay at the monastery the whole time?"

"No, only a couple weeks. Afterward I went to a Benedictine abbey in Yorkshire. There I added in some meditation and occasionally attended morning prayer. Then I made a pilgrimage to Canterbury Cathedral, where I stayed in a lodge on the grounds." I closed my eyes, remembering. "In my room I moved my prayer book from inside the closed drawer to the top of the nightstand, cried only every other night, and began attending evensong. By the time I got to Oxford, I was saying the prayers in my prayer book daily and crying less frequently." I patted Bogie's head. "I was also missing my sweet dog and craving human companionship, laughter, and tea with scones, jam, and gobs of Devonshire cream."

"I love Devonshire cream! We had cream teas all the time when we lived in England. Yum." Dorothy licked her lips. "We should have tea and scones together one of these days. Maybe we could even have a ladies' afternoon tea at church?"

"Did someone say tea and church?" Patricia Beacham appeared before us, looking as if she had stepped out of the pages of the Coldwater Creek catalog in her multicolored maxi dress and light cardigan. "That's a great idea. We used to do teas regularly, but we haven't had one in a few years."

"Why is that, anyway?" Dorothy asked.

"Don't you remember? The great Ethel and Marjorie debacle?"

"Oh yes. I had pushed that unpleasantness out of my mind. So far out of my mind I'd forgotten all about it."

I looked from one to the other. "Would you like to share with the class?"

"Let's just say two strong-willed women—each with very distinct ideas about how things should be done, and each who believes her way is the right way—should never be cochairs of an event," Patricia said.

"Talk about a recipe for disaster." Dorothy grimaced. "As I recall, I don't think Ethel or Marjorie spoke to one another for an entire year afterward."

Sadly, I had seen it before in church. People become possessive of their small patch of power and do not want to concede it to anyone else. Differences of opinion escalate into clashes and hurt feelings. Priests often find themselves moderating conflicts between parishioners privately so that no one undermines the health of the church.

"They eventually made up though, right? I remember at the rectory Marjorie calling Ethel a dear friend."

"Yes. Thanks to Father Christopher," Patricia said. "He talked to them both individually and jointly. I have no idea what he said, but whatever it was, he persuaded them to bury the hatchet, and they were good friends again until the day Ethel passed."

"So, after that, did Father Christopher put the kibosh on having another ladies' tea?"

"Oh no. Nothing that drastic. I think both Marjorie and Ethel didn't want to chance endangering their friendship again, so they steered clear of holding another tea."

"Weren't there other women in church who could have organized one?"

"Not this woman," Patricia said. "I was working full-time until two years ago and already juggling several things. I promised myself, and my husband, I wouldn't commit to anything else."

"Lottie was always Marjorie's right hand behind the scenes," Dorothy said, "but she's never been very good at being in charge."

Bingo. Here's my chance to do something for the women of Faith Chapel. "Well, I happen to be very good at being in charge, so I'll take on that role. Once I get Father Christopher's blessing, of course. In fact," I said, thinking aloud, "what if we made it a classic English tea? Dorothy, since you lived in Merrie Olde, you could guide us to make sure everything's authentically English."

Dorothy's face lit up like a kid hearing the ice cream truck. "I'd love to. Cucumber sandwiches and scones are a must, of course— genuine English scones, with jam and cream." She scrunched up her nose. "Not those big old dry things they serve in all the coffee shops today. I'll make my lemon squares, and I'm sure I can get the other Episcopal Christian Women to pitch in. Ooh, maybe Marjorie will make her wonderful curried chicken salad." Dorothy turned to Patricia. "Remember when she brought it to Ethel's reception?"

"How could I forget?" Patricia patted her nonexistent stomach and groaned. "I had four of those little sandwiches and two of your delicious lemon squares. Not to mention one of Lottie's decadent brownies. I was bloated for days."

"Well, I may be a lousy cook, but I make great sandwiches," I said. "In fact, my sister-in-law has a wonderful recipe for ham sandwiches with an apricot cream cheese spread. They're delicious." I frowned. "Although I'm not sure exactly how English they are."

"As long as they're savory and don't have crusts, that's fine," Dorothy said. "We could have ham, chicken, or salmon, or maybe even egg salad."

As we brainstormed different food ideas, all at once I had a brain wave. "What if we asked the men of the congregation to serve us?"

"That's a great idea," Patricia said, in her role as senior warden of the vestry. "Harold can be in charge of the male brigade, and I'm sure a couple of the vestry members will be happy to help too. We can also put out a call for volunteers."

Just then, a familiar-looking middle-aged man strode up to us. *No time like the present.*

I stuck out my hand and smiled. "Hi, I'm Pastor Hope. I remember seeing you at church this morning, but we didn't get a chance to meet. Would you like to serve the women of Faith Chapel?"

"Be happy to." He shook my hand. "Randy Thompson. At your service."

"This is my son, Randy Junior," said Dorothy proudly. "Randy, we're talking about having a ladies' tea and getting the men of the church to be servers."

"Count me in. As long as I don't have to wear a frilly apron." Randy glanced at his watch. "Mom, we really need to get going."

"Oh, of course. I don't want to be late for my granddaughter's birthday party." She turned to me. "Now Pastor Hope, I'll talk to the ECW women this week and see who'd like to help with the tea." She squeezed my hand and sent me a gentle look. "And thank you so much for what you shared earlier." Dorothy said her farewells and then picked up her cane, linking her arm through her son's and beaming up at him with love and pride as they departed.

"I can see why Father Christopher calls her the sweetheart of Faith Chapel," I said. "She's a doll."

"Yes, she is. Everyone loves Dorothy." Patricia frowned. "Except Stanley. He wasn't a fan."

"Why in the world not?"

"She wouldn't put up with his crap and called him out on it publicly a few times—usually when he was putting down his kids. Dorothy is a retired first-grade teacher. She taught both Todd and Samantha and wouldn't stand for anyone bullying *her* kids."

"Good for her."

The more I learned about Stanley, the more I understood why someone might have wanted to take him out. The million-dollar question was who. Or maybe, as I was beginning to realize, the more likely question was, who wouldn't? Figuring out the identity of his killer was going to be much harder than I'd first thought.

Patricia and I chatted about the tea and some church business. As we were doing so, a silver-haired couple passing by smiled and nodded at us. "Sergeant Beacham." The man saluted Patricia before they moved on.

"Sergeant? You didn't tell me you were in the military."

"Police. Was. I'm retired, which is why I can be on the vestry now. For years my work schedule wouldn't allow it."

I stared at Faith Chapel's senior warden. With my mouth open, apparently.

"Better watch out," Patricia said. "You'll catch flies that way."

My mother used to say that. She would also say, "Do you have a bee in your bonnet, missy?" She had a host of expressions handed down from her mother, which she loved to apply to my sister and me. Like, "I have a bone to pick with you, young lady," and my personal favorite, "You better learn how to cook, 'cause it takes face powder to catch a man but baking powder to keep him." That was her response when I called to share the news of my engagement. I never did learn to cook, but David didn't care because he loved to cook, as did his sister, Virginia.

I returned my attention to Patricia. "Did you and Harold meet on the police force?"

"Yes, ma'am. Thirty-seven years ago. He was my partner in the Sacramento PD. Harold didn't take too well to a woman partner at first, but I soon set him straight."

"I'll bet you did." I grinned. "How long have you been retired? And how come Harold didn't retire at the same time?"

"In answer to your first question, two years. As for the second, good question." She expelled a sigh. "I've been after Harold to slow down and relax for ages now. It's not as if he needs to work. He could have retired at sixty-five with a full pension, but not my husband. The man is seventy-three and he keeps on going, like the Energizer Bunny. He has a perfectly good deputy who could step in and take over, but Harold has a hard time letting go."

"Most men do." I sang a snatch of "Let it Go" from *Frozen*.

"You should join the choir," Patricia said. "They could use another soprano."

Two boys ran past then, kicking a soccer ball on the grass. Bogie's ears perked up. Then a family of four appeared. They spread a blanket on the ground and plopped down on it, and the mother opened a picnic basket and began handing out sandwiches. A young couple, arms entwined and eyes intent only upon each other, strolled by. Just another bucolic Sunday afternoon in small-town America. I could get used to this.

Soon another couple appeared—a white-haired one. Grandparents, I assumed, as I watched them swinging their granddaughter, in jeans and pigtails, between them. When they caught sight of Patricia, they smiled and waved. Then they saw me. The couple hesitated, smiles faltering. The woman leaned over and whispered something to the man. They did an abrupt about-face and headed the other way. "But Grampa, I wanna see the lady who kilt the King," the little girl whined, swiveling her head around to look back at me.

Now I knew how Cary Grant felt in *To Catch a Thief* when everyone, including his love interest, Grace Kelly, accused the retired cat burglar of stealing jewels. Not quite on the same level as murder, though. I sifted through my mental movie database for a better example. Ashley Judd in *Double Jeopardy*. Except no way was I going to wind up in prison for a crime I did not commit. I definitely was not going to accelerate a car off a ferry into the ocean in a daring escape attempt—I'm a lousy swimmer.

"Don't let them get to you," Patricia said. "As one-half of the lone black couple at Faith Chapel, I know firsthand that folks here take their time with acceptance."

How much time? Before or after I lost my job? But I didn't want to be a whiner. Especially not to the vestry senior warden. I redirected the conversation. "I noticed there isn't much diversity in church. Is Apple Springs predominantly white?"

"Pretty much. There are a couple other black families in town, but they attend First Baptist. There are a few Latinos over at St. Mark's, the Catholic church, but we only have two Asian families here. The Wongs are Buddhists and Mr. Lee is an atheist."

"Do you know what they all eat for breakfast too?"

"Pretty much. Let's see." Patricia thought for a moment. "The Johnsons over at First Baptist have waffles on the weekends, while their friends, the Montgomerys, usually go for omelets. The Garcias like their bacon and eggs, but the Martinez family prefers pancakes. Mr. Wong likes his French toast, but Mrs. Wong prefers English muffins and fruit. And Mr. Lee has oatmeal every day except Saturday, when he mixes it up with a Danish and coffee."

"Remind me to hide my Cap'n Crunch."

"When you live in a small town for any length of time, you know everything about everybody."

"Obviously." I unzipped my hoodie as the sun warmed the square. "Speaking of, what's the story on Todd and Samantha's uncle?"

"James Brandon? He's a great guy. Really good real estate agent and a perennial bachelor, like his look-alike George Clooney. Like George was, I mean. James just hasn't met the woman of his dreams yet." Patricia gave me a speculative look. "Or has he?"

"Not me." I held up my hands. "I'm not looking for romance."

"Then why did you ask what the story was on him?"

"I meant his backstory." I glanced around to make sure no one could overhear. "Do you think he could have killed Stanley?"

"Are you playing Nancy Drew?"

"Trixie Belden. Nancy drove a convertible and always had to run to her rich father for help. I am just trying to clear my name and keep my job. Kind of hard to do when everyone thinks you whacked the richest guy in town."

"Not everyone."

"I appreciate the vote of confidence, but you're in the minority."

"I'm used to that," Patricia said dryly, "but I'm not the only one."

"Huh?"

She looked around as well, and upon seeing a woman two benches over engrossed in a book, she lowered her voice. "I'm not the only one who thinks you didn't kill Stanley. A little birdie told me he was most likely killed the night before you found him."

"Then I'm no longer a suspect?" I stopped myself from doing a fist pump and yelling out "Yes!" but barely.

"Not officially. By the way, that tidbit is between you, me, and this bench."

"Got it. But back to my original question. From what you know of Todd and Samantha's uncle James, do you think he could have killed his brother-in-law?"

"I don't think so. James is a really nice guy. He's not the murdering type. Although . . ." A thoughtful look crossed her face. "He did get into a terrible fight with Stanley years ago when his sister Lily died. Attacked him at her funeral, in fact. James went a little crazy—started yelling and punching Stanley in the face. Stanley never was one to back down from a fight, so of course he fought back. Harold and I had to pull them apart. I thought James was going to kill Stanley."

"That's what I'm sayin'."

"But that was over twenty years ago. He was crazy with grief over the loss of his sister. Why would he kill Stanley now?"

"Good question."

Patricia's attention was diverted by a beefy bald man in a tan suit crossing the street. "He's certainly got a spring in his step these days."

"Who?"

"Don Forrester." The bald man saw Patricia and waved. She smiled and waved back, saying under her breath, "Stanley's ex-partner in the law firm. For my money, he's someone more likely to consider as a potential murderer than James Brandon. Stanley ruined Don. He lost his practice, his wife, and his reputation." Retired cop Patricia then informed me of the most common motives for murder: money, passion, and revenge. "It took Don years to recover. It was a long, hard slog for him, but over time, he built his practice back up. Rumor is he also started seeing someone recently, although I don't know who."

"Wait." I stared at her. "You know what everyone in town eats for breakfast, but you don't know their love lives?"

"People tend to be more discreet about their relationships than their food choices."

"So, do you think this Don guy's a serious suspect?"

"*There* you are. I've been looking everywhere for you."

We both jumped at the police chief's voice, which made Bogie bark.

"Shh, Bogie. It's okay."

"Darling, you startled us."

"I noticed. Sounded like an intense discussion you two were having." Harold Beacham joined us on the bench, crossing his khaki-clad legs. "Did I hear the word *suspect*, or did my ears deceive me? I'm hoping it's the latter."

Pinocchio has nothing on me. I cannot tell a lie. Although my nose doesn't grow, it does turn red and my face gets all blotchy whenever I tell an untruth. Since becoming a priest, I have given up lying altogether, and not just for Lent. "Your ears didn't deceive you, Chief. I'm trying to figure out who could have murdered Stanley."

"Aren't you a bit young to be playing Miss Marple?"

"Trixie Belden," I corrected him. "I'm trying to clear my name."

"Please leave that to the police. No offense, Pastor Hope, but how about you stick to pastoring, and I'll stick to investigating?"

"Sweetheart," Patricia interjected, smoothly changing the subject. "I hope you don't mind, but I've offered up your services to Hope."

"You what?"

"We want to have a women's tea at church and have the men of Faith Chapel serve us. I told Hope you'd be delighted to be in charge of the male servers."

Harold sent a wry glance at my T-shirt and affected an English accent. "Just call me Carson." He stood and gave a bow. "One lump or two?"

Chapter Six

After the Beachams left, I decided to take the long way home. As Bogie and I wandered the outskirts of Apple Springs, I mulled over what Patricia had said about James and his fight with Stanley all those years ago. Adding that to what James himself had revealed to me, could it be he didn't want to see history repeat itself and had killed Stanley before he had a chance to destroy his niece's life as well? Then I thought of what Patricia had said about Don Forrester and how the most common motives for murder were money, passion, and revenge. Based on what she and Susan over at the diner had said about Stanley ruining his former partner, Don Forrester certainly had the revenge factor going for him. Could money also be a possibility? As far as I knew, Stanley and Don were the only two lawyers in Apple Springs. With Stanley now out of the way, Don Forrester would be the only game in town, legally speaking.

Bogie strained at the leash, putting an end to my conjecturing. I noticed an open field before us dotted with massive oaks and squirrels, his favorite toys. "Okay, boy." I unclipped his leash. "Go have fun."

He streaked across the field, heading for the nearest tree and a play date with his furry friends. I watched as two gray squirrels skittered up the trunk of the live oak, keeping up a constant stream of chatter. Bogie hurtled himself at the tree as the noisy duo toyed with him, scampering just out of his reach. Eventually he planted himself at the base of the tree and stared upward, his big brown eyes following their every movement. The squirrels put on a show for Bogie, the larger one playing a game of catch me if you can. The larger squirrel scurried around to the back of the tree, then back to the front, as his chattering pal on the branch above him cheered him on. Bogie followed, barking and circling the tree in a furious attempt to keep up with his bushy-tailed buddy.

David and I used to laugh together over Bogie's squirrel obsession. All my husband had to do was say "Squirrel!" and Bogie would be out the back door like a rocket, racing to our huge pecan tree and barking at the trio of red squirrels that called it home.

Home.

Ready to go home, I whistled, and Bogie came running. Exiting the field, we found ourselves in a small cemetery, and I realized we'd wound up on the grounds of Faith Chapel behind the annex. Christopher had mentioned that the church had a graveyard, but I had missed seeing it when I was last at the chapel crypt. Something about finding Stanley's dead body.

I have always loved cemeteries. When I was young, my parents would take us once a month to put flowers on my grandparents' graves. After paying my respects, I would wander among the graves with my sister, reading the headstones. My girlish heart was touched by the lasting testaments and tributes to those who had

63

gone before, and I would imagine what my headstone might say one day. One thing for sure, it wouldn't be just *beloved wife and mother*—I had more exciting plans for my epitaph. Like dancer, artist, actor, Nobel Peace Prize winner . . .

On our honeymoon, David and I spent a couple of days in Normandy, where we visited the American Cemetery at Omaha Beach. Nothing could have prepared us for the terrible beauty of row after row of thousands of white marble crosses on a hill high above the English Channel. Afterward, we paid our respects at the nearby Bayeux War Cemetery, wandering among the graves of fallen Englishmen, Scots, and Canadians. There the epitaphs were more detailed—often with scriptures or lines of poetry. We saw a few that said, *Greater love hath no man than this; that a man lay down his life for his friends,* but the one that made me weep was *To the world—a soldier. To us—the world.* I recalled those poetic remembrances as I walked through Faith Chapel's graveyard with its mix of old and new headstones. Some of the weather-beaten tombstones told the hard life story of the early days:

Sarah Brown, age 18. Anna Brown, age one day, 1867. Forever united.

Richard Chamberlain, age 1 year, 5 months, 25 days, 1869.
Henry Chamberlain, age 11 months, 29 days, 1870.
Mary Chamberlain, age 17 days, 1870.

A banner over the family headstone of the three Chamberlain children—Marjorie's ancestors, I assumed—read *Lost on earth to bloom in heaven.* I knelt and prayed.

Bogie barked, interrupting my meditations.

A dark head popped out from behind a massive oak a few feet away. "Hey. How's it goin'?"

As I rounded the tree, I saw the head was attached to a teenage girl with a familiar colorful sleeve tattoo and an open sketchbook in her lap. She introduced herself as Riley Smith and apologized for not being able to talk to me at church this morning.

"Megan and her mom got into it, and she needed me."

"I understand. We all need friends we can vent to." I glanced down at the sketchbook. "You're an artist?"

"I wish. I'm just messing around."

"Could I see?"

"They're not very good."

"I'd still love to see them. I always admire people who can draw. I can't draw to save my life. Even my stick people bow their heads in shame." I had scratched *artist* off my imaginary tombstone ages ago.

Riley handed me the sketchbook hesitantly, then focused her full attention on Bogie, stroking his fur while I checked out her art. He rolled onto his back, offering her his stomach, and she scratched his tummy, sending him into dog ecstasy.

I looked at the sketch she was working on—a meticulous charcoal rendering of Faith Chapel with the town of Apple Springs spread out below it and the cemetery headstones in the foreground. As I looked closer, I noticed a fairy peeking over the top of one of the headstones, adding a touch of whimsy to the peaceful scene.

"Wow. This is really good." I turned the page. The next sketch was also of the church grounds, only this time from a different angle. A gorgeous unicorn stood in the center of the graveyard, a mischievous wood nymph on its back, plaiting its mane. Fairies fluttered in the air above the unicorn. It could have been an illustration out of a fairy tale. "These are amazing.

This one makes me want to jump on the unicorn's back and fly off to Neverland."

"Really?" Riley blushed.

"Really. You're very talented. These could be in a children's book. How long have you been drawing?"

"Since I was a kid."

The next sketch was a colored pencil drawing of flowers, hearts, and dragonflies. I glanced at her arm and then back at the sketch. "This is your tattoo."

"Yeah. I knew what I wanted, but the guy didn't have any examples in his shop, so I drew it out for him."

"How cool is that? Do you mind if I look closer at the real thing?"

"Sure." She extended her arm to me.

I scrutinized the vivid ink. A water lily formed the centerpiece of her tat, with vivid green and blue dragonflies flying among trailing fuchsia vines entwined between pink hearts and purple canna lilies. "Gorgeous."

"My grandma had this dragonfly lamp she loved, and I was always fascinated by it as a kid, so drew my inspiration from it."

"That inspiration served you well. How long have you had your tattoo?"

"Six months. It was my eighteenth birthday present to myself."

"My stepdaughter did the same thing when she turned eighteen." I smiled, remembering. "Emily had wanted a tattoo since she was fifteen, but since you can't get one until you're of legal age, she asked us for one as a gift for her eighteenth birthday. Her dad was squeamish of needles, so I took her to the tattoo parlor instead."

"You did? Cool. My mom would never do that."

"Neither would mine. My mother wouldn't even let me wear makeup in high school, much less get my ears pierced." I glanced at Riley. "Are you out of school already?"

"Not yet. A few more months before I graduate. I was held back freshman year." She grimaced. "I suck at math."

"I hear ya. I almost didn't get my bachelor's because I kept failing the requisite math test. Luckily, there was a bonehead math class at the community college my final semester that I passed. Barely." I hadn't used algebra or geometry since, but I kept that fact of life to myself, figuring Riley's parents wouldn't appreciate my telling her that at this so-close-to-graduation juncture.

"Have you been at Faith Chapel long, Riley? Does your family also attend?"

"Nah. They're Baptists. I was raised Baptist, but their music's too happy-clappy for me, so I started coming here with Megan last year. I like the whole liturgy thing. It's cool."

Be still my Episcopal heart.

Riley locked her big dark eyes on mine. "Can I ask you something?"

"Anything."

"Did you kill Stanley King?"

I met her eyes with a steady gaze. "No."

"That's what I thought. I mean, he was a real creep and all, but you didn't even know him. Why would you murder the dude?"

"Exactly. I take it you weren't a Stanley fan?"

"God no!" She blushed. "Sorry. I mean gosh no. He was a pig. Always hitting on every woman in sight, even though he was hella old. Gross." She made a moue of disgust.

My priestly radar went up. "Did Stanley ever hit on you?"

"Yeah. A couple times." She waved it off. "But I told him where to go. Then he hit on Megan, though, and she totally freaked, especially since he used to date her mom. Really creeped her out. She wasn't even seventeen yet. The guy was a real perv."

Good thing Stanley was no longer around. If he were, I would have given him a piece of my mind, and my fist, and then reported him to Harold Beacham. I wondered if anyone ever had. "Did Megan tell her mom about Stanley coming on to her?"

"Are you kidding? Her mom would lose it. Or worse, not believe her. They have their issues. Bonnie's uber-protective with lots of rules—I think 'cause she's a single mom—and Megan has a hard time following all the rules, so sometimes she lies to her mom. Nothing big," Riley added hastily. "The normal stuff. You know. Like saying she's done her homework when she hasn't, or about where she's going, what time she got home. Things like that."

I knew all too well. Emily had gone through her own rebellious teen phase—lying to us about where she had been, what time she had gotten home, and falling for a bad-news boyfriend. Thankfully, she outgrew all that and went on to college and got her degree. Emily was now married to a great guy—a lieutenant in the Air Force—and living in Germany with him and our three-year-old granddaughter, Kelsey.

"Stanley was a total douchebag." Riley's thick eyebrows met in a scowl. "So mean to his kids. Did you know his son Todd's this really amazing artist? You think I'm good, wait until you see some of Todd's stuff. It's epic." A fangirling smile replaced her scowl.

Someone has a crush.

"Todd used to have this cool studio in town where he'd let the art students come and hang out and work on their stuff. Even our teacher painted some of her watercolors there." Riley's scowl returned. "Then his dad kicked him out. Said he needed the space, but it's still sitting empty. That creeper didn't need it. He was just punishing Todd. The scumbag."

"Do you know Todd very well?"

"Kind of." Her cheeks turned pink.

"He seems pretty tight with his sister."

"Yeah. They're like best friends, I guess."

"What about his dad? I understand they didn't get along?"

Riley snorted. "God no. Sorry, I mean gosh. Todd hated his dad. I would have too if he had been my dad. Stanley King was the biggest control freak around. When Todd moved out, his dad couldn't stand it. Didn't want his son to have his own life, so he did all these things to sabotage him."

"Like what?"

"Like putting him down all the time in front of other people, telling him he had no talent, and taking back the car he'd given him for his birthday. The worst thing, though, was two days before Todd was set to have his first art show at the studio, Stanley pulled the plug and kicked him out. Can you believe it? What an a-hole." She blushed. "Sorry, Pastor."

"That's okay. I've heard worse."

"Todd was so upset. He'd been working day and night to have enough pieces ready for the show, but because his dad is such a jerk, suddenly he had no place to exhibit them. Todd had to cancel the show. He was devastated."

"I can imagine. I would be too." *How could a father be so cruel?* I was beginning to get a clearer picture of Stanley King, and it wasn't pretty. No wonder someone had done him in. The question was, could it have been his own son?

"What about Samantha? Do you know her too? How did she get along with her dad?"

"I don't really know her, but Todd said Stanley thought of his daughter as his property and tried to make her his arm-candy substitute wife whenever he had parties."

Bogie nudged Riley to keep petting him. "Sorry, boy. Was I not paying attention to you?" Riley plowed her fingers through his thick fur and scratched his back. "I know you're not supposed to dis the dead and stuff, and I prolly shouldn't say this, but to tell you the truth, I'm glad the guy's dead. He made his son's life and many others' a living hell." She swiveled her head, looking around, and said in a stage whisper, "I think I know who killed him."

Be cool. Don't overreact. "You do? Who?"

"That lawyer guy Don Forrester."

"What makes you say that?"

"Because last Thursday I was sketching here after school, and I heard loud voices in the crypt. There was a lot of yelling, but I couldn't hear what they were saying. Then there was this crash or something, and a few minutes later I saw Don leaving in a hurry."

"What time Thursday?"

"Five forty-five," she replied instantly. "I know because I had to be home for dinner at six and kept checking my phone so I wouldn't be late."

That would go along with the confidential tidbit Patricia had shared with me earlier about Stanley's murder occurring the night before I found him. "You're sure it was Don Forrester?"

"Totally. I'd recognize that bald head anywhere. He's a deacon at First Baptist, and he's been to our house for dinner lots of times. Don's been dating Bonnie, Megan's mom, too. They're trying to keep it on the down low, but we've seen them together a few times." Riley glanced at me. "Everyone knows Bonnie used to date Stanley, but then he dumped her. Who knows? Maybe Stanley started sniffing around Bonnie again and Don got jealous and whacked him."

Or maybe Bonnie found out about her creepy former boyfriend hitting on her underage daughter and lost it. Maybe she told her current boyfriend Don, who'd been ruined by Stanley years earlier and still bore a grudge, and Don finally snapped at this last straw and took care of his former partner permanently.

"Did you tell the police this?"

"No."

"Why not?"

Riley looked down, affecting an absorbed interest in her silver thumb ring. "I didn't think they'd believe me."

"How come?"

"I did something dumb and got in trouble last year." She ducked her head. "Swiped a pair of earrings at the mall down in Sacramento. Stupid. I know. They didn't even cost ten bucks. It was a one-time thing, but everyone in town heard about it. It was like I was walking around with a scarlet letter *T* on my chest." She slapped her sketchbook shut. "Megan's mom already doesn't like me very much. If I went around saying her boyfriend killed someone, she'd probably make Megan stop hanging out with me."

Riley checked her phone and scrambled to her feet. "Gotta go. I have to babysit my brother, and Mom has a cow if I'm late." She gave me a shy smile. "Thanks for liking my drawings."

As I walked home, I added the information Riley had revealed to what I'd already learned. Don Forrester and Stanley King had obviously had a fight in the crypt, but had that fight ended with Don bashing Stanley in the head with Ethel's urn? What about James Brandon and his clear hatred for Stanley? I recalled Samantha's words in the diner. "What if someone finds out?" *Finds out what? That she killed her father?* Then there was Todd King. Stanley had treated his son like dirt and seemed to take great delight in humiliating him. Had he humiliated Todd enough to the point where his son couldn't take it anymore and finally snapped?

My head swirled with all the possibilities. Don Forrester. Todd King. Samantha King. James Brandon. Who was the guilty one?

By the time I got home, my head was throbbing. I popped two ibuprofen and gave Bogie his afternoon treat. Then I made myself a cup of PG Tips and sat down at the kitchen table with a pad of paper and a plate of shortbread.

Is this how you plan to lose those fifteen pounds? my dietary conscience snarked.

Shut up. Certain indulgences are exempt. You will have to pry my cold dead hands off my Walkers shortbread before I give it up. Then I thought of Stanley's cold dead hands and began making a list of suspects and motives. I've always been a list girl. They help me organize my thoughts. Seeing things on paper helps me figure them out. As I mused over all I had seen and heard over the past couple of days, one name rose to the top of the list.

Don Forrester.

Chapter Seven

Monday morning found me back at church at eight a.m. This time Father Christopher was waiting for me in his office with coffee and homemade apple strudel.

"Courtesy of Lottie Wilson," he said, extending a fragrant slice across a stack of papers on his desk. "She makes the best apple strudel in town, much to Marjorie's dismay."

"Thanks. That looks and smells delicious. No coffee for me, though. I'm a tea girl all the way." I held up my portable electric kettle. "Have kettle, will travel." Looking around for a place to plug it in, I couldn't see any outlets due to the massive stacks of papers and folders everywhere.

The rector's ears turned rosy. "Sorry. I'm a bit of a pack rat. Ethel used to keep me in line, but since she passed, the piles keep growing. I can't seem to find anything."

"That's okay. You are looking at the organizing queen. I'll have this sorted in no time. Meanwhile, I can set the kettle up in my office instead."

"Um . . . well . . . we've kind of been using your office as a storage room." His ears turned pinker. "I meant to have it cleared out before you came, but with one thing and another, that didn't happen." Christopher's cherubic face brightened. "There is a credenza in the reception area, however, where Ethel always kept coffee and tea supplies for visitors." He bounded out of his chair and I followed, strudel and kettle in hand.

The credenza was hidden beneath boxes and more mounds of paper. Christopher shifted a few boxes to the floor and transferred some of the stacks of paper to Ethel's old desk. "Aha!" he said, triumphantly holding up a dusty box of Lipton with fake creamer packets peeking over the edge. "What'd I tell you?"

Good thing I brought my own tea and milk. I wiped off the credenza and plugged in my electric kettle. While I was setting up my tea things, I told Christopher about my encounter with Riley Smith and how taken I had been by her drawings.

"She let you see her sketchbook? I'm impressed. It took me weeks before she'd show me any of her art. Riley's usually pretty private."

"It's a girl thing. By the way, when we were talking, Riley mentioned she had some problems last year with shoplifting?"

"Typical teenage stuff. High school girls daring each other to see what they can get away with. The other girls managed to get away with it, but Riley didn't. She was mortified." Christopher looked thoughtful. "I've often wondered if maybe she wanted to get caught to show Megan Cunningham—who can be quite susceptible to peer pressure—the dangers of following the in crowd. Riley's a smart girl. She and Megan are best friends, which makes Bonnie nervous, particularly since Riley covered her entire arm with a tattoo. I told Bonnie not to judge a book by its cover—tattoos have become a form of expression among young people

today." He grinned. "Although most of my fellow old coots in
congregation don't share my elevated artistic awareness. To th
tattoos still mean Hells Angels, prison, and drugs."

"Good thing they can't see mine, then."

"You have a tattoo?"

I nodded. "A small cross and a bird in flight on my lower bacl
David loved Lynyrd Skynyrd's 'Free Bird.'"

"What a lovely way to honor him."

"I thought so. He also loved *Pirates of the Caribbean*, but I
didn't think Johnny Depp's face on my back—or front—would
be quite the thing."

Christopher belly-laughed. "I'm glad we hired you, Hope. You
are exactly what Faith Chapel needs. Some fresh young blood to
breathe new life into this dusty old place full of dusty old folks
and shake things up a bit."

"Too bad so many think I shook things up too much by killing one of those same dusty old folks."

After we finished our tea and coffee, we got ready to head out
on the weekly calls to visit the sick, housebound, and lonely.

"I like to do the pastoral calls on Monday," Christopher
explained, "but since you're now in charge of those, feel free to
switch the day of the week to whenever you like. Although I must
warn you, our mainly blue- and white-haired congregation is used
to Mondays—that's when I've done them for the past thirty-three
years." He grinned. "Before me, Father Henry visited on that same
day for two decades. The parish isn't too big on change."

Ya think?

"I'll stick with Mondays. I think a tattooed woman priest with
a black eye suspected of murder is enough change for now."

75

Father Christopher chortled and pulled out a box of Twinkies from his desk drawer. "Our first stop will be the Jacksons, Bethann and Wendell. You'll like them. They're a little unusual, particularly Bethann, but very nice." His eyes twinkled. "They love their Twinkies."

"I know. We've already met."

"You have?"

I pointed to my eye, now beginning to turn purple and yellow. "Remember? Bethann accidentally bopped me with a garden gnome my first day on the job."

"Oh that's right. Which one was it again? Buddy Holly? Bobby Darin?"

"Elvis."

"Figures. She's had problems with him in the past. He likes to remind everyone he's the King."

I stared at him.

"Don't worry." Christopher chuckled. "I'm not going around the bend. Bethann never had kids, so she looks upon her gnomes as her children."

"Famous children, apparently."

"She's a singer, or was, a long time ago. She named her garden gnomes after her favorite singers." Christopher got a pensive look on his face. "When Bethann first moved to Apple Springs, she told me she got into drugs when she was touring with her girl group in the sixties and had a hard time kicking them. Years later, by the time she finally did, they had scrambled her brain some. As a result, sometimes she gets confused and loses touch with reality. Bethann had a pretty rough life before Wendell," he said. "If she chooses to cope by sometimes living in a fantasy world, who am I to deny her?"

Who indeed? I knew there was a reason I wanted to work with this man. When I first met Christopher at seminary, his reputation for compassion had preceded him. Since then, I had heard many stories of his kindness and his reaching out to *the least of these*, as Jesus told us to do in the Gospel of Matthew. "Good to know. Thanks for filling me in."

As he drove us to our first pastoral call, I said, "I hear the Jacksons had some kind of yard issues with Stanley?"

"Yes. Stanley took great pride in his home and formal landscaping, and Bethann's colorful eclectic style clashed with his upper-crust taste." Christopher frowned. "He always called her poor white trash and tried to buy them out a few times, but the Jackson home has been in Wendell's family for generations, and they weren't about to leave. Stanley then threatened them with frivolous lawsuits—even had them cited for having a rooster in their yard."

"A rooster?"

"Yep. The Big Bopper. They also had a couple hens, Tammy and Gidget," he said fondly. "Bethann was kind enough to share their eggs with me. Apparently, however, it's against the law to have a rooster within city limits, so they had to get rid of Bopper. Honestly, though? I think it was just a smoke screen for Stanley's hatred of their Big Mart yard design choices."

Garden gnomes, *Grimms' Fairy Tales*, and plastic flowers would not be my first choice of yard decoration either, but to each his own. The clutter is what got to me. So. Many. Gnomes. My minimalist mother forever ruined me—I can't abide clutter and mess. Makes me twitch. Like Christopher's office, for instance. All the church offices, in fact. When we finished our pastoral visits for the day, first thing I planned to do was clean out my office and set it to rights. Then I would begin on the other offices, which made me wonder. "How come you haven't filled Ethel's clerical position?"

"It's hard to imagine anyone replacing Ethel," Christopher said. "Besides, our budget will only allow part-time."

"I'm surprised none of the parishioners have volunteered to help out."

A dull flush crept up his neck. "Uh, well, Marjorie has." His words rushed out in a torrent. "Except she doesn't know anything about computers, and Ethel had the Sunday bulletin all set up on the computer. Besides, the altar guild and ECW keep Marjorie pretty busy. I didn't want to overload her. She is eighty-two, after all."

What wasn't he saying? Could it be the old occupational hazard they'd warned us about in seminary? When members of the flock develop a crush on their spiritual leader?

Christopher babbled on. "Thankfully, Patricia stepped up and took over doing the bulletin after Ethel passed. Although she can't do it next month, since they're going on a long vacation with their kids and grandkids then."

I offered to take over organizing and putting together the Sunday bulletin until the requisite clerical help arrived. You would have thought I had offered to donate a kidney the way Father Christopher responded. It all made sense when I later learned that my boss is intimidated by the computer and is only comfortable with email and writing his sermons in Word.

"Well, here we are." He pulled up in front of the scene of my close encounter of the Elvis kind. As we walked through the metal arbor studded with plastic Technicolor daisies and other fake flowers of a color not to be found in nature, I noticed the King off to one side in the front corner of the yard. *Am I imagining things, or did he give me a dirty look?* We approached the arched Hobbit-style front door beyond the *Grimms' Fairy Tales* yard.

Before Christopher could knock, Bethann flung open the door, clad today in a screaming-orange minidress with white polka dots and the ubiquitous white go-go boots. "Welcome to our humble home, Father Christopher and"—she hesitated a moment—"uh, *Mother* Hope?"

"Pastor Hope is fine."

"Oh good. I felt kind of funny callin' you mother." She let loose a girlish giggle. "I've known a few mothers in my time, and you don't fit the bill." Bethann ushered us through the door. "Y'all come right on in now." She led us into the living room, where wall-to-wall bubblegum-pink shag carpet tickled my ankles. Atop the scratchy carpet sat a white sofa covered in protective plastic. Two avocado Naugahyde club chairs sat opposite with a retro blond coffee table between them and a fuzzy pink ottoman off to one side. A garden gnome carhop waitress on roller skates sporting a Pepto Bismol–pink uniform and hoisting a tray with a burger and a shake completed the sixties tableau.

A Pepto Bismol–pink garden gnome. On roller skates. With shades. Oh. My. Eyes. *Should have brought my sunglasses.*

Christopher handed Bethann the box of Twinkies.

"Thank you, Father." She kissed him on the cheek. "You're always so thoughtful. Now y'all make yourselves comfortable, and I'll be back in a jiff with refreshments." She disappeared down a hallway covered in lime-green shag carpet.

Father Christopher sat on one of the avocado chairs and indicated I should do the same. Nodding his head to the couch, he mouthed, "Plastic's slippery."

Probably stuck to bare thighs in summer too. I sank into the other Naugahyde chair, turning my head to take in the rest of my surroundings. A floor-to-ceiling wall of shelves across the room overflowed with hundreds of record albums, while a vintage TV and hi-fi system took pride of place next to the record wall. Above the TV hung a collage of framed photos, where a grouping of three vintage black-and-white pictures caught my eye. A beautiful young blonde with beehived hair, false eyelashes, and white lipstick beamed back at me. *To Wendell, with love, Bethann* was scrawled across the bottom. The other two publicity stills showed our hostess standing in front of two other beehived blonde-haired women, her hand on her hip. Across the trio of photos, a banner proclaimed *Bethann and the Blondelles.*

"Ah see you've found my braggin' wall." Bethann returned with a plate full of Twinkies and Hostess cupcakes. "Wendell insisted on putting those old photos up."

"'Course I did," he said, following his wife with a tray of retro soda bottles: Bubble Up, grape Nehi, Orange Crush, and Coke. "I fell in love with you when the Blondelles played Sacramento in 1966. I will never forget how you signed that photo for me after the concert and kissed me on the cheek. You smelled like heaven."

"That was my Shalimar, honey. It's my signature fragrance."

"Don't I know it?" He winked at us and said, "I get it for her every year on her birthday." Wendell, who was wearing a beige-and-white-striped polo with his ubiquitous beige pants today, set the tray down on the fuzzy ottoman. "Take your pick. Although, Pastor, you may have to arm-wrestle Father Christopher for the grape Nehi."

"No, she won't." Christopher's hand snaked out and grabbed the purple soda. "Sorry, Hope, I need my weekly Nehi fix."

"No problem, Father. We all have our addictions."

Inwardly I groaned. *Did I really just say that, knowing Bethann's history with drugs?* Thankfully, she didn't seem to notice. I settled for the Orange Crush, telling myself it was the closest thing to orange juice and a far better option than Tang. "So how did you two lovebirds get together?" I asked.

Wendell handed his wife the Coke, taking a swig from his Bubble Up before answering. "I first saw Bethann in person at that concert." His eyes took on a faraway look. "She was the most beautiful woman I'd ever seen, with the most amazing voice. I couldn't believe my luck when I ran into her thirty years later at the snack bar of the G.I. Joe convention in Virginia."

"G.I. Joe convention?" My head swiveled from one to the other. "I didn't know there was such a thing. What were you doing there, Bethann? Do you collect Army figures?"

"Pardon me, Pastor," Dell interjected in a professorial tone, "but Joe wasn't only Army. The military years ran from 1964 to 1968. Although we think of Joe as a soldier, all figures and uniform sets were either the Action Soldier, Action Pilot, Action Marine, or Action Sailor. In 1969 they started transitioning away from the military background of G.I. Joe to the Adventures of G.I. Joe and then the Adventure Team."

I stared at the walking, talking G.I. Joe encyclopedia. *Who knew?*

Bethann giggled as she broke a Twinkie in half. "You get my Dell going on Joes and he'll never stop. To answer your question, Pastor, I was at the Barbie convention on the other side of the center. The Coke was out at our snack bar, and all they had was that awful Tab cola that tastes like something the cat drug in." She shuddered and took a long pull of her Coke. "I walked to the other end of the building, passing G.I. Joes left and right to get to another snack bar, and guess who was there?" She stared at her husband, eyes brimming with love. "My Dell." Bethann batted her false eyelashes at him. "Of course, he wasn't my Dell yet."

"Oh yes I was, honeybunch. I was your Dell ever since the first time I met you. It just took me three decades to find you again, and once I did, I told myself I was never going to lose you."

"And you never will, sugar." She planted a big kiss on her husband's lips.

"How long have you two been married?"

"Twenty years," Dell said. "Next month will be our twentieth wedding anniversary. We're going to renew our vows at church and then have a big blowout in our backyard to celebrate."

"Ah can't wait!" Bethann said. "Now that mean ole Stanley's gone, we can have one heckuva party. We'll invite Todd and Samantha too—they're not nasty like their daddy was. Samantha always stopped and talked to me when she saw me out front." She frowned. "Bless her heart. Sami's had some problems, but her biggest problems were with that mean ole father of hers. There were a couple times she was fixin' to run away, but somehow or other Stanley always found her before she got too far and brought her back. Poor thing."

Interesting. I tucked that piece of Samantha-and-Stanley information away to examine later. "Bethann, I love all your southern expressions. I met another southern belle down the street from me recently. Liliane Turner?"

"Shoot, honey, Liliane's about as southern as I'm tall cotton. Ah'm the real southern belle. She just plays one on stage."

"Tall cotton?"

"That means rich in the South."

"Where exactly are you from? I've been trying to place your accent. Tennessee?"

"No, honey, that's Dolly country." Her face lit up like Clark Griswold's house in *National Lampoon's Christmas Vacation.* "You ever been to Dollywood? It's amazin'. Wendell took me for our tenth anniversary. Y'all should go sometime." She scratched her beehive. "What'd you ask me again, Pastor?"

"I was wondering where you're from."

"Oh, that's right. You'll have to excuse me. I get forgetful every now and then." Bethann giggled. "I'd forget my head if it weren't screwed on. Good thing Dell's here to fill in the blanks. But before I go down another cotton-pickin' rabbit trail, lemme answer your question. I was born and raised right outside of Biloxi, Mississippi. Em-eye-ess-ess, eye-ess-ess, eye-pee-pee-eye," she recited in a singsong voice. "Or as I like to call it, the armpit of America." She wrinkled her nose. "Summers down in Biloxi were so humid, everythin' smelled. Biloxi's claim to fame is its military base. On the weekends my girlfriend Suellen and I would go into town and sneak into the NCO Club with our fake IDs so we could meet some of those good-lookin' soldier boys. We hoped one of 'em might be our ticket out of Biloxi."

Bethann's face clouded. "I guess you could say I was tryin' to follow in my mama's footsteps. She run off with a GI when I was nine, and my daddy like to went crazy afterwards, takin' it out on all of us with his belt—and other things," she said quietly. "As soon as I could, I hightailed it out of there. And then I was 'discovered' in a li'l honky-tonk and the rest is history."

Before she continued with the rest of that history, I jumped in. "As a singer, Bethann, I'm surprised you don't sing in the choir. It looks like they could use another soprano."

"Now y'all don't take this the wrong way, Pastor. Father. I don't mean no offense, but that music's too old-fashioned for me. I'm more of a doo-wop girl." She jumped up and belted out "Soldier Boy" for our benefit, demonstrating that she still had quite the voice.

We all clapped, and Dell gazed at his wife with stars in his eyes.

"Bethann, Wendell," Father Christopher said, bringing them back down to earth, "I was concerned when you weren't in church yesterday."

"Ah know, Father. Ah'm sorry. Dell's gout was flarin' up."

"Now, honey, let's not be telling fibs to our priest." Her husband caressed her cheek. "Truth is, Father, we didn't want to hear folks go on and on about what a good man Stanley was now he's dead. Stanley King was an awful human being. I know it's not Christian of me to say, but I'm relieved he's gone. He was very mean to my Bethy and hurt her feelings. If I was younger and stronger, I'd have given him a real thrashing. As it was, all this seventy-eight-year-old body could do was yell at him." His beige countenance reddened. "And you know what Stanley did after that? He laughed and walked away."

Bethann patted her husband's hand. "Let's not talk about that now, sugar. Let's think about happy things." She turned to me. "Pastor, would you like a tour of our home?"

"I'd love one—as long as there are no gnomes lying in wait around corners to bop me on the head."

She giggled and held up three fingers of her right hand. "Scout's honor. Petula's in the kitchen, but she's not high-strung like Elvis."

Chapter Eight

After Bethann showed off her vintage-sixties kitchen, she led me down another hallway. "We call this our higgledy-piggledy house, 'cause it's been added on to over the years and goes all over the place." She came to a door in the hallway and opened it with a triumphant flourish. "This here is Barbie's room. Isn't it pinkiful?"

"It certainly is." The room even smelled pink—the spun-sugar pink of cotton candy, which I realized emanated from a nearby unlit jar candle. Bethann's Barbie room featured the same pink shag carpet as the living room, but here the walls were Pepto Bismol pink as well. A petite pink crystal chandelier hung from the sparkly pink ceiling, and pink floor-to-ceiling shelves held Barbies of every shape and size. So. Many. Barbies.

Bethann proudly gave me a doll-by-doll tour. "This here's Western Barbie, and Day-to-Night Barbie, and Enchanted Evening Barbie—don't you just love her white gloves and tiny white fur stole? Then there's Kissing Barbie, Wedding Day Barbie, and Malibu Barbie." She proceeded to show me a host of other Barbies whose names I couldn't keep track of.

"I don't think I've ever seen so many Barbies in one place before."

"Shoot, honey, then you haven't been to a Barbie convention."

Another item to add to my bucket list.

Leaving Barbie world, Bethann nodded to another closed door across the hall. Dell's G.I. Joe room, she said, adding that he would want to give me an in-depth tour of all his Joes, so it would be best to save that for another visit.

Thank you, Lord.

When we returned to the living room, Father Christopher and Wendell were discussing the legal threats Stanley had made against the Jacksons and their home in the past.

"It's our property!" Bethann burst out. "He had no rights to it. We don't live in one of them fancy communities with all those DOA rules and such."

"That's HOA, honey," Dell said. "Homeowners' association. DOA means dead on arrival."

"I'm always getting those alphabet words mixed up." Bethann giggled. "But I guess it means Stanley's DOA, huh? Now that that old sourpuss is no longer with us, I have a confession to make." She leaned in and said in a stage whisper, "Once I let all the air out of the tires of that fancy Lexor of his."

"Lexus," Father Christopher said.

"Lexus-shmexus. Nothin' beats a Caddy in my book."

* * *

"I always leave the Jackson home with a smile on my face," Christopher said as we exited the gnomey front yard.

"And Twinkies and grape Nehi in your tummy. Should I order some for the office?"

"Oh no. I don't want too much junk food around tempting me. My once-a-week indulgence is plenty."

As we walked, I told Christopher about my idea for the English tea. He gave me his blessing and brought me up to speed on the rest of our visits. Next, we were going to see Bob and Velma Hastings. Bob owned the barbershop on Main Street, Christopher informed me.

"He fell and broke his hip a couple months ago, and although he's almost fully recovered now, his wife, Velma, is mostly a shut-in, with Parkinson's and lymphoma." My boss stopped abruptly on the sidewalk. "I need to warn you, though—Bob's the one who stormed out of the service when you were speaking. He's old-fashioned. Doesn't believe women should be priests, and they certainly shouldn't preach in church."

"He must have been a good friend of Stanley's."

"Stanley didn't have friends, good or otherwise, but he and Bob definitely shared some similar opinions." Christopher pulled a face. "Very loud opinions. They were both on the same page about 'the fairer sex.' I tried to remind them that Jesus treated women as equals, but I wasn't very successful. My prayer is that once Bob gets to know you and sees you in action, he'll come around. Shall we give it a shot?"

"Why not? What's the worst that can happen? Besides the tar and feathers, that is?"

We turned the corner and approached a buttery yellow cottage with a manicured lawn. Gorgeous red camellia bushes hugged the front of the house, window boxes brimmed with pansies, and sunny daffodils reminded me of England and Wordsworth. *I wandered lonely as a cloud, that floats on high o'er dales and hills, when all at once I saw a crowd, a host of golden daffodils . . .*

Christopher knocked. A few minutes later, the robin's-egg-blue door swung open to reveal a beaming Bob Hastings holding on to his walker. Quite a difference from the surly man I had seen at church.

"Father Christopher, right on time." Then he saw me. Sparks flew from his faded blue eyes as they locked on to my dog collar. His hands shook as he gripped his walker. "What is *she* doing here? I will not allow that woman—that affront to the church—into my home."

Well, all righty then.

"Now Bob—" Christopher began.

"It's okay." I laid my hand on his arm. "You go ahead. I'll catch up with you later."

"Are you sure?" He sent me a concerned look.

"I'm sure."

My job was to provide spiritual comfort and care to parishioners who needed it. With this congregation, much of that comfort would involve the elderly and sick. Forcing myself on a frail old man adamantly opposed to women priests, and with an ailing wife to boot, would do more harm than good. That didn't mean Bob Hastings's deep-seated antagonism didn't rankle, even sting, but now was not the time to show that. I hitched up my big-girl pants and told Father Christopher I would meet him in the square when he was finished. Then I nodded to the elderly man. "Mr. Hastings. Please give your wife my best. She's in my prayers."

As I turned and walked away, I took deep breaths in and out. I've never been big on conflict, thanks to my upbringing with a rageaholic father. I used to quake at the prospect of any kind of discord and went out of my way to avoid it. Over the years, however, I've learned how to manage my response to conflict and not let it get the best of me. Arriving at the square, I sat down on Dorothy's husband's memorial bench, pulled out my phone, and texted my San Francisco sister-in-law.

Guess what? The good old boys club is alive and well in Apple Springs.

I paused before hitting send. Did I really want to whine to Virginia?

Of course you do. She's your oldest friend, and you don't know anyone else here well enough to join you in your whinemobile. You can't whine to anyone at Faith Chapel. Even senior warden Patricia. As her pastor, it would be inappropriate to dis one member of the church to another.

That's one of the reasons our bishop always encourages his priests to have friends outside the church to confide in. My go-to person has always been Virginia. I hit send.

Within seconds, her response appeared.

Virginia: *No! Say it isn't so. Thank God you told me. I thought we would NEVER figure that out.*

Me: *Funny.*

Virginia: *Did another good ol' boy walk out on you?*

Me: *No. The same one who left in a huff yesterday wouldn't allow me to darken his door today. Once Barber Bob saw me, he nearly burst a blood vessel. Good thing he wasn't giving someone a haircut. Talk about a close shave.*

Virginia: *Ba-dum-bum. So what happened?*

Me: *He wouldn't let me in his home, so I left. Guess he thought I'd contaminate the place.*

Virginia: *Probably afraid you'd give his wife ideas. LOL.* She added a wink emoji. *Some men can't handle a strong woman. But other than that, how's it going?*

Me: *Good. I spent more time with the Elvis-gnome couple earlier and I've been learning more about some of the townspeople. I think I might have a good lead on a possible suspect.*

Virginia: *Beehive woman and Beige man?*

Me: *Yes. Their names are Bethann and Dell and they're actually quite sweet. Eccentric, but sweet.*

Virginia: *Eccentric seems to be the word of the day for Apple Springs. So, which one is your suspect?*

Me: *Neither. Well—the husband might be, but there's someone else who seems a lot more likely. He—*

"Hi, Pastor Hope."

I looked up from my phone to see two women from the congregation whom I recognized as the altos who had joined Dorothy's standing ovation when Christopher introduced me. Could I remember their names, though? Not a chance. The joys of midlife. "Hi there. How are you?"

"Fine," said the tall, older one. "We wanted to say how happy we are you're at Faith Chapel. It's great to have a woman priest."

"Thank you." I sent her a winning smile, hoping it would off-set the fact that I had forgotten her name.

"Long overdue," said her shorter, younger pal, who introduced herself as Judy. "It's about time we had some female leadership in church. Seems Apple Springs is always a day late and a dollar short. It takes us a while to catch up with the rest of the world."

You want to pass that on to Bob the barber?

Her tall pal, who revealed that her name was Jeanne, said, "Pastor, I don't suppose you sing, by any chance? You may have noticed our choir's pretty thin."

"Except for Ed," Judy said.

Jeanne snorted. "He's loud enough to carry the bass section by himself. Now, if we could only get him to sing in tune."

"Elizabeth tries, but it's like banging her head against a brick wall. She's hoping to find another bass soon to try and balance him out."

The choir director, Elizabeth Davis, and I had met during cof-fee hour yesterday but had not gotten a chance to talk much. I was looking forward to tomorrow's staff meeting, where I would hope-fully get to know her better. As we were the only two women on staff, it would be nice to share a comrades-in-arms kinship.

"Well, I'm not a bass, but I do sing, although it's been a few years since I was in choir."

"That's okay. It will come back to you. It's like riding a bike," said Judy, who seemed to have an affinity for clichés. "Are you an alto or soprano?"

"Soprano."

"First or second?"

"First. I don't read music that well, so I need to stick to the melody."

"Works for me," Jeanne said. She grinned and high-fived a beaming Judy. "Now the women will be evenly matched. We need to start hunting for some men."

"I've been doing that for years," Judy said, "and come up empty-handed."

"Nuh-uh," Jeanne said slyly. "What about Stanley?"

Stanley? Inwardly I did Bogie's Scooby impression—*Aarug?*—while outwardly I maintained my pastoral composure. Here was the perfect opportunity to learn more about the dead Mr. King from someone who might have known him intimately.

Judy blushed. "As I said, I came up empty."

"Stanley King? Did you two date?"

"If you can call three dates dating."

"What was he like?"

"Very charming. At first. Flowers, fancy dinners out, compliments out the wazoo, the whole nine yards. When Stanley turns his attention on you, he's laser-focused. Makes you feel as if you're the only person in the world. It was all a game to him though, a game I caught on to quickly. Once I did, the real Stanley came out." Judy made a face. "The nasty, narcissistic player without an ounce of empathy. The charm disappeared in a New York minute. After that, whenever I saw him, he acted as if I didn't exist, which was fine by me. I really dodged a bullet there."

"Stanley didn't." Jeanne winked.

"Huh?" Judy's forehead creased. "He was shot? I thought someone hit him over the head with Ethel's urn."

"You're so literal. It was a joke."

Judy stuck out her tongue at her fellow alto before turning to me. "Elizabeth will be over the moon to learn we have a new soprano."

"As over-the-moon as Elizabeth gets," Jeanne said. "She's what you'd call reserved."

The two altos then filled me in on choir details, including what to expect from our choir director. Elizabeth Davis might be distant in her social interactions, Judy said, but when she put on her director's hat, she was a stern taskmaster who pushed them hard and demanded excellence.

"Works for me," I said. "I like to be challenged." After a few more minutes of polite chitchat, the double-Js left.

I then returned my attention to my phone to discover multiple texts from Virginia.

Virginia: *He what? Don't leave me hanging after saying there's a likely suspect in the murder.*

Me: *You there?*

Virginia: *Everything okay?*

Me: *Sorry. Everything's fine. Can't talk now. I'll call or text you later.*

I leaned back against the bench and thought about my morning so far. When I woke up today, I had not expected to join the choir. I've always loved to sing, as did David. It was one of the things that drew us together—that and our love of old movies. We had been in choir together at St. Luke's, but when David got so sick, we had to drop out. After he passed, I couldn't face rejoining the choir and not seeing David in his familiar seat in the tenor section. This was a new church, though. A new choir. And I was ready—no, eager—to sing again.

Then I thought of Bob Hastings, and my good mood dissipated. How was I ever going to get him and others like him to accept me? I might have to face the fact that they never would, and I would have to make my peace with that. I couldn't force it, but neither was I going to turn tail and run because some old guys got their boxer shorts in a twist. As we had learned in seminary, not everyone in church is going to love you. It's a fact of clerical life.

One of those church people who did not love me walked past just then—Marjorie Chamberlain, in a yellow-and-orange-checked polyester pantsuit. She pretended she didn't see me and kept right on walking.

Chapter Nine

I felt the need. The need for tea. Maybe even a piece of Susan's yummy pie.

Pie? Seriously? After the junk food you had at the Jacksons?

It was only half a Hostess cupcake, I reminded my dietary conscience. *I didn't even eat the whole thing. It would have been impolite to refuse, especially during my first pastoral visit. The last thing I need is any more negative commentary.*

Susan looked up from wiping down the counter as I entered the nearly empty diner, which smelled of bacon, cinnamon, and coffee. "Looks like someone needs some liquid refreshment."

"Got any margaritas behind the counter?"

"Sadly, no. I'd offer you a good cup of coffee, but since you're the tea queen, why don't you take a load off while I go get you some boiling water?"

I sank into the back booth where I could gaze upon Cary Grant—always a good way to improve my mood. *North by Northwest* is one of my favorite Grant-Hitchcock collaborations. I used to wish I were Eva Marie Saint hanging from Mount Rushmore with my leading man of choice. However, gazing at Cary didn't help this time.

Susan returned, steaming kettle in hand. "Now what happened to give you such a hangdog expression? I thought priests were always supposed to be mellow and beatific like Bing Crosby."

"Easy to be beatific when you're male and not the spawn of Satan." I pulled out my PG Tips and dropped it into the cup. "I just came from the Hastings'."

"Ah, that explains it." Susan poured the steaming water into my cup. "Bob's—how shall I put this nicely? A chauvinist. He's usually fine with me because I know my place. After all, I make and serve food—the best job a woman can have, after being a wife and mom." She dropped into the seat across from me. "But when I dared to challenge him as a contender for president of the rotary club a few years ago, he about blew a gasket."

Sounds like my parents. When my mom and dad learned of my decision to become an Episcopal priest, they went ballistic. Called me a heretic and said I was going against the natural order of things. I invited them to my ordination, although I knew they wouldn't come, and they didn't disappoint me.

I snapped out of my walk down unhappy memory lane when I noticed Susan's lips moving.

"Think of yourself as the spiritual Obi-Wan facing off against Darth Vader," she was saying.

"Bob Hastings isn't Darth Vader. I'm not sure I'd even consider him a stormtrooper." *Actually, he reminds me more of Yoda, with his wispy head and big ears*—but I didn't say that aloud.

"You're right. Stanley King was actually Darth Vader. Or some other kind of alien life-form." Susan snapped her fingers. "That's it. Stanley was that ancient evil alien, and you're Sigourney Weaver. Ripley was such a badass. Remember that last scene when she blasted that freakin' alien into deep space?"

"Don't forget *Aliens* when she was protecting the little girl Newt and said, 'Get away from her, you you-know-what.'"

"You can't say the b-word?" Susan glanced at my collar. "Oh yeah, I guess you can't."

Although there is no official rule in the Episcopal Church against profanity and bad language, most priests avoid it. It was easy for me not to indulge because of how I was raised. I've shed much of my repressive upbringing, but some of it still clings to me like plastic wrap. "I can't say the f-word either—and not the f-word you're thinking of," I confessed. "It wasn't allowed in our house. We had to either say *toot* or *pass gas*. Actually, I prefer what they say in England—break wind."

Susan snorted. "Okay, Dowager Countess. Or is it Lady Hope?"

The bell over the entrance jangled, and I looked up, expecting to see Christopher. Instead, in walked my number-one murder suspect in a gray suit and red power tie heading straight for me.

The lawyer strode over, gave me a huge smile, and stuck out his bear paw of a hand. "Welcome to Apple Springs, Pastor Hope. Sorry I haven't had a chance to meet you yet. I'm Don Forrester, Baptist and attorney-at-law, although not necessarily in that order." He released a hearty laugh. "May I join you?"

"Of course." *Saves me having to come up with an excuse to seek you out.* I motioned for him to sit.

Before he did, the jovial lawyer clapped his beefy hand on Susan's shoulder. "Susan, could I have a cup of joe and some of your fabulous blueberry pie?"

"You got it."

Don smiled and waved at someone across the room, then gave a thumbs-up to a middle-aged man at the counter before sliding into the booth across from me. He turned his full attention on me, giving me a megawatt smile, which revealed blinding white teeth. "So, what do you think of our little town so far?"

I think you must have a great dentist.

"I really like it. Apart from the obvious first-day debacle, of course."

He tilted his head to one side, the way Bogie does when he's confused.

"Finding Stanley King dead in the columbarium and being accused of his murder?"

A scowl replaced Don Forrester's smile. "I won't pretend I'm sorry that ass—pardon my French, Pastor—piece of sh—I mean jerk, is dead. He got what was coming to him."

"That seems to be the prevailing opinion. Still, it's disconcerting to be thought of as a murderer."

"Why the hell—excuse me, heck—would you kill Stanley? You didn't even know him, did you?"

"No. I met him once."

"Well then."

Susan reappeared with his pie and coffee. "Here you go." To my dismay, she lingered. "How's it going?"

"Can't complain, can't complain."

I sipped my tea and listened with half an ear as the two caught up on the latest town gossip, trying to think of a way to bring the conversation back around to Stanley so I could casually grill his former law partner.

Susan beat me to it. "Pretty shocking about old Stan-the-man, huh? I don't think our sleepy town has ever had a murder before, has it?"

"Not that I know of," Don said, greedily forking down a mouthful of pie.

"So who do you think did it?" She leaned in and lowered her voice. "Some jealous husband? A spurned lover? Business associate?"

Don choked on his pie. He grabbed his coffee and took a big gulp as his face turned red.

"Are you okay?" I hoped I wasn't going to have to give him the Heimlich. I knew how—I'm certified in first aid and CPR—but Don was a big guy, and I wasn't sure I'd be able to wrap my arms all the way around him.

He took another gulp of coffee. "I'm okay. Went down the wrong way."

Susan brought him a glass of water, which he downed.

"Better?"

"Much. If you'll excuse me for a minute, I think I'll go to the little boys' room."

"Knock yourself out," Susan said. "Sure you're okay?"

He nodded.

We watched after him as he headed to the back of the diner.

"Well played, my friend, well played. Do you think he thinks you're hinting he may have murdered Stanley?"

"Maybe." Susan leaned in and whispered. "But also I was tired of looking at those teeth. The guy beams all the time like he's frickin' Santa Claus or something. And even more so now that his ex–business partner's kicked the bucket."

The bell over the front door jangled again. Father Christopher entered and looked around. Spotting me, he smiled and hurried over. "I thought you might come here for some fortification." Then he noticed the half-eaten pie and coffee opposite me. "I'm sorry. Am I interrupting?"

"Not at all. Have a seat." I scooted over. "Don Forrester will be back in a minute."

Susan held up the coffeepot. "Coffee, Father? And pie?"

"I'd love a cup of coffee, but no pie today." He patted his pot-belly. "I've had my fill of sweets this morning."

"Well, that's a first."

"I need to keep my boyish figure."

Don returned but did not sit back down. He dropped a ten-dollar bill on the table and said he had to leave for an appointment. The lawyer made his farewells and left, considerably less jovial than when he'd arrived.

Christopher filled me in on the Hastings visit, and we discussed the upcoming vestry meeting and myriad church-life details until we couldn't put it off any longer.

"Are you ready for this, Hope?"

"Yep. Let's do it."

Our final pastoral visit of the day was with Todd and Samantha King to discuss their father's funeral and burial arrangements. Christopher had given me a heads-up that the siblings would probably be unpleasantly surprised at what their father had arranged.

Dealing with the bereaved is a tricky situation and can often turn ugly. Particularly when it comes to funeral arrangements. Sometimes one family member has a plan in mind while another has a very different idea. Trying to manage the needs of each family member requires tact and diplomacy. In this case, however, Stanley had not left much to chance. His instructions were quite clear.

As we walked, Christopher told me how Stanley liked to play games with people. His latest game had been to tell his children he was going to cut them out of his will and leave all his money to the church instead.

"And did he?"

"I have no idea. As far as I know, they haven't read the will yet, but I can't imagine Stanley would have left his children high and dry. They were Kings, after all, and he wanted to leave a legacy."

Most people consider their children their legacy, I thought. Stanley, however, from everything I had learned about him, defined himself by his affluence. *It would not surprise me one bit if he wanted to leave Apple Springs some sort of lasting monument of his wealth.*

Passing the Jacksons' gnome wonderland, we continued around the corner to Stanley's mansion. A tall boxwood hedge separated the two houses, blocking Stanley's view of Bethann and Wendell's higgledy-piggledy home and yard. We climbed the wide stone steps of the Italianate mansion, and Christopher rang the bell.

Samantha opened the door, wearing skinny jeans and a black tee. "Father Christopher. Pastor Hope. Thank you for coming." Although her eyes were red-rimmed, she seemed more composed today. She led us into the foyer, where I noticed a framed picture of Stanley and world-renowned opera singer Luca Giordano on the entry table, with Stanley holding a program from *La Bohème*. My favorite tenor. His version of "Nessun Dorma" always gives me chills.

"Was your father an opera lover?"

"Nope." Todd joined us, clad in a Pink Floyd T-shirt, board shorts, and flip-flops. "What the King loved—besides money and himself—was being part of the elite rich and famous, and documenting it for everyone else to see."

"Todd, please," Samantha said.

"What? I'm just telling it like it is." He nodded at the wall behind us.

I turned around to see a collage of framed photos of Stanley King and various luminaries: Ronald Reagan, Steve Jobs, Joe Montana, Clint Eastwood, Arnold Schwarzenegger, Mary Kay Ash, and Vanna White. Interesting that the only two women on the celebrity wall were the founder of a cosmetics empire famous for its coveted pink Cadillacs and a pretty blonde who pushes letters on TV for a living. "That's quite a collection."

"Yes, my father was very proud of his wall of fame," Samantha said.

"Prouder than he was of his offspring. Notice my sister and I didn't make it onto good old Dad's wall," Todd said. "We're in good company, though. Meryl Streep and Gloria Steinem didn't make the cut either. He met them at a fund raiser where he was spouting his usual sexist crap, and they eloquently cut him down to size." He grinned. "One of the highlights of my life."

"Why don't we go into the living room?" Samantha led us into the large, celery-green high-ceilinged room with coved ceilings, crown molding, plush Oriental carpets, and a massive marble fireplace. In front of the fireplace stood a tall man, his back to us, gazing at something on the mantel. He turned as we entered, and I saw he had been looking at a silver-framed photo.

"Father, you know Uncle James, but Pastor, I don't think you two have met."

"We have, actually. Yesterday, when I was walking my dog." No basketball shorts today, though. James Brandon was wearing gray dress slacks and a black button-down shirt, which highlighted his gray-flecked hair. *If I was in the market, I might take a second look, but I've never been a big shopper.*

Samantha sent her uncle a questioning glance.

"Nessa-the-Brave went into full-on protect mode against the reverend's big Lab."

"My big *chicken* Lab. Bogie hid behind me while Nessa warned him off her turf."

"I'd like to have seen that," Todd said.

James glanced at my eye. "I like the purple and yellow."

"Shall we all sit?" Samantha said. "Would you like iced tea or coffee? Father, I've got your favorite French roast and chocolate pie from Suzie's."

"Sounds heavenly."

I watched in surprise as Christopher accepted the piece of pie he had turned down at the diner not ten minutes ago. Probably to fortify him for the difficult task ahead. With that in mind, I accepted one as well so as not to be rude.

As we ate, we made small talk about the weather (mild, with the potential for a cold snap), James's Realtor job (encompassing Apple Springs and nearby Sutter Creek as well), Todd's art (he was working on some new pieces for a client), Samantha's return to school (for a teaching credential), and their beautiful home. Much to my surprise, I learned that the Italianate mansion had formerly been Marjorie Chamberlain's ancestral home.

"I can't believe Marjorie sold this place," I said, looking around. "She's so proud of her heritage, I'd have thought nothing could move her from her family home." Marlon Brando's Godfather popped into my head. *Maybe Stanley made her an offer she couldn't refuse.*

"You obviously didn't know the King," Todd said. "He always had to have the best and the biggest. Chamberlain House was the best and biggest stately home in town. He bought it as a wedding present for my mother years ago."

James scowled. "Lily hated it. This place was way too big and grand for her. She would have preferred something smaller and simpler. She always called it the prisoner's palace."

"Mom knew what she was talking about." Todd shot his sister a meaningful look. "Right, Red?"

"That's another story for another day," Samantha said. Setting down her half-eaten piece of pie, she looked at her uncle, who gave her an encouraging nod. "Uncle James has been a huge help in all of this." Her voice trembled. "I don't know what we'd have done without him. Thank you," she said to him as she retrieved a piece of paper from the table beside her.

"You're welcome, sweetheart. Any way I can lend a hand, you let me know."

"Nice to have you back in the palace again, Unc," Todd said. "How many years has it been since you were last here?"

"Quite a few, but that's in the past. Time to look forward now."

"I agree." Samantha took a sip of water and cleared her throat. "Father, Todd and I have been talking, and as he was a longtime member of Faith Chapel, we know Dad would like to have the funeral at church. We're hoping maybe the choir could sing his favorite hymn, 'Amazing Grace,' and we'd like Elizabeth Davis to sing 'Pie Jesu.' Dad always said she had the most beautiful voice." Samantha consulted her notes. "Afterwards, we'd like a reception in the parish hall, followed by a private family interment as we place Dad next to Mother in the columbarium." She looked over at her brother. "Did I miss anything?"

"Nope. You've got it pretty much covered, Red."

Father Christopher looked distinctly uncomfortable. I had never been more grateful not to be the one in charge. I watched closely to see how Christopher was going to handle it and sent up a quick prayer for him.

"Samantha. Todd." My boss tugged at his collar. "I'm afraid your father has made other arrangements."

"What?" Samantha said.

"What kind of arrangements?" Todd asked.

The rector cleared his throat. "Well, for one thing, Stanley has a burial plot in the church cemetery beside the fountain."

Samantha paled and James scowled.

"Are you frickin' kidding me?" Todd said.

"I'm afraid not. He also has a headstone ordered that he picked out online a few years ago."

"Online?" The siblings exchanged incredulous looks.

"He found an online company that makes headstones you can preorder," Christopher said. "He told them what he wanted, and it should be ready within the next couple days. All that remained

to be added was the date of death, which I sent to them at your father's request after he passed."

Tears pooled in Samantha's eyes. "But he should be next to Mother. She was his wife."

"Like that ever mattered to him before," James, who was sitting in the chair next to me, said under his breath.

"We should have known the chapel crypt with its simple plaques was good enough for our mother, but not the King," Todd said.

"I'm sorry." Father Christopher looked wretched. "I tried to talk him out of it, but he was adamant."

The tears Samantha had been trying to hold back spilled down her cheeks.

Todd clenched and unclenched his fists. "What other surprises does the King have in store for us?"

Christopher consulted a piece of paper he had pulled from his pocket. "As you'd suggested, he wants Elizabeth to sing 'Pie Jesu,' but he wants to follow it up with a recording of Frank Sinatra's 'My Way.'"

Todd snorted. "Figures. Did he also want a marching band with dancing girls in short skirts to lead the graveyard procession?"

* * *

"Well, that was fun," I said as we descended the stone staircase after Christopher shared the remainder of Stanley's detailed funeral arrangements with the King family. "What's next? Sticking bamboo shoots under our fingernails?"

We opted to forgo the bamboo shoots in favor of work. Back at the church, Christopher returned phone calls and I set about

cleaning and organizing the chaos and clutter better known as my office. Removing my clergy vest and setting it to one side, I rolled up my sleeves and donned a large apron I had brought from home. Then I dug in.

The first thing to go was a broken TV-VCR combo, followed by three rickety folding chairs. Next, I discarded an old bowling ball, vacation Bible school posters from the nineties, and a worn men's tennis shoe. Not a *pair* of shoes—*one* lonely, tired, beat-up old shoe. I found two coatracks in decent condition, so I moved one to the reception area and kept the other. Then came piles and piles of boxes—some half full with old clothing or papers. I condensed a few of the boxes until I had four large empty ones, which I marked *Keep*, *Save*, *Dump*, and *Maybe*. Then I started filling them.

A popular cleaning book recommends thanking each item for its service before discarding it, but that was not going to happen. I'm all for manners, but I'm never going to thank some smelly old shoe. If I did that for every item, I would be here until Christmas. As I worked, I prayed I wouldn't find any critters nesting in the piles of junk. Bugs and spiders I can handle; rodents are something else altogether. As much as I hate stereotypes, I have to admit that rats and mice freak me out. All my degrees, training, and professional expertise fly out the window in the face of creatures with long skinny tails. Including possums. I scream like a girl if I see one. As far as I'm concerned, possums are simply big mentally challenged rats.

Picking my way through the mess, I cleared a path to my desk, also piled with boxes. I removed the boxes and stacked them next to the desk. Then I tossed a dead plant, some dusty pens, and

packets of hot chocolate that had expired seven years ago. As I sorted through the boxes, I found stacks of old bulletins going back a decade. I kept ten of each and dropped the rest into the recycle box.

Half an hour later, Christopher wandered in. "Wow! I'm going to start calling you Wonder Woman."

"Nah. I've never been good with a whip, and I'd probably get my metal cuffs caught on my vestments when I tried to deflect gunfire. Besides, these hips would never fit into Wonder Woman's costume. Although I can kick some serious cleaning butt, if I do say so myself."

"That you can." He glanced down at the discard box. "Hey, that's my old bowling ball. I've been looking everywhere for it."

"You have? For how long?"

"A few months. Well . . . maybe a year or more."

A scripture from Matthew floated through my head—*Do not store up for yourselves treasures on earth*—but I decided not to quote it to my boss just then. "The rule of thumb in organizing is if you haven't used something in more than a year, you get rid of it. Unless you love it or it has great sentimental significance."

Christopher picked up the ball and cradled it to his chest. "Both of the latter," he said. "I'll take this to my office." Then he noticed the box of discarded bulletins. "You're throwing away bulletins? What if someone wants to look up something from a past service?"

"Some of those bulletins go back twenty years, Father. I've pulled ten from each year to archive, but we don't need more than that." I smiled to soften my cleaning-commando stance. "Unless you plan to wallpaper your office with them?"

"You're right. I know. Ethel called me a hopeless pack rat. She was always after me to get rid of stuff too."

"I'm happy to carry on her tradition. Do you know how long ago she started posting bulletins online?"

"Maybe four or five years ago?"

"Well, there you go. We have an online record if anyone wants to go back and look at an old issue."

Christopher protested that some of the older members did not know how to use computers or even own one, which was why they always printed out hard copies. I reassured him that past bulletins would always be available for members in the archives.

Changing the subject, I said, "I was surprised to learn the King mansion used to be Marjorie's. I wonder why she sold her beautiful family home. Especially to Stanley. They weren't close, were they?"

"No. I don't think anyone was close to Stanley." Christopher set the bowling ball down and perched on a nearby chair. "As I recall, there were some serious structural issues and other major repairs at the time that Marjorie couldn't afford to make. I believe she was having some financial difficulties at the time as well—bad investments her husband had made or something." A pained look crossed his features. "She was quite distraught at having to sell her home. I found her crying over it once. Only once, though. Marjorie is made of strong stuff. She comes from sturdy pioneer stock, you know."

"I know. Too bad she can't transfer some of that sturdy stock to Samantha King. I'm glad she and Todd have their uncle for sup-port." I looked at Christopher. "I understand James and Stanley got into a fight at Lily's funeral?"

"Yes. James blamed Stanley for her death, and not without some cause. Lily was so young when she got married. I think she was looking for stability and a father figure more than a husband. She found both—at first—in Stanley, but it wasn't long before he became abusive."

"He beat her?"

"No. Stanley was too smart for that. Instead, he abused her mentally and verbally. Things were better for a while after she had Todd—Stanley Todd King Junior."

I stared at him. "Todd is Stanley Junior?"

"Not anymore. Once he was old enough, Todd dropped the Stanley, which, as you can imagine, did not go over well." Christopher expelled a sigh. "Father and son have always been at loggerheads. Before Todd turned three, Stanley was back to his old verbally abusive tricks. To cope, Lily lost herself in pills and booze." He shook his head as if trying to dislodge the memory. "After the fight at her funeral, Stanley kept the kids from their uncle, but Todd started sneaking off to see James when he was a teen."

"How about Samantha? Did she sneak off to see her uncle too?"

"A few times, but when Stanley found out and flew into a rage, she stopped. Until she turned eighteen. Then she'd visit James with Todd, but always on the sly."

And I thought my family was dysfunctional.

Chapter Ten

Opening my front door, I kicked my shoes off.

"Hey, watch where you're throwing those gunboats. You could knock a person's eye out."

"Virginia?"

"The one and only."

I flung my arms around my sister-in-law, who had popped up from my red toile wingback. "What are you doing here?"

She hugged me to her generous bosom. "I thought you could use some moral support."

Bogie nudged his head between us, wanting attention. I knelt down and gave him a hug, ruffling his fur. "Did you know Auntie Virginia was coming?"

As I looked at my sixty-year-old sister-in-law in her sleek black pants and white button-up shirt, unbuttoned to show just a hint of voluptuous cleavage, my heart swelled. Virginia always reminded me of a slightly older Kristin Chenoweth—tiny but mighty, only with auburn hair. From the moment David first brought me home to meet his older sister, Virginia had welcomed me with open arms and made me part of the family. Eighteen years my senior, she had started out as a surrogate mother to me, but over the years had become my friend. My best friend. I could always count on her to support me and have my back.

That fact was never more evident than during the final leg of my English monastery tour when I was mourning David. Virginia surprised me at my single-bed churchy lodgings in Oxford and spirited me away to the Randolph, the sumptuous five-star hotel in the heart of the city. There we luxuriated in king-size beds with eight-hundred-thread-count sheets, room service, and our choice of spa offerings. After a full day of seaweed wraps, hot-rock massages, and mani-pedis where we caught up and laughed over Virginia's latest goofy romantic escapades, we enjoyed the most decadent tea of my life.

That evening when we got back to our room, my sister-in-law sat beside me and clutched my hands in hers, her vivid green eyes bright with tears. "Hope, it's time to come home. You can't shut yourself off from the world. I know you're hurting, but I'm hurting too." Tears spilled down her cheeks. "I don't know what it's like to lose the love of your life, because I've never had that, but Davy was my baby brother—my favorite person in the world." She choked back a sob. "His death broke my heart, but one thing I know for sure: he would want you to go on living." Her nose ran and dripped into her D cups.

"Um, you might want to clean up your cleavage." Extricating my hands from hers, I grabbed a tissue from the bedside table.

Virginia took the proffered tissue and began dabbing at her chest. "You ruined my big speech," she said, pouting. "I practiced it the whole flight over."

Now as I looked at my sister-in-law and best friend, I wondered one thing. "How did you get in here, anyway?"

"I threw myself on your neighbor Nikki's mercy. You told me she had an extra key in case of emergency. I told her I'd driven all the way from San Francisco and was in desperate need of a bathroom; otherwise I was going to burst." She grinned. "I think my doing the pee-pee dance convinced her. She was going to call you to make sure it was okay, but I told her I wanted to surprise you. Once I showed her photos of us on my phone along with a recent text from you, that did the trick." Virginia plopped down on the sofa and kicked off her three-inch stilettos to admire her pedicure. The woman has the tiniest, daintiest feet of anyone I've ever known—size four and a half. I'm a nine and a half, and she never lets me forget it.

I stuck my foot alongside hers. "It looks like my foot had a baby."

"A very pretty baby." She wiggled her coral-polished toes.

"So, when I was texting you earlier, you were here all along?"

"You got it, Sherlock. If you'd checked Find My iPhone, you'd have seen me at Twenty-Seven Clover Lane, but since you never use that handy-dandy feature, I knew my secret was safe." She got up and poured me a glass of Chardonnay. "Here. You look like you could use this."

I relieved her of the glass and took a sip as I headed down the hall to my bedroom, unbuttoning my clergy vest as I went.

Bogie and Virginia followed. "So, what's the latest on the dead rich guy? Do the cops still think you did it?"

"So much for small talk."

"I believe in cutting to the chase. You know that."

"Yes, I do. It's one of the things I love about you." Bogie jumped on my bed and did his usual three-circle rotation before settling down on top of the pillows and regarding us with a sleepy eye. "To answer your question, no. At least I don't think so." Opening the closet door, I shed my clerical garb and pulled on a pair of black jeans and David's old Beatles' *Abbey Road* T-shirt.

Virginia perched on the edge of the bed. "So spill. Got any clues, Trixie?" My sister-in-law well knew of my childhood love for Trixie Belden. She had replenished the young-adult novel collection my ultra-strict, ultra-religious, patriarchy-focused parents had thrown out when they discovered teen-sleuth Trixie was "way too independent for her own good."

I sniffed the air. "Wait. Is that what I think it is?"

"Yep. Your favorite. Chicken marsala."

I raced to the kitchen, lifted the lid of the stove-top skillet, and inhaled deeply. Virginia is an amazing cook. Recently retired, my sister-in-law had run a successful catering business in San Francisco for years. Her stuffed pork tenderloin was renowned throughout the Bay Area, and her chicken marsala is the best I've ever had. She can make an amazing meal out of nothing, as evidenced by the countless times she's whipped up something from my forlorn fridge and spartan cupboards.

"And that's not all," Virginia said. She opened the nearly empty fridge to reveal a white pastry box stamped with a familiar logo and tied with string.

"Ooh, you went to Stella's?" I threw my head back and did my best Marlon Brando yell. "Stella!" The iconic Stella Pastry and Café in San Francisco's North Beach has the best cannoli around, bar none. The crunchy outer pastry shell dusted with powdered sugar and the creamy ricotta filling studded with chocolate chips is heaven. I'd never had cannoli until I met David and his sister, but once I tasted my first bite, I could understand why Clemenza said in *The Godfather*, "Leave the gun. Take the cannoli."

"Dinner's not quite ready," she said, turning the flame down low and removing the lid. "It needs to simmer for about fifteen minutes."

We sat at the kitchen peninsula, where Virginia had set out bruschetta topped with fresh tomatoes, goat cheese, and basil. As we drank our wine and nibbled on bruschetta, I filled her in on life in Apple Springs. Then she brought me up to date on her latest escapades in online dating. Virginia had tried one site but discovered it catered to a younger crowd and was too raunchy for her, so she'd recently registered on a site that catered to those over forty. As she was telling me about an interesting fifty-eight-year-old prospect, the doorbell rang.

"Who could that be?" I slid off my barstool.

When I opened the door, there stood diner owner Susan Jacobs holding a foil-wrapped plate.

"Hey there." Susan extended the plate. "I heard about Stanley's latest dirty dealings with his kids and knew you had to be the bearer of bad tidings, so I thought you could use a pie to take the edge off." Then she noticed the wine in my hand. "Although it looks like you're already covered in that department."

"Actually, Father Christopher was the one who had to break the unwelcome news." I invited Susan in.

"I already took him a pie. Chocolate. His favorite. I brought you apple, since you went into fits of ecstasy over your last piece."

"Is that right?" Virginia's voice behind me said.

Uh-oh. Now I'm in for it. My sister-in-law is justifiably proud of her homemade apple pie. Many have called it the best apple pie in the City. It was the go-to dessert choice on her catering menu, and several customers had standing orders for it. I introduced the two women.

"Is this the sister-in-law who's not supposed to know I make the best apple pie you've ever had?" Susan said with a wink.

I sent Virginia a weak smile. "I love you."

Virginia's green eyes bored into Susan's. "I feel a Bake-Off coming on."

"Bring it on."

Both women looked at me expectantly.

I held up my hands. "I'm not judging it. *Judgment is mine, saith the Lord.*"

"There she goes, bringing her work home again," Virginia said, teasing me as she always does about my professional calling. "Don't you know you're not supposed to talk about religion or politics in polite company?"

"Sorry. Occupational hazard." I ushered them both to the kitchen table. "Thanks so much for the pie, Susan, but you didn't have to go out of your way to bring it over."

"It's not out of my way. I live two doors down. In fact, I have a bird's-eye view of your backyard from my upstairs bedroom window."

"You do?" I stared at her. "You never said."

"You never asked. I was going to mention it, but then we got sidetracked talking about Stanley."

"The dead Stanley?" Virginia asked.

"None other. The topic on everyone's lips, which would thrill him no end." Susan noticed the bubbling skillet on the stove. "I should go. I don't want to interrupt your dinner."

"Not at all," Virginia said. "In fact, why don't you join us? There's plenty for three."

"Are you sure? It smells amazing. Better than the Lean Cuisine I have waiting for me at home."

"You're married to a cook," I said. "Why on earth would you eat a TV dinner?"

Virginia gave a knowing nod. "Sounds like a case of the cobbler's children having no shoes."

"You got it," Susan said. "Besides, it's Mike's poker night. On poker night, I eat TV dinners in the den and snuggle up with a favorite old movie. Tonight it was a toss-up between *Breakfast at Tiffany's* and *You've Got Mail*."

"Well, you're in luck," I said, "because I happen to have both."

Virginia groaned and laid her head down on the table, sliding a look at Susan. "Don't tell me you're an old movie buff too?"

"Yes, ma'am. Considering Hope's current situation, though, I think we should switch from a romantic comedy to a murder mystery. How about *Double Indemnity*?"

"Nope," I said. "Barbara Stanwyck was guilty in that movie. I'd prefer one where the heroine is innocent." I set another plate as Virginia brought over the chicken marsala, baby red potatoes, and steamed broccoli. My mouth watered at the tantalizing aromas of my favorite meal. I took a bite, and a moan escaped.

Virginia nodded at my chicken. "Would you two like to be alone?"

"I can't help it. This is like heaven on a plate."

"This is pretty amazing," Susan said. "I don't suppose you share your recipes?"

"Not usually, but sometimes I make an exception. Let's talk once I taste your apple pie."

As we ate, Susan asked about Virginia's former catering business, while Virginia in turn quizzed Susan on how long she and Mike had been in town and how they liked owning a restaurant—something she had considered doing. While the two foodies talked, I focused my attention on enjoying every bite of my chicken marsala. After dinner, I cleared the table and took the dishes to the sink.

"You know," Virginia said, "rather than watching a movie, I think we should spend the time figuring out a strategy."

"Strategy for what?" I rinsed the plates and stuck them in the dishwasher.

"Clearing your name and figuring out the real killer. You know, in most whodunits, it always turns out to be the least likely suspect. Who would that be in this bucolic small town?"

"Dorothy Thompson," Susan said without hesitation.

"Sweetheart Dorothy?" I stared at Susan.

"She said the least likely suspect. That's definitely Dorothy."

"Who is this Dorothy?" Virginia asked.

"The sweetest little old lady in town. There's no way she could have killed Stanley."

"You never know." Virginia put on her reading glasses and pulled a small notebook from her purse. "What was her relationship to the deceased?"

"She didn't have any relationship with Stanley," Susan said, "other than attending the same church he did and teaching his kids years ago."

Virginia scribbled in her notebook. "Did she ever have any problems with the deceased?"

"Just the same ones everyone had with Stanley."

"And what would those be?"

"An overall dislike of his all-around assholiness," Susan said.

"Virginia, the woman is eighty-one, less than five feet tall, has advanced osteoporosis, and walks with a cane," I said. "No way could she have bashed a man who was at least a foot taller than her in the head with a heavy urn. Besides, what would be her motive?"

"Then give me some other options."

Susan began ticking off names on her finger. "Don Forrester. James Brandon. Todd King. Samantha King. Wendell Jackson."

The same names I had written on my list. With the exception of Wendell. I pulled out my notepad from the kitchen junk drawer and handed it to Virginia. "And maybe Bonnie Cunningham. Stanley used to date her, and I hear he hit on her daughter Megan when she was sixteen."

"Are you serious?" Susan's eyes flashed. "That pig. If Bonnie ever found out, she would have punched his lights out. Our local florist may be on the prim and proper side, but she's a mama bear when it comes to her daughter. And if Bonnie didn't deck Stanley, Albert would have."

"Albert Drummond?" I recalled my Henry Fonda–ish admirer from coffee hour.

"Yep. Bonnie's father. He's not as frail as he looks. The man is a Korean War vet. Got a purple heart for saving some of his men during combat. I wouldn't expect him to do any less to protect his granddaughter from Stanley."

Virginia scrawled down Albert's name. "That's quite the list," she said, setting down her notebook and going to the fridge.

"Before we go any farther, though, who's ready for dessert? Susan? Hope?"

"Yes, please," I said.

"Cannoli or apple pie?" My sister-in-law fixed me with a challenging look.

Bethann's Twinkies never looked so good. My mouth was watering for my favorite cannoli that Virginia had brought all the way from Stella's. Yet not to choose Susan's homemade pie would be rude. Finally I took a page from King Solomon, who in ancient times, when he was faced with deciding which of two women was the mother of a baby both claimed to be theirs, ordered the baby cut in half so each woman could have a part of him. The real mother, not wanting her child to be killed, of course, told Solomon to give the baby to the imposter. "I'll have both, please, but can you cut the cannoli in half and give me only a sliver of pie?"

Virginia opted for the pie. After a few bites, she had to grudgingly admit that Susan's was "a smidge" better than hers.

We continued our discussion of the possible murder suspects, and as we talked about Wendell, I mentioned that his wife Bethann had been the lead singer of a sixties girl group back in the day.

Virginia squealed. "Bethann and the Blondelles? You didn't tell me your Elvis-gnome Bethann was *the* Bethann from the Blondelles. I almost wore out their record *Raindrops, Bubblegum, and Daisies*, playing it over and over again when I was ten." My sister-in-law sent me a beseeching look. "I want to meet her. Do you think if I bring my record next time I come, she'll sign it for me?"

"Sure, and if you're nice, she might introduce you to Petula Clark and Bobby Darin too."

Chapter Eleven

Tuesday I didn't need to be at work until eleven, so I decided to get some housecleaning done first. I inherited my clean gene from my neatnik mother. I also inherited her need to have music blaring while she cleaned. Unlike my neatnik mother, however, who loved the Statler Brothers, I preferred to get down and dirty to Abba. Scrolling through my playlist, I started mopping the kitchen floor to "Waterloo." I was vacuuming the living room and rockin' out to "Dancing Queen" when the music abruptly stopped.

"Hey!" I turned around to see Virginia setting my phone down and picking up hers.

"What have I told you about that bubblegum stuff?" she said. "You need to listen to some *real* music." She scrolled through her phone and pressed play. Suddenly Tina Turner blared out "Proud Mary." "Oh yeah," Virginia said, cranking up the volume.

We jammed to Tina as I continued vacuuming and Virginia dusted. Between the music and the vacuum cleaner, we couldn't hear anything else. Like the doorbell. Which is how I wound up coming face-to-face, or rather face-to-butt, with a disapproving Marjorie Chamberlain and her pal Lottie. As I was wildly gyrating my hips in a pathetic white-girl-can't-dance attempt to emulate Tina, a scandalized "Well I never!" caused me to whirl my still-shaking hips around.

"Marjorie. What are you doing here?"

She started to answer, then clapped her hands over her ears. I shut off the vacuum and made a motion to Virginia to turn down the music.

Once she had, Marjorie, who was wearing a lime-green pant-suit, said primly, "Dorothy told us about your ladies' tea idea, so we came to discuss it with you." She frowned at my flushed, sweaty face and then looked over at a glistening Virginia in her V-necked tank, which displayed her ample cleavage. "The question, though, is what are *you* doing, Pastor?"

"Killing two birds with one stone. Getting our aerobics in and cleaning the house at the same time."

Lottie giggled. "That looks like a fun way to clean house. I love Tina Turner." She sang a snatch of "Let's Stay Together" and busted a move.

"Go, Lottie."

Marjorie pursed her lips at her friend. "Remember your age, dear, and your brittle bones. If you're not careful, you could fall and break a hip."

Lottie immediately stopped dancing. "You're right, of course. Pastor, would it be okay if we sat down?"

"Of course," I said, ushering them over to the couch. "Why don't we all take a seat." I introduced the two older women to my sister-in-law and offered them something to drink.

Virginia smiled at Lottie and Marjorie. "We've also got some of Susan's great apple pie, if you'd like."

"No, thank you," Marjorie said, averting her eyes from Virginia's glistening bosom. "We can't stay long." She turned to me as I settled into my toile wingback. "Pastor Hope, I know you're a busy woman with a lot on your plate," she said briskly. "I've come to relieve you of some of that burden. I will be happy to take over the ladies' tea so you can concentrate on your work—particularly all those dear souls requiring pastoral care. That is your main ministry, correct?"

Lottie fidgeted uncomfortably, but Marjorie plowed on before I could answer. "For years, Ethel Brown and I did a lovely ladies' tea at Faith Chapel, so I have all the necessary recipes, linens, china, and silver. It's quite a lot of work to put on a proper tea—too much work for you." She delivered a condescending smile. "I know you recruited dear Dorothy as a sort of de facto adviser, but Dorothy's never put on a major event such as this, and I think it would be way too much for her. She does make some lovely lemon squares, however, so that can be her contribution."

I'd like to make a contribution to you, Marjorie, but I don't think you'd like it. Sensing Virginia bristling opposite me and about to let loose on my cradle-Episcopalian parishioner, I jumped in before she could.

"Thank you so much for your kind offer, Marjorie. I appreciate it, but I'm really looking forward to organizing the tea. It will give me a good chance to get to know all the women of the church." A trickle of sweat left over from my Tina-dancing dripped between my shoulder blades. Pushing my spine against the back of my chair, I trapped the trickle with my T-shirt blotter before it could drip down into my capris.

"I'm glad you stopped by, though. I was planning to call and ask if you'd like to head up one of the committees. I haven't gotten everything all figured out yet, but someone will need to be in charge of food, someone else the decorations, and I'm sure there's other things as well. I know you've done tons of teas over the years, and I'd love to have your help and expertise." I sent her the sweetest pastoral smile I could.

Apparently, help was not in Marjorie's vocabulary, however. She huffed out, followed by Lottie, who mouthed to me behind her friend's lime-green polyester back, "Sorry."

"Well, that went over like liver and onions," Virginia said.

Chapter Twelve

Wednesday morning when I met Elizabeth Davis, the quiet fiftyish choir director during our staff meeting, she was, as altos Jeanne and Judy had predicted, pleased to get another soprano. "I'm so happy you've joined the choir," Elizabeth said in a soft voice as she clasped my hand between hers. Her words of welcome belied the dispirited expression in her eyes, however.

Faith Chapel's choir director was a slight, pale woman with a slender swan neck and espresso-colored hair shot through with strands of silver and pulled back in an elegant chignon. It was obvious that she had once been a beauty, but something—the vicissitudes of life, perhaps?—had worn that beauty down. A lacy network of fine lines covered her ivory face, while deep-set dark circles under her hazel eyes made her look perpetually sad and tired.

"I've always loved to sing," I said, hoping talk of music would cheer her up. "But I have to warn you, I don't read music very well. I can tell when the notes go up and down and when I'm supposed to hold a note, but I wouldn't know a *G* from a *W* if it came up and bit me in the diaphragm."

A flicker of a smile crossed Elizabeth's careworn face. "That's okay. You don't need to know the alphabet to sing. Watch me and listen to the singers next to you."

"Will do. The good news is, after I hear a song a couple times, I've got the melody down and I'm good to go."

"Perfect."

"Now if we can get another tenor and bass, the choir will be at full strength once again," Christopher interjected.

"Yes," Elizabeth said. "Luckily, the altos can help with the tenor parts, but we're definitely hurting in the bass section. If only George hadn't defected to the Baptists last year."

"I tried to get him to stay at Faith Chapel, but the siren song of the dark side was too strong." Christopher winked, and we laughed. The laugh transformed Elizabeth's tired face. I determined to do my part to make her laugh more often.

Christopher got an odd look on his face. "And of course we lost Stanley's bass too."

My head swiveled from one to the other. "Stanley King was in choir?"

He nodded.

"Until he died?"

"No. He dropped out last year, right before our busy Christmas season, leaving us in the lurch." Elizabeth's pale lips compressed. "Stanley wasn't a team player." She turned to the rector. "Father Christopher, would you like to finalize the musical selections for the rest of the month now?"

*   *   *

That night I attended my first Faith Chapel choir rehearsal, bringing the total number of choir members to eight: three altos, three sopranos, a lone tenor, and Ed, the loud, out-of-tune bass. I was the youngest member at forty-two.

At rehearsal everyone was friendly and welcoming—too friendly when it came to bass Ed, who went in for the too-long, full-on body hug. I quickly rotated into the patented side hug I had perfected for occasions like this. One choir member who was not very friendly was Rosemary, the older soprano next to me, who apparently viewed me as some kind of threat. When I stumbled over a couple of passages in the anthem, she took great delight in pointing out my errors to the rest of the group, all under the guise of innocent confusion.

Rosemary raised her hand during one particularly difficult passage in the Latin anthem scheduled for Sunday. "Elizabeth, isn't that a G?"

"Yes."

"Just checking. Thanks. Oh, and isn't the word *sincero* pronounced *sin-chair-o*?"

At break time, the two J altos came up to me, beaming. "Pastor Hope, we're so glad you've joined us," said tall Jeanne.

"Yes, we are," short Judy said. "Already the soprano section is sounding fuller."

Rosemary, standing behind Judy, stiffened at the remark.

"Did you hear the news about Stanley?" Judy continued in a stage whisper.

"No. What?"

"His Rolex watch was apparently missing from his wrist, which makes the police think his murder may have been a robbery gone bad."

Inwardly I did a mental fist pump, while outwardly I maintained my cool, unruffled composure. If Stanley's death truly was a result of a robbery gone awry, people would stop suspecting the worst of me and give me a chance and my job would be secure.

"Well, I wouldn't be at all surprised if Samantha King killed her father and stole his watch," Rosemary snarked. "Everyone knows she has terrible gambling debts."

"That's true," echoed her soprano shadow Helen.

"After all," Rosemary said, "with daddy gone and his kids set to inherit his fortune, Samantha's now sitting pretty."

"That's an awful thing to say." Judy swung around and scowled at her. "That poor girl has been through enough. She doesn't need you starting new rumors about her."

Rosemary flushed, but before she could reply, I interjected, "Rosemary, do you think you might be able to help me with the anthem sometime before Sunday? I'm struggling in a few places, and I can see you really have it down."

"Certainly." She favored me with a magnanimous smile. "I'd be happy to help, Pastor. I know it can be a bit overwhelming when you're new."

Elizabeth clapped her hands. "Okay, everyone, break's over. Back to work."

The rest of rehearsal went well, and afterward I lingered to talk to our choir director, but she was in a rush. Again. After our staff meeting earlier today, I had invited Elizabeth to lunch in an attempt to get to know her and do some woman-to-woman workplace bonding, but she had excused herself by saying she had another appointment and hurried off. Now when I tried to talk to her, she rebuffed me again.

"I'm sorry, Pastor, but I have to dash. I have to get up early for work, and I still have a bit of a drive ahead of me."

*   *   *

As I walked home, I wondered why Elizabeth seemed intent on not spending time with me. Could it be she also thought I might have killed Stanley, even after the latest news of the theft of his watch and police suspicions of a robbery? Or was I being paranoid? Then I remembered what she had said earlier about Stanley's quitting choir and not being a team player. Elizabeth, like much of Apple Springs, seemed to be firmly in the not-a-fan-of-Stanley camp.

At Suzie's I stopped for a cup of tea and found Virginia and Susan laughing together in a booth. Apparently, they had gotten over their competitiveness from the night they met.

"What's so funny?" I asked, sliding in next to my sister-in-law.

"Oh, we were swapping terrible-customer stories. How was choir?"

"Nice. It felt good to be singing again."

"How's Elizabeth as a director?" Susan asked.

"Great. She really knows her stuff. I've never seen anyone so sad, though."

"Really? What's the scoop on her, Susan?" Virginia asked.

"No gossip, please," I said, holding up my hand in a stop motion.

"Hope's being PC—pastorally correct—but I'm not as pious," Virginia said. "So spill, please. Hope, shut your ears."

I knew I should excuse myself and get up to use the restroom, but I really wanted to know Elizabeth's backstory as well. Maybe then I could help in some way.

Yeah, right. Keep telling yourself that, Pastor Do-Good. It's not like you're not dying of curiosity yourself.

Susan leaned in and lowered her voice. "Elizabeth went through a really bad divorce. It crushed her. She adored her husband, but evidently he was a real player who cheated on her all the time. Apparently, he skipped town with some bimbo and left her holding the bag financially. She lost everything and had to start all over—that's why she's working two jobs now. Besides choir director, she's also got some part-time government job in Sacramento she commutes to every day."

"Men can be such pigs," Virginia said.

My sister-in-law had dated her fair share of males of the porcine persuasion. She used to tell me I got the last good man with her brother.

Susan stood up. "I assume you want your usual water for tea?"

"Yes, please."

"Any pie?"

"No, thanks. If I keep eating how I have these last few days, I won't be able to fit into my vestments. I don't think the congregation would appreciate a priest who's bursting at the seams." The song from *Carousel* played in my head. Unlike June, I did not want to be busting out all over.

"I can think of a couple people who'd probably appreciate it a lot," Susan said dryly before she left to get my hot water.

Virginia filled me in on all the things she'd done today while I was at work. She had decided to stay a couple of days to check out the town, keep me company, and make some of her mouthwatering home-cooked meals in place of the peanut-butter-and-banana sandwiches and salads-in-a-bag I usually lived on. "Well, Hope, your Apple Springs is quite a cute little town. It's got some nice houses for sale. I had a Realtor show me a few."

"What?" I stared at my sister-in-law. "Are you thinking of moving here?"

"Maybe. You never know. If I sold my condo in the City, I could make some serious bank and buy a house outright here." She sent me an innocent look. "At least that's what the real-estate guy James said. He's quite the hottie, by the way. I like that whole George Clooney vibe he's got going on." She leaned over and whispered. "He even gave me a first look at this gorgeous Italianate house he said will be going on the market soon."

"The Kings are selling their family home?"

"Shhh. That's not for public consumption yet. I just thought you might find it interesting." She sat back with a satisfied smirk.

Had I been Spock, I'd have arched a high eyebrow. "You're sleuthing, aren't you? You have no plans of leaving San Francisco and moving here. That was a ploy to investigate James Brandon. Right?"

"Maybe. Or maybe I really am considering leaving the rat race and moving here to Mayberry now that I'm retired and I decided to kill two birds with one stone." She leaned in and said, "And speaking of killing two birds, did you know Stanley's wife Lily was barely seventeen when they got married?"

"Seventeen?" I knew California had no minimum age requirement for getting married, unlike most states where the age is eighteen. I had discovered this in my last parish when a pregnant sixteen-year-old wanted to marry her twenty-year-old boyfriend. I counseled them not to rush into marriage, since she was so young, but they got a court order and parental consent and were legally married. "How in the world did you find that out after just one afternoon with James?"

"You know me," Virginia said, exaggeratedly batting her lashes. "I have my ways."

True. My sister-in-law never met a stranger. People tell her everything.

Susan reappeared with my water. "What'd I miss?"

"Did you know Lily King was only seventeen when she married Stanley?" I asked.

"No. Stanley always said she was eighteen. Although he was in his forties when they tied the knot, so in my book that still makes him a perv."

"Another reason James probably hated him," I said. Would her younger brother have tried to stop Lily from marrying Stanley?

Virginia's voice intruded on my thoughts. "In other news, I heard a certain mansion might be going on the market soon."

"I thought that wasn't for public consumption."

"Susan's not public. She's our friend."

"That's right," the diner owner said. "And I know how to keep my mouth shut. Unless I'm bribed with filthy lucre. Then all bets are off."

I stirred my tea and took a sip. "Well, I happen to have some interesting—and helpful—news as well."

"Spill." Virginia's eyes sparkled as Susan slipped into the booth beside her.

"Apparently, a Rolex watch was missing from Stanley's body, leading the police to suspect his death could have been a robbery gone wrong."

"That's not news," Susan said. "That was all over town two hours ago."

"Sure was," Virginia said. "I don't even live here and I heard about it."

"Great. I go to rehearsal for a couple hours, and when I come out, the whole place is abuzz."

"Better get used to the small-town rumor mill," Susan said. "No one's secrets are safe."

"Good thing I don't have any, then. What I want to know, though, is if the Rolex theft story is a rumor or a fact."

"Why not get it straight from the horse's mouth?" Susan inclined her head to Harold and Patricia Beacham, who had just walked through the door.

The Beachams headed our way, and I introduced them to my sister-in-law, who piped up, "So, we hear the dead guy's watch was stolen and it looks like a robbery gone bad. Does that mean Hope's off the hook?"

The police chief frowned, but his wife said, "Honey, it's all over town already. You might as well fess up."

"Pastor Hope has been off the hook for a while. The estimated time of death was several hours earlier than the time she was found in the crypt with the deceased. And yes, Stanley's Rolex watch was missing, so robbery is a possible motive and one of the lines of investigation we're pursuing."

One of the lines? It didn't sound like it was the main line. And the time of death had been several hours earlier than Friday morning? How many hours was *several*? I thought back to what Riley had told me in the cemetery about hearing loud voices in the small chapel and then seeing Don Forrester leave in a hurry the evening before I discovered Stanley's body. I scooted out of the booth. "Could you excuse us, please? I need to talk to the chief for a moment. Harold, do you mind if we go outside?"

"Not a problem." He kissed Patricia on the cheek. "I'll be back in a minute, sweetheart. Could you order me a cup of coffee, please?"

As we walked to the door, I could feel all eyes on me. Virginia's, in particular, were boring a hole in my back. I knew I'd need to give her the scoop once we got home.

Once we were outside, the chief said, "I guess you're going to give me a piece of your mind for not letting you know you weren't a suspect." He quirked an eyebrow. "I had the feeling, however, that someone had already passed on that information to you."

"That's not what I want to talk to you about. I knew I didn't murder Stanley, and I knew you'd realize that pretty quickly as well. You're no dummy."

"Thanks for the compliment. I think."

I scanned the vicinity, then stepped closer to the chief. "I think I know who killed Stanley King. You said he was killed several hours before I found him in the columbarium Friday morning, right?"

He nodded.

"How many hours?"

"You know I can't reveal those specifics."

"What if I guessed a certain time frame? Say, maybe between five and seven p.m. the night before?"

Harold narrowed his eyes. "What made you come up with that specific time period?"

"Because at five forty-five Thursday evening, someone heard yelling in the columbarium, followed by a loud crash. Moments later Don Forrester was seen leaving in a hurry."

"Who told you this?"

"I'm not at liberty to say. It was revealed to me in confidence, but I thought it was information you'd want to know." I patted myself on the back for my investigative prowess. Trixie Belden would be proud.

Chapter Thirteen

M y idea for the English tea was running into some resistance. Not the actual tea itself, but the fact that I was in charge of it. Father Christopher had given his blessing and carte blanche to do whatever I wanted, within a specific budget, but I was getting pushback from some of the women in the congregation. Led by Marjorie, naturally.

After her earlier unsuccessful attempt to take over the tea, Marjorie Chamberlain let it be known around church how she felt about being "pushed out to pasture" by the new, young "upstart" priest. A few of Marjorie's pals in Faith Chapel's women's group, whom Dorothy had approached to see if they would bake or make sandwiches, rebuffed her and told her in no uncertain terms that it was disgraceful to cast Marjorie aside "like an old shoe."

Invited to speak to the ECW group at their monthly luncheon, I talked up the tea and said how much I hoped they would all attend and that some would lend a hand, but the battle lines were clearly drawn. None of Marjorie's cronies would help, except for Lottie, who volunteered to assist me in any way she could. That was a surprise. I knew how tight the two women were and that wherever Marjorie went, Lottie went. At the same time, I was pleased to see Lottie coming out of Marjorie's shadow.

After Virginia left Thursday morning to return home, the tea-planning committee, made up of Patricia, Dorothy, Lottie, and me, met at the diner to go over plans. Patricia reported that Bonnie Cunningham, owner of Bonnie's Blooms, had volunteered to do the flower arrangements at cost. Patricia offered to provide pink tablecloths, in two different shades, left over from her daughter's wedding the year before.

"Reminds me of Julia Roberts' wedding in *Steel Magnolias*," I said, affecting a southern accent. "'My colors are blush and bashful. I have chosen two shades of pink—one is much deeper than the other.'"

"Great chick flick," Patricia said. "Sally Field made me cry."

"I liked Shirley MacLaine as Ouiser." I recited, "'You are evil and you must be destroyed.' Anyway, now we need to decide about the food. Dorothy, since you lived in England, would you head up the food committee?"

"Me?"

"Yes. Why not?"

She sent a doubtful glance at her cane, propped against the table. "Are you sure?"

"I have complete confidence in you, Dorothy."

"Me too," Patricia said. "Why don't you tell us about the teas in England and what they ate there?"

"Well, it was always a nice mixture of sweet and savory."

"Savory?" Lottie quirked an eyebrow.

"Salty or spicy rather than sweet. Finger sandwiches usually, or in the winter, something hot, like soup or quiche. Since it's

spring, though, I think we should have three kinds of sandwich
Cucumber sandwiches are a must, and one or two with some ki
of meat filling." Dorothy's face fell. "I was counting on Marj
rie's delicious curried-chicken salad, but I guess that's not goir
to happen now." She shot a hopeful look to Lottie. "Do you thin
there's any chance Marjorie might come to the tea?"

Lottie, who was taking notes, shook her head. "You know how
Marjorie is when she gets her dander up."

I heaved an inward sigh. I knew I had really stepped in it with
Marjorie and needed to make amends. She was a longtime member of the congregation, after all, and from one of the founding
families, while I was the new girl in town. *Correction. New priest.*
I determined to try yet again to smooth things over with Marjorie.

Patricia offered to make salmon-salad sandwiches, which she
had served to great success at her recent book club luncheon.

"Perfect," Dorothy said, turning to me. "Didn't you say your
sister-in-law gave you a recipe for ham sandwiches with an apricot
cream cheese spread?"

I nodded.

"Yum," Lottie said. "Sounds delicious."

"Okay," Dorothy said, eyes agleam, "then we've got our three
sandwiches: cucumber, ham, and salmon-salad. Now we need to
decide on two kinds of scones. I recommend the classic English
scone—I have a great recipe from when we were stationed over
there—and another with some kind of fruit, usually currants, rai-
sins, or blueberries." Our former resident of Great Britain then
explained that a classic English tea needs to be served on a three-
tiered tray with savory offerings on the bottom, scones in the center, and dainty desserts on top.

Luckily, Dorothy and I both had a couple of the three-tiered English china trays at home, and Patricia said she'd order one online. Dorothy suggested that she and Patricia could go to some of the antique stores in nearby Sutter Creek to hunt for a few more.

"Please say you'll make your amazing lemon squares, Dorothy," Patricia begged.

"If you want, but we'll need something chocolate too."

Lottie shyly offered to make her triple-chocolate brownies. "Everyone always seems to love those."

"What's not to love?" Patricia said. "Best. Brownies. Ever."

"Thank you. I was thinking, to make them more petite and tea-like, I could bake them in mini-muffin tins and maybe add a dollop of whipped cream with a cherry on top."

Patricia groaned. "I'll have to wear a loose dress that day, since there's no way I'll be able to button my pants after all that."

"You and me both," I said, determining to increase my daily walking between now and the tea.

Dorothy tapped her chin. "Now let's see . . . we still need one more petite sweet for the top tier."

Susan, who had stopped by our table several times during the planning meeting to fill coffee cups and water glasses, asked, "Do you have to be a member of Faith Chapel to get in on this tea action? If not, I could make mini fruit tarts. They're like my pies, only smaller and cuter."

"Really, Susan?" Dorothy and Lottie chorused.

"You'd do that?" I said. "That would be amazing. Thank you."

"As long as you don't make me join your church club."

"Not on your first visit," I said quoting another *Steel Magnolias* line. I looked at Susan. "You've given me an idea . . ." I

turned to the rest of the planning committee. "What's to say our tea needs to be only for Faith Chapel? What do you think about maybe making it a community-wide event and opening it to all the women in town?"

"I love that idea!" Dorothy said.

"So do I," Patricia said. "We've been wanting to have more community events, but we'd have to run it by Father Christopher and the vestry for approval."

"Of course." *Oops. Way to forget going through the church's chain of command,* Pastor *Hope.* I really needed to work on my tendency to blurt out whatever popped into my head in the moment.

"I think it's a wonderful idea," Patricia continued, "but we should discuss how many women to invite. If it was Faith Chapel only, we'd probably have twenty tops."

"Less than that if Marjorie and her pals don't come," Dorothy said.

"What's the maximum the parish hall will accommodate?" I asked.

"Sixty," Patricia said. "And that's tight."

"So maybe we limit it to the first fifty women who sign up?"

We discussed selling tickets to recoup the cost, with Susan weighing in on what we would need to cover the cost of food and Lottie, who lived on Social Security, worrying that it might be too much. Finally, we agreed on keeping the costs down as much as possible by asking church members to donate food or go in with others to donate some of the ingredients.

"Remember, we want to make this an outreach to the community," I said.

"As long as you don't try and convert everyone," Susan said.

"No, we'll just make everyone stand up on one leg and recite the Nicene Creed while balancing a teacup on their head."

* * *

Munching on a peanut-butter-and-banana sandwich at home, I crunched numbers for the tea. Father Christopher had said the church had a few hundred dollars in its discretionary fund and he thought a hundred or so could be earmarked for tea costs, pending vestry approval. Meanwhile, he gave me a twenty-dollar bill as his contribution. I pulled out the notepad I kept in the top kitchen drawer to scribble a few notes and saw the list of murder suspects I had created, with Don Forrester at the top. Probably useless now, since the police were investigating the unknown-robber angle. Although . . . that didn't mean I couldn't find out some background on Apple Springs' now lone lawyer.

When I did a Google search, the first thing that popped up was Don Forrester's law office website with a photo of the ever-beaming lawyer. I clicked through the pages, but nothing jumped out—standard boring business stuff. The next Google entry showed a picture of him on his church's website leading a camp-out with the First Baptist youth group. Then I searched for Don on Facebook. I found his profile and didn't notice anything out of the ordinary other than his liking Snoop Dogg and Wayne Newton. I scrolled through his entries, but Don didn't post often. When he did, it was usually a plug for his law firm or links to funny YouTube videos.

I entered a new Google search, typing in *Don Forrester and Stanley King*, which resulted in a plethora of entries—many of them going back to when the two had shared the law practice of King and Forrester. As I scrolled through several inconsequential items, one entry at last caught my eye. I clicked on the article from the *Apple Springs Bulletin* and discovered that Stanley King had been named as the correspondent in the divorce suit Don had filed more than a decade ago against his then-wife Debbie.

One more reason for Don to hate his old partner.

After spending most of the spring day inside, I felt the need to go outside and get my hands in the dirt. I had a couple of new rosebushes I was eager to get in the ground. Pulling on my gardening sweats, I headed to the backyard and the ancient shed in the far corner, followed by Bogie. I rooted around in the shed, looking for a shovel within the dark interior. An ominous creak froze me in place. What was that? I heard a rustling. My heart clenched. Another creak. More rustling. Then something ran across my foot. I squealed and backed out of the shed in time to see a huge rat streak across the yard to the overgrown ivy covering the fence in the far corner, a barking Bogie hard on its heels.

"No, Bogie, no!"

My mortal enemy scampered up the fence and onto an adjacent tree in the next-door yard as Bogie continued to bark below. I watched, heart still racing, as the hideous disease-carrying rodent leapt from a tall branch onto the phone wires high above and scurried away.

Bogie rejoined me, panting and trembling. Kneeling down, trembling myself, I cuddled him to soothe both my jangled nerves and his. "Good boy, chasing that ugly old rat out of here. You showed him." Stroking his head, I stared into his chocolate velvet eyes. "Thank you for protecting us." He licked me on the nose.

Then I filled his outdoor water bowl, squared my shoulders, and headed to the shed again. This time I made a lot of noise as I approached, stomping my feet and loudly singing "Mamma Mia" to frighten off any other creatures who might be lurking inside. I picked up a nearby stick and banged on the shed walls before I entered. Then I waited. Nothing. No sound. No movement. All was still. Flinging the door wide to let in more light, this time I quickly found a shovel, spade, and some old metal loppers before slamming the door shut and making sure it was firmly secured. Then I made my way over to the spot where I intended to plant the rosebushes at the back of the yard, currently possessed by what might once have been a hedge but now more closely resembled the Incredible Hulk on a rampage.

You can do this.

I took a deep breath and began whacking off dead branches from the overgrown hedge, which I could now see had once been individual bushes before they all grew together in a tangled mess. Ten minutes later, as Bogie stretched out on the grass nearby, basking in the late-morning sun, I began to dig up the first bush with the shovel. *You've got this. You're a healthy, strong, independent woman. What did that seventies women's anthem say? Hear me roar!*

As I worked, perspiration dripped down my back and blisters began to form on my hands. Sweat trickled into my eyes, and I paused to wipe it away with the hem of my T-shirt. My womanly roar receded to a whimper, but I continued digging. Half an hour later, I was rewarded with a pop. *Yes!* I set the shovel down and tugged on the trunk, but it refused to budge.

Think maybe it might have been a good idea to soak the ground first, Sherlock?

Oh shut up, I told my inner nag.

I dug deeper, and this time Bogie joined in. "No, no," I scolded, until I saw that Bogie was a good digger. *Many paws make light work.* Moments later, I heard another pop. I tugged on the trunk again. This time it gave some. We both dug some more. More popping. More digging. More tugging. At last, the recalcitrant trunk gave way as I yanked it, causing me to stagger backward and Bogie to release a concerned yip. I tossed my Incredible Hulk nemesis to one side, then raised the shovel high over my head and swayed back and forth as I sang "We Are the Champions."

"Love that song," a familiar voice said.

Bogie barked, and I spun around to see Susan in denim capris and a red T-shirt advancing toward me with an icy pitcher and two glasses.

"I saw you working away from my upstairs window and thought I'd better bring you some lemonade." She set the pitcher and glasses down on a rusting bistro set the former owner had left behind, then knelt down to scratch the backs of Bogie's ears.

I motioned for Susan to sit as I gulped down the refreshing liquid. Then I sank into the other bistro chair and fanned my face with my hand. "Thanks. I was dying."

"I figured that. I'm guessing you're not used to manual labor." She pushed her dark hair behind her ear.

"Not so much. I can deadhead and plant six-packs with the best of them, but David was the one who did all the heavy lifting and digging. I'll get the hang of it, though."

Susan flexed a sturdy bicep. "If you need help, let me know." She took a drink of her lemonade. "By the way, I hear you're joining the Downton Divas."

"Looking forward to it. I loved that show."

"Who didn't? Other than my husband and most men."

David had not been like most men, for which I was grateful. Masterpiece Theatre had been our Sunday night TV tradition, and we always snuggled in and watched *Downton Abbey* together, as well as all the Masterpiece mysteries.

Susan's voice interrupted my memories. "Word on the street is you're also a woman of means."

I choked on my lemonade and sputtered. "Woman of means?" Yes, David's life insurance, split between Emily and me, had left me comfortable, but not wealthy. Thanks to the sale of our home, I'd netted enough to buy my Apple Springs bungalow.

Susan held up her hands in mock surrender. "Not my words. I couldn't care less how much or how little money you have, but you bought Harry's house outright, and real estate's not cheap in these parts."

"Cheaper than the Bay Area. Especially when the house is twelve hundred square feet and in need of work."

"True dat."

I lifted an eyebrow.

"Did that sound as ridiculous to your ears as it did to mine?"

"Pretty much."

"That's what I get for trying to speak my kids' language." Susan held up her right hand. "I solemnly swear: those words will never pass these lips again." She pretended to spit them out.

When we stopped laughing, I asked, "How many children do you have? Do they still live at home?"

"Bite your tongue. We are empty nesters at last, thank God. I love my kids, but I thought they'd never leave. Jennie and Jeremy are twenty-five and twenty-seven, respectively. Jeremy and his wife Amanda gave us our grandchild, Jason, who will turn three in a couple months—thank goodness. I adore Jason, but they don't call them the terrible twos for nothing." She shuddered.

"Is Jason your only grandchild?"

"No. Jennie and her husband Brian have given us a beautiful granddaughter, Julia. Eleven months. Mike is completely besotted. Turns to total mush whenever she's around. I have to fight him for the chance to even hold her." She took a drink of her lemonade.

If David were still alive, I would probably have had the same problem with our granddaughter, Kelsey. Not for the first time, I thought of what a wonderful grandfather David would have been. He had been an amazing, involved dad to Emily, and I wouldn't have expected any less with his only grandchild. Sadly, though, he got to see Kelsey only twice before he succumbed to cancer.

I shook off the bittersweet remembrances and returned to the present. "I checked out Don Forrester online last night and learned something. Stanley had an affair with Don's wife?"

"Yep. Poor guy got hit with a double whammy. First Stanley cheated him out of the law practice, and then Don discovered Debbie was cheating on him with Stanley. Broke his heart, and he filed for divorce."

"What happened to his ex-wife?"

Susan's mouth tightened. "She thought Stanley was going to marry her, but he played her like a violin. Stanley used Debbie to get Don's private business files, and once he had them, he executed some shady behind-the-scenes maneuvering to push Don out of the firm. Once that was a done deal, Stan dropped Debbie. Last I heard, she had moved to the Midwest some—"

Bogie interrupted Susan by proudly depositing something at our feet.

I lifted up the object. "Good boy! You found a bone. Want to play fetch?" I raised my arm to throw, but Susan halted my hand midair.

"That's a human bone."

Chapter Fourteen

"Human?" I dropped the bone, but Susan snatched it up before Bogie could. "You have got to be kidding me."

"Nope." She was busy examining the bleached object. "I think it's a metatarsal."

"Metatarsal?"

"Foot bone."

"How do you know?"

"I studied archaeology and went on a few digs back in the day."

Digs. I jumped up from my chair and sprinted over to the hole I had dug, with Susan and an excited Bogie right behind me. Bogie tried to burrow down into the hole again, but I held him back, then knelt and peered into the earthy pit he'd enlarged while we'd been engrossed in conversation.

I saw white.

Susan, who had also dropped to her knees to peer inside the hole, saw it too. "More metatarsals," she breathed, as she rocked back on her heels. "That's someone's foot."

"There's a dead body in my yard?"

"More like a skeleton." Susan got to her feet and brushed off her hands. "We'd better call Chief Beacham."

* * *

Ten minutes later, I looked up to see a brawny man in a kilt striding across the backyard toward us. Definitely not the police chief. "Did you call Braveheart?"

"Hal must be busy on another call. That's his deputy, Dylan."

"Does he always dress like that?"

"Only for special events. I think there's a Celtic festival somewhere nearby today. Dylan's the best stone thrower around."

"Good thing I don't live in a glass house."

"It's a Highland competition. Like the shot put."

"Ah."

"Sorry, Dylan," Susan said as the sandy-haired deputy joined us.

"That's okay, business before pleasure." He smiled and extended his hand to me. "Dylan MacGregor."

"Hope Taylor."

Braveheart quirked a shaggy eyebrow. "The same Hope Taylor who found Stanley King's body?"

"Guilty. Unfortunately."

"Bodies seem to have a way of following you around."

"Not until I came here. Are you sure the name of this town isn't Death Valley?"

"Now that you're here, we may have to change it." He grinned.

Susan handed the kilt-wearing Dylan the bone. "Looks like a metatarsal to me."

He turned it over in his hands, closely examining it. "Sure does." Then he pulled on a pair of gloves, grabbed the shovel, and approached the hole. Fifteen minutes later, he set the shovel down. He had carefully dug out the next two overgrown bushes that formed the hulking hedge and moved them aside.

Susan and I joined the deputy at the hole, which was now a wide trench, and peered down, where we beheld a mass of white. Bogie began barking and squirming even more, eager to get at the bounty of bones. "No boy, that's not for you."

"Definitely human." Dylan MacGregor frowned. "I'll need to call Stu Black."

"Do you think the butler did it?" I joked. Glancing back at my bungalow, I said, "Although this place isn't large enough to require a butler. Maybe it was a jealous husband who did in his unfaithful wife, buried the body, and told everyone she'd run off with the milkman."

"Traveling salesman," Susan murmured.

"Huh?"

"Harry Guthrie's wife left him for a traveling salesman," Dylan MacGregor said curtly. "Sixty years ago."

"Seriously?" I whistled, and squeezed Bogie in surprise. He yelped in protest. "Sorry, boy." I turned to Susan and caught a dismayed look that she was exchanging with the deputy. "I'm going to take him inside. Be right back."

When I returned after placating Bogie with a couple of Milk-Bones, Braveheart was on his smartphone.

"Is he still talking to the medical examiner?"

"Nope, an archaeologist who consults with him. She'll have to come out too."

"Why?"

"This could be a Native American burial site. A Miwok cemetery was discovered down the road about a decade ago, and they've found a few smaller sites in the area since then."

"Well, that would be better than having my house predecessor be a killer." I shivered at the thought of a murder being committed in my backyard, or worse yet, inside my house. It was bad enough finding a dead body at church, but having one on my property gave me the creeps.

"The only person Harry ever killed was me. At dominoes," Dylan said, overhearing. He shoved his phone into a furry purse-thing with tassels hanging from a chain at the waist of his kilt and stalked off.

I turned to Susan, bewildered.

"Harry was like a grandfather to Dylan," she said softly. "He took him under his wing after his dad died when he was a kid. Watched him while his mom was at work and taught him cribbage and dominoes. Dylan really loved that old man."

Way to go, Pastor Compassion. Great way to endear yourself to the local law. I determined to keep my mouth shut from then on.

The deputy returned from his car with a roll of yellow crime scene tape and some wooden stakes, which he proceeded to shove into the dirt around the grave perimeter.

"Wait! What are you doing?" *So much for keeping my mouth shut.*

Before Dylan could answer, a turquoise tornado enveloped me. "Oh mah dear, are you all right?" Liliane Turner embraced me, wafting waves of Tabu. "We were having brunch at my house and saw the police car and thought maybe something had happened to you, so rushed right over."

"I'm fine." I gently extricated herself from Liliane's spindly but surprisingly strong arms before the spicy, too-sweet fragrance knocked me out. "But thanks for your concern."

"I told you that you were overreacting, Lil," said Dorothy, whose fuchsia lipstick perfectly matched her button earrings and silk blouse. "Pastor Hope is perfectly capable of handling herself. She's not some damsel in distress in need of someone to rescue her."

Patricia hugged me hello.

"Love your outfit," I said, admiring her retro-looking black-and-white polka-dotted dress. "Especially with the red belt. Very Audrey Hepburn."

"I was thinking more Sophia Loren," Liliane said.

"Thank you. Hal said it reminded him of Lucille Ball."

"I love Lucy!" Dorothy said. "Especially the chocolate-factory episode."

Liliane giggled. "When they were stuffing all those chocolates in their mouths."

"Lucy looked like a tick about to pop," Patricia said.

Peals of laughter rang out.

"If you ladies are finished with your garden party now—" Deputy Braveheart began.

"It *is* a party, Mommy! I told you!" Maddie, my almost-four neighbor advanced into the backyard, holding her mother's hand. "I wanna play!" Then she caught sight of the yellow police tape, which the others had overlooked in their *I Love Lucy* bonding. "Hey, what's that?"

Dylan, Susan, and I closed ranks to block the grave from the little girl's sight. Catching on, Nikki scooped Maddie up in her arms and turned her back on the police tape. "Hey Maddie-boo, guess who's going to give someone a zerbert?" She planted her lips on her daughter's tummy and blew a raspberry, which caused Maddie to shriek in delight.

"Do it again!"

Nikki blew another raspberry. Then another, with Maddie shrieking and giggling all the while.

Susan strode over to the mother-daughter duo with a huge smile. "Hey, we're going to move the party over to my house. Who wants some lemonade and cookies?"

"I do, I do!" Maddie said.

"I do, I do," Nikki echoed.

"You funny, Mommy."

"There's plenty for everyone," Susan said over her shoulder to us as the threesome departed.

Once the trio disappeared from view, Patricia turned to Dylan and me, hands on her hips. "Now what in the world is going on?"

The deputy exhaled an exasperated sigh. "We found a skeleton in Harry's—I mean Pastor Hope's—backyard."

Dorothy and Liliane gasped.

"So this area is off-limits until Stu Black and Doc Linden arrive to examine it."

"The archaeologist?" Liliane asked, peering around Dylan to try to see into the hole.

He nodded. "Most likely it's more Miwok bones like they found down the road."

"Harold's going to hate having missed this," Patricia said. "Two bodies in one week? What are the odds? That's more crime than Apple Springs has seen in the past decade." She sent me a mischievous smile. "Thanks, Hope."

"What can I say? Some people attract mosquitoes. I seem to attract bodies."

The deputy's furry purse-pouch buzzed. He pulled out his phone and glanced at the text. "That's Doc Linden. I'm going to meet her out front. Be right back." He fixed the women with a stern stare. "And stay away from the grave site." Dylan jogged away, kilt flapping.

"I declare, that man has the nicest legs," Liliane said, in full-on Scarlett mode.

"He has the nicest everything," Dorothy said.

"Except temper."

"Temper? Dylan?" Patricia sent me a surprised look. "Dylan's one of the most even-tempered men I know. He rarely gets bent out of shape."

"Well, I guess I bent him." I could feel my face flushing. "Apparently I dissed his surrogate grandpa when I joked that the guy who lived here before me may have knocked off his wife and buried her in the backyard."

Liliane and Patricia exchanged looks.

"Sorry. I was kidding. Some of you may have been friends of his."

"Yes," Dorothy said. "I've known Harry all my life. We went to the same school, although he was a couple years ahead of me. He had his faults, like all of us, but Harry was a good guy, especially in his later years."

Liliane arched a painted eyebrow.

"What? Look how kind he was to Dylan when his father passed away."

"He sure had a temper when he was young, though," Liliane said. "Quite the jealous streak too. Remember when he punched Tom Shelton for staring at Betsy?"

"That was years ago."

"Harry and Betsy were high school sweethearts," Liliane explained. "They were crazy about each other. Everyone knew they were going to get married."

"And did they?"

"Oh yes," Dorothy said. "Betsy was the love of Harry's life, and he was hers." She frowned. "At least that's what we thought. That's why it was such a shock when she ran off with a traveling salesman a couple years after they were married. It nearly killed Harry."

"Or"—Liliane paused dramatically, eyes wide beneath her thick-mascaraed lashes—"was it poor Betsy who was killed? No one evah saw her leave, and you can bet in a small town like this, someone would have seen something."

"Here we go," Patricia said. "Lady Macbeth in action, resurrecting ancient rumors."

"Make fun of me all you like," Liliane snapped, losing her accent. "All I know is my mother said no traveling salesman stopped at our house the week Betsy disappeared."

*   *   *

While the medical examiner and forensic archaeologist examined the bones in my backyard, we all gathered over at Susan's house. Everyone was eager to discuss who might be in the grave, but Maddie's presence inhibited them. Luckily, Susan's husband Mike arrived with his grandson Jason and took the two kids into the kitchen to make root beer floats.

The moment the door closed behind Mike, Liliane burst out, "I'll bet you anything that's poor Betsy down in that grave, and Harry killed her in a fit of jealousy all those years ago."

"That doesn't sound like the Harry I knew," Susan said. "He was a nice, sweet old guy."

"I agree," Nikki said.

"You didn't know him in his younger days."

"Harry would never have hurt Betsy," Dorothy said. "He adored her."

Liliane snorted. "Lots of men who supposedly adored their wives apparently wound up killing them. Do the names Scott Peterson or Drew Peterson ring any bells?" She turned to retired cop Patricia. "Don't police say most murders are committed by family members or someone the victim knows?"

"Much of the time, yes."

"See. What'd I tell you?"

"But let's not rush to judgment," Patricia cautioned. "They don't even know how old the bones are yet. They could have been there for a hundred years or more. There was a huge Native American presence in this area, so they might well be Miwok remains like Dylan said. Let's wait until we get the report from the archaeologist before jumping to any conclusions."

"How long will that take?"

"It depends. Could be a couple days. Could be a couple weeks."

"Well, I still think it's going to be Betsy," Liliane said. "You mark my words."

Nikki shook her head. "I don't think so. Harry was a doll. He was always kind and gentle with Maddie. I can't see him doing something like that."

"Maybe it's one of Marjorie's ancestors," Dorothy suggested.

"Marjorie?" I glanced at my favorite parishioner.

"Yes. Didn't you know her family owned your house long before Harry?"

"No. I wonder why Marjorie never said anything."

"I think she's embarrassed by the fact. Back then, it wasn't much more than a shack. Marjorie wanted to bulldoze it years ago, but Harry talked her into selling it to him when he got his first job. He fixed it up and made it what it is today."

Complete with sparkly harvest-gold linoleum. I had a feeling that was Harry's wife's touch. Most men I know aren't into glitter.

Liliane rested her pancaked chin on her hand. "If I recall correctly from what my grandmother said, Marjorie's great-granddaddy Richard was originally from someplace back east. He came out west during the gold rush like hundreds of others, hoping to strike it rich. When that didn't pan out, he settled here and became a banker, banking everyone else's gold. Did quite well for himself."

"I remember that story," Dorothy said. "I heard his mother moved out here to be with him after her husband died. After Richard Chamberlain became a successful banker, they left his original home—now yours, Pastor—and he built the grandest mansion in town, Chamberlain House."

"That's right." Liliane's eyes sparkled. "He left his mother in charge of furnishing it, and she imported marble from Italy, chandeliers from France, and Oriental rugs from Turkey. They spared no expense to make it the biggest and best house in Apple Springs."

"I still find it hard to believe Marjorie sold that house," I said. "I know it needed repairs, but you'd think she could have gotten a loan. Marjorie would have found some solution to hold on to her family home."

"That's what we all said at the time," Liliane said. "It like to killed her when she sold it to Stanley all those years ago. Everyone was so shocked when she did. That house was her pride and joy." A sly look stole over her heavily made-up features. "I always wondered if Stanley might have had something on her that forced her to sell."

"On Marjorie?" Patricia said. "Like what?"

"Oh, I don't know, but that's how Stanley was. You know—always poking around, finding embarrassing stuff out about folks and then using it against them." Liliane's mouth set in a grim line.

"Like he did with poor Gus Clayton, who used to own the general store," Dorothy said. "Once Stanley spread the word about Gus liking to wear his wife's dresses, he and Roberta couldn't hold their heads up in town. Had to sell out and leave."

"Let me guess," I said. "They sold the store to Stanley?"

"For a fraction of what it was worth," Liliane said.

"I wonder what in the world Stanley could have had on Marjorie that caused her to give up her family home?" Patricia mused.

"No idea, but I hear Stanley's kids are planning to sell the house," Nikki said.

"Ooh, if that's true, you can bet Marjorie will be first in line to snap it up," Dorothy said.

"Do you really think so?" Patricia asked. "At her age?"

"What do you mean, *her age*?" Liliane said, a dangerous glint in her eyes.

"No offense. I'm just saying that's a lot of house and grounds to maintain. Mine is half the size, and it's all I can do to keep up with it. I'm about ready to downsize."

"Best decision I ever made," Dorothy said. "I love my cute mother-in-law cottage. It's neat and compact and easy to keep clean, and best of all, no yard work."

Yard work. That was my cue to leave and see what was happening in my backyard. I found Chief Beacham conferring with Dylan, the kilt-wearing deputy.

"We need to stop meeting like this, Pastor," Harold said with a teasing glint in his eye. "Did you make a habit of stumbling over dead bodies in your last parish too?"

"No. Just sea lions."

Then I noticed a slight woman with glasses and a chin-length gray bob squatting in the hole. Harold introduced me to Abigail "Doc" Linden, the forensic archaeologist. She informed us that the skeleton needed to stay put for now and that no one must disturb the site. In the past, she said, looters had stolen native artifacts like beads and arrowheads from graves and sold them on eBay. If the remains were Native American, which she could determine upon a more extensive on-site examination, members of the local tribe—in this case, likely Miwok—must carefully remove the bones and rebury them on tribal land in a sacred ceremony. If the bones were not Native American, she would then remove them from my yard and take them to the lab for carbon dating to establish how old the body was.

"So I guess this means I can't let my dog in the backyard?"

"Absolutely not." Doc Linden gave me a horrified look.

"I think the pastor was kidding," Harold said.

*　*　*

That night as I washed the dishes from my grilled-cheese dinner, I looked out the kitchen window and noticed the yellow tape around the grave fluttering in the breeze. *Who are you? What's your story, and how did you get in my backyard?* Then I said a prayer for the unknown skeleton who had once been a person.

I stayed up late watching *The Best Years of Our Lives* and ugly-crying as I always did at the part where small-town-boy Homer, who has prosthetic hooks in place of the hands he lost in World War II, is being tucked in by girl-next-door Wilma, his fiancée. Homer had nobly tried to release Wilma from their engagement after his injury, so when she kisses him and says, "I love you and I'm never going to leave you . . . *never*," I start sobbing.

It seemed I had just fallen asleep when Bogie awakened me with frenzied barking. Glancing blearily at the nightstand, I saw the digital clock glowing one thirty. "Shh, Bogie. Settle down." He continued to bark, standing on his hind legs, his front paws on the bedroom windowsill. "What is it, boy?" I got up and went to the window in time to see a dark figure hurrying away from the backyard grave.

I called the police, but by the time Deputy Braveheart arrived, the figure was long gone. He checked out the site with his flashlight, however, and said the skeleton had not been disturbed.

"I wouldn't worry about it," Dylan said. "Probably just kids trying to score some souvenirs."

"Thank you. That makes me feel so much better."

"We aim to please, ma'am." He tipped his hat and left.

Did he really just call me ma'am?

Chapter Fifteen

F riday night I attended my first Downton Divas get-together
over at Liliane's Victorian. After she proudly took me on a
tour of her southern-inspired home, complete with a cluttered
den full of *Gone With the Wind* paraphernalia, we rewatched the
Downton Abbey Christmas episode from the end of season two—
the one where Matthew proposes to Mary as the snow falls gently
around them.

I wiped away tears.

"So romantic," sighed Liliane afterward.

"Magical," Dorothy breathed.

"I'm surprised she didn't freeze to death in that sleeveless
gown," Susan said.

"Leave it to Susan to break the mood." Patricia set down her
teacup.

"I save my romantic moods for Mike," Susan said with an
exaggerated leer.

Liliane passed around a plate of Pepperidge Farm Milanos,
and I excused myself. Washing my hands at the bathroom van-
ity with gold taps, I marveled at the frilliness surrounding me.

Tasseled cords tied back shiny satin window curtains boasting six ruffled tiers in descending shades of lavender. The same satin ruffles repeated on the shower curtain, the curtain beneath the sink, the tissue holder, even the wastebasket. Textured damask lavender wallpaper covered the walls, and gold sconces held china figurines of women in hoopskirts holding parasols. Drying my hands on the ruffled, satin-edged towel, I escaped the frilly claustrophobia and returned to the Downton Divas.

"Okay, now that we've all—or rather, *most* of us have"—I slid a glance at Susan—"swooned over Matthew and Mary, can we talk about the women's tea for a few minutes? Do you mind, Liliane?"

"Go right ahead."

I informed the group that, as of that afternoon, we already had nineteen sign-ups, and that was just Faith Chapel parishioners. Once we opened the tea to the whole town (providing I got Father Christopher's and the vestry's permission to do so), we might easily triple that number. Since the round tables in the parish hall seated eight, if we kept to our original plan of ending sign-ups at fifty, that would give us six full tables with two women left over.

"So if you get the full fifty women, why don't you just seat four tables of eight and three tables of six?" Susan asked. "Problem solved."

"Not quite," I said. "We're going to need more table hostesses now." I held up my hand, ticking off on my fingers, "Dorothy, Patricia, Lottie, and I are each hosting a table. That's only four. We still need three more women to serve as table hostesses."

"Well, by my count, you've got two more right here," Susan said dryly, pointing to herself and Liliane. "What do you say, Lil? I'm game if you are."

"Count me in."

"So sign us up." Susan cut her eyes at me. "Unless we need to get baptized or something at your church first?"

"Oh no, as long as you say the secret password, you're in."

"Secret password?" Liliane asked.

"Sorry. I meant passwords. Plural. All you need to do is recite the Ten Commandments. Then you can be an official table hostess. Isn't that right, Patricia?" I sent our senior warden an innocent look.

"Oh yes. And of course the commandments must be in order." Dorothy giggled.

"Oh, y'all are funnin' us," Liliane said. "Pastor Hope, you should do stand-up comedy."

Susan tilted her head at me. "I wouldn't quit your day job if I were you."

We discussed what was necessary to host a table, explaining to Susan and Liliane that linen tablecloths, napkins, water pitchers, and fresh-flower centerpieces would be provided by the church but each table hostess needed to bring her own teapot, china, glassware, and cutlery for each table member.

"And decorations," Dorothy added. "We're going to award a prize for the best-decorated table," she said excitedly. "I can't wait to see everyone's pretty china and how they decorate."

A competitive gleam lit Susan's eyes. "Me either."

"We're still one table hostess short," Patricia reminded us.

"Don't worry," I said. "I have someone in mind." That someone was Marjorie. Time to take the high road. Visiting Marjorie and making amends had been on my to-do list for some time now, but other more urgent things kept popping up and taking precedence.

Who are you kidding? Face it, Hope—you're chicken.
Don't sugarcoat it, I told my conscience.

It was too late to see Marjorie tonight, so I vowed to pay her a visit first thing in the morning. Clicking on my phone calendar to tap in her name, I saw I already had another morning appointment. One I couldn't miss or reschedule—Stanley King's funeral.

*   *   *

Stanley's funeral was the most uncomfortable funeral I had ever attended. I had officiated at funerals before where feuding family members had to be seated as far away from each other as possible to keep the peace. I had even assisted at a funeral where wife number one was on one side of the aisle casting dirty looks at wife number two on the other side. Then there was the time I conducted a funeral where the deceased was laid out in an open casket wearing his lucky bowling shirt, sporting an odd smirk, and clutching his favorite bowling ball, ready to throw a final strike.

None of those funerals were as awkward as Stanley's, however. The weather was perfect, the music was beautiful, and the setting was lovely. Faith Chapel had undergone an extensive and thorough cleaning—paid for by the deceased, thank you very much. The pews gleamed with a patina of polish, the stained glass sparkled, and the altar dripped with flowers. White roses, Asiatic lilies, gladiolas, chrysanthemums, and Queen Anne's lace filled the sanctuary, while a spray of white roses, orchids, and lilies covered the casket. There was awkwardness, though, among the assembled mourners who had come to pay their last respects.

First, nobody wanted to do the eulogy. In his funeral instructions, Stanley had chosen a pal from the rotary club, who also headed the local Toastmasters group, to deliver his tribute. However, the "pal" had said he had to be out of town on an important business trip the same day as the funeral—one that could not be rescheduled. Father Christopher had then asked Todd and Samantha if either of them wanted to say a few words about their father, but they also declined. He then approached various community leaders and church members, including Stanley's fellow traditionalist, Barber Bob, but everyone had an excuse as to why they couldn't deliver the eulogy, so it was left to Father Christopher.

Then at the last minute, choir director Elizabeth begged off singing "Pie Jesu" due to strained vocal chords. Although soprano Rosemary volunteered to take her place, Stanley had left strict instructions that he wanted a professional vocalist, not "some second-string choir member," singing at his funeral. Instead, Elizabeth played a CD of Sarah Brightman performing the famous requiem. When "Pie Jesu" ended, per Stanley's instructions, Sinatra's "My Way" filled the church.

Todd and James sat stone-faced, Samantha looked shell-shocked, and the rest of the assemblage exchanged incredulous looks and whispers. When Sinatra finished, I read the Twenty-Third Psalm and assisted Father Christopher with the rest of the service.

* * *

"Well, that cost a pretty penny," Bonnie Cunningham murmured, nodding to a massive cascading flower arrangement of orchids and roses on a table in the foyer of the King home. "Nearly a thousand bucks, I'd say."

"You didn't do the flowers?" Lottie asked.

"No. He used some fancy Sutter Creek florist. Not that I'd have done his funeral anyway."

A middle-aged woman stopped to admire the floral display. "I know Stanley had a lot of faults," she said, "but he could be quite the charmer."

"That's how he sucks—excuse me, sucked—people in," Bonnie replied. "The charm wore off quickly."

"Ain't that the truth," alto Judy said.

We moved into the large living room. The same way Bonnie's Blooms was not good enough for Stanley, the parish hall was not grand enough for his funeral reception. Stanley had arranged for the reception to be held at his home—a home that apparently few of the townspeople had been inside, at least since he'd bought it from Marjorie two decades earlier.

Father Christopher said that back in the day, Marjorie used to entertain a lot at the mansion. She would host diocesan events, vestry dinners, ECW luncheons, Easter egg hunts for the children of Faith Chapel, and a legendary annual Christmas Eve open house. Once Stanley took ownership of Chamberlain House, however, he allowed only a select few inside the inner sanctum.

"He was probably banking on the curiosity factor alone to get people to show up," Lottie said in a stage whisper to Marjorie, who looked like she had been sucker-punched at being in her former home.

Don Forrester entered and strode up to Bonnie. He linked his arm with hers and kissed her on the cheek. She rewarded him with a blush and a tremulous smile. Don glanced around the room. "It's been a long time since I've been here, but I see Stan's taste in art hasn't changed." He nodded behind me. I turned to see a small painting I had missed the last time I visited. The oil canvas showed a man who bore a faint resemblance to Stanley dressed all in black on a red background smirking and flipping a bird.

"How rude!" Marjorie said. "You call that art?" She accepted a glass of red wine from a passing waiter and took a big gulp.

The server was part of a catering crew from a celebrated Napa winery who worked the crowd, serving wine and platters of coconut shrimp, mini beef Wellingtons, smoked salmon, bacon-wrapped scallops, chicken skewers, and crab puffs. I noshed on the hors d'oeuvres while chatting to parishioners and keeping a watchful eye on the crowd, wondering which of the guests might be Stanley's murderer.

I zeroed in on Don whispering to Bonnie. Interesting that they had chosen Stanley's funeral to make their debut as a couple. As I watched, Todd King, who looked uncomfortable in a navy suit, made his unsteady way toward the romantic duo. Uh-oh. Was he drunk and on his way to tell off his father's former partner?

Christopher must have had the same thought. He caught my eye, and we both headed through the crowd toward the trio.

Todd snagged a glass of wine from a passing server and drained it in one gulp. Then he clapped his hand on Don's back. "Hey, bro," he said loudly, "good to see ya. Glad you could make it." Todd gave a slight bow to Bonnie. "Lookin' good, Bonnie. Happy to see your taste in men has improved."

Before Bonnie could reply, Christopher appeared beside them. "Hi, Todd. Could you show me where to find the dessert? My sweet tooth has a powerful craving."

"Sure, Father, no prob. Follow me." A wobbly Todd led Christopher to a round table near the front of the room covered in a cornucopia of sweets, including assorted cheesecakes, truffles, Texas sheet cake, and platters of oversized cookies.

"Mind if we sit down and have some coffee with our dessert?" Christopher asked.

"Prolly a good idea." Todd sank down in a nearby chair and loosened his tie.

Taking the chair across from him, I munched on a chocolate-chip cookie as Todd and Father Christopher exchanged small talk. From my seat, I had a perfect vantage point of the foyer, where I spotted Marjorie looking around wistfully at her former home. She ran her hands lovingly across the mahogany banister of the wide staircase. Then she glanced upward and wrinkled her nose in distaste at the two oversized, elaborate chandeliers.

I agreed. One crystal chandelier would have been plenty. Maybe I could use that as a bonding moment when I talked to her and asked her to be a table hostess—hopefully during the reception.

Marjorie rejoined the group in the living room as Samantha motioned for Todd to join her by the fireplace.

"'Scuse me, Father. Pastor. Duty calls." Todd stood up carefully and navigated his way through the crowd to his sister's side, snagging another glass of wine from a passing server as he did.

Samantha gave him an uncertain look, but Todd gave her arm a reassuring pat. James, who was standing nearby, sent his niece an encouraging nod. Samantha cleared her throat and offered a tentative smile to the funeral guests. "My brother and I would like to thank you all for coming," she began.

"That we would," Todd interrupted, raising his glass. "In fact, why don't we have a toast? To dear old dad. We are gathered here to celebrate, *not* your lousy life, but your passing from it. Freedom!" he said, channeling Mel Gibson in *Braveheart*. Todd drained his glass and, as he did so, lost his balance and almost fell. James gripped his elbow and kept his nephew upright, then led him from the room, a flushed Samantha following.

After a moment of shocked silence, a murmuring swept through the crowd.

"He just said what everyone else was thinking," muttered a gray-haired man in front of me.

"Maybe so," said his female companion, "but how tacky to say it aloud in front of everyone. That boy needs to learn to hold his liquor. Looks like he's following in his father's footsteps."

"Not entirely. I heard he and his sister are unloading this place and it's going on the market soon. King wouldn't like that—this was his Hearst Castle."

As they moved away, I turned to see Marjorie staring openmouthed after the duo. I started to walk over to her, but James Brandon reentered the room at that moment, and Marjorie made a beeline for him.

I circulated through the crowd, making sure to stop and chat with all the Faith Chapel parishioners. Then I spotted Dorothy Thompson sitting alone on a burnished-leather love seat in front of a massive potted palm. "Dorothy, did you come by yourself?"

"Oh no, Pastor, Randy brought me. He went to get me some dessert and coffee. Have a seat." Once I did, she leaned over and whispered, "Isn't this place something else? I'd sure hate to have to clean it."

"Me too." We chatted about the grand mansion for a few minutes and then fell into a companionable silence.

A voice I recognized as Rosemary's from choir intruded fr
behind the potted palm. "Well, I don't care what anyone say
she said in a stage whisper. "I mean, take a look at this place! I
probably worth at least a couple million. I'll bet you anythin
Samantha did her father in so she could inherit."

"No. Do you really think so?" said a second voice I identified
as fellow soprano Helen. "I thought they said it was a robber?"

Rosemary snorted. "What would a robber be doing in the
columbarium? I'm telling you, the killer was someone Stanley
knew, and who knew him better than his own daughter?"

I coughed to indicate our presence, and the two sopranos
made a fast exit.

Randy Thompson returned, carrying a cup of coffee in one
hand and a plate in the other, which he deposited on the table in
front of us. "Mom, I got you a piece of cheesecake," he said.

Dorothy did not respond.

We both looked at her, concerned.

"Mom, are you all right?"

She started. "I'm fine. Sorry, I was woolgathering." The troubled expression in her eyes belied her words, however.

"You sure?" Randy asked.

"Yes. I'm just not big on funerals. In fact, I'm a little tired. Can
you take me home now? I'd like to take a nap." Dorothy wrapped
the cheesecake in a napkin and tucked it into her capacious purse.
Mother and son made their farewells, then left.

Wondering if Dorothy's distressed look was due to memories
of losing her husband or something more, I determined to pay her
a pastoral visit that week. Then, deciding I had stayed long enough
to fulfill my pastoral obligation, I also left. As I walked down the

stone steps, a slight movement at the corner of the house caught my eye—a blonde woman's hair blowing in the wind. Continuing down the sidewalk, I turned right when I got to the street. That's when I glimpsed Don Forrester and Bonnie Cunningham pressed up against the side of Stanley's house, making out like two teenagers.

Chapter Sixteen

S unday after church, I headed to Suzie's for lunch.

"Don't tell me, let me guess," Susan said as I walked through the door. "You want boiling water for tea, right?"

"Nope. I'm going to mix it up a bit today. I'd like iced tea and a BLT, please."

"Way to live on the edge."

"I'm Episcopalian. That's as edgy as we get."

When Susan left, I pulled out my phone and started scrolling through my emails to make sure nothing urgent had come in. I answered a question about the women's tea, filed the reminder about tomorrow night's vestry meeting, and downloaded the latest pictures from Emily in Germany.

"Aw, who's the cutie-patootie?" asked Susan, as she set down my iced tea.

"My granddaughter Kelsey."

"She's adorable, but you're too young to have a granddaughter. What are you? Forty, maybe?"

"Forty-two. Kelsey is my stepdaughter Emily's child. Emily was fifteen when I married David."

"Fifteen? I'll bet that was fun."

"The first year was no walk in the park. Can you say hormone city? But by her senior year, Emily and I had become good friends."

"You're lucky. My daughter hated me her senior year and could not wait to go away to college. To be honest, I couldn't wait for her to leave either. It wasn't until she'd been gone nearly a year that she finally realized I wasn't the evil ogre she'd made me out to be." Susan shuddered. "I'm so glad those teen years are over."

"Ditto."

Riley Smith and her BFF Megan Cunningham entered the diner.

Good one, God.

Susan left to take another order, and I smiled at the two teens as they approached.

Megan mumbled a greeting and slipped into the booth behind me, while Riley lingered. "Hi, Pastor Hope. I hear you found another body."

"Yep. What are the odds, right?"

"At least this one's an old skeleton and there's no blood and stuff."

"Thank God for small miracles."

"It was cool seeing you in the choir today. I didn't know you sang."

"Only in a group where I can blend in."

"I liked the music," Riley said. "Latin's cool."

"Have you ever thought about joining choir?"

She snorted. "Nah. Too many old folks." Then she realized what she had said and clapped her hand over her mouth.

"I hear you. I'm actually the youngest in the group. We could use some more singers, though, especially in the tenor and bass section. If you know any guys who might be interested, let me know."

"Will do." Riley gave me a half wave good-bye and rejoined Megan.

Susan reappeared with my BLT and fries and went to take the teens' order. As I bit into my sandwich, I overheard Megan say they wanted to split a burger and fries, with two Cokes.

"Just water for me," Riley interjected.

"Chill," Megan said. "I told you I would pay."

"I know, but I don't want you to keep paying for me."

"It's no big deal. I got my paycheck Friday."

"You're so lucky you have a job. I can't find anything in this town."

"The only reason I have a job is because my mom needs cheap labor at the flower shop," Megan said. "Trust me, stripping roses after school isn't my idea of a good time. I keep getting pricked by thorns."

"Send me into that briar patch. I don't care what I do, I need to find a part-time job."

Turning around in my booth, I said, "Sorry, but I couldn't help overhearing. Riley, do you have experience typing and filing?"

She nodded. "I type ninety words a minute and used to do my dad's filing when he was working from home."

"Riley's a whiz on the computer, Pastor Hope," Megan said. "She's always helping me out with technical stuff."

"Have you ever used graphics software programs or worked on websites?"

"Totally. I created websites for some friends and the art department at school. I've also done posters and graphics to promote school events."

"Well, I can't promise anything, but I might have a clerical job for you. How would you feel about working part-time at the church?"

"Serious? I'd love it! Cool."

"I'll need to check with Father Christopher and run it by the vestry, but why don't you bring your résumé by the church one day this week for us to review?"

"I'll bring it by tomorrow," Riley said, eyes shining. "Thank you so much for this chance, Pastor Hope. You won't regret it." She scrambled out of the booth.

"Where are you going?" Megan asked.

"I need to update my résumé."

"Right now? What about lunch?"

"I'm not hungry. You can have my share."

"Hang on. I'll go with you."

Five minutes later the teens rushed to the exit with their boxed lunch to go, bumping into Harold and Patricia Beacham at the door.

"Whoa, slow down there." Harold reached out to right Megan's Coke before it spilled.

"Thanks," Megan said.

"Sorry, Chief. Mrs. Beacham." Riley flushed.

"That's okay," Patricia said. "Tell your folks hello for me."

The girls left, and Susan greeted the Beachams. Spotting me, they smiled and walked over.

"Care to join me?"

Harold glanced at my plate. "Looks like you're about finished."

"Looks can be deceiving. I haven't had dessert yet."

The couple slid into the booth across from me, and Susan arrived to take their order—the fried chicken special for Harold and a chef's salad for Patricia.

No wonder she stays so slim and trim. You sure you still want pie? my dietary conscience asked.

"Susan, what kind of pie do you have today?"

"Apple, cherry, and chocolate."

I ordered cherry and caught up with the Beachams. Patricia and I shared the latest pictures of grandkids on our phones while Harold talked about an upcoming fishing trip with his son and oldest grandson. Susan delivered our food, and Harold attacked his fried chicken, mashed potatoes, and gravy with gusto. Patricia tucked into her salad, and I enjoyed my warm cherry pie with the scoop of vanilla Susan had added. Patricia asked questions about the tea and I responded on autopilot, my mind elsewhere. I waited until the chief was almost finished with his meal before I pounced.

"So what's going on with Stanley's murder investigation? Have you got any leads on who the robber might have been, or do you think he's long gone?"

"He?" Harold said, lifting an eyebrow. "What makes you think it was a he?"

"Nothing. I guess I assumed . . ."

"Pastor, are you getting sexist on me?"

"Certainly not." Then I saw he was teasing. "Okay, I deserved that. Do you think the thief—male or female—is someone local, or a stranger? Although," I mused aloud, "what would make a stranger visit the columbarium? It's not like it's a tourist destination or anything. Doesn't make sense. No, it must be someone local. What about Don Forrester?"

Harold sighed. "I talked to Don, and he admits he and Stanley had a fight in the columbarium on the night Stanley died. Stanley said some nasty things about someone Don cares about, so he punched him in the nose and Stanley went down, hitting his head on the altar."

"The altar? But there was no blood on the altar. At least not when I arrived the next morning. Although . . . I suppose Don could have cleaned it up before he left."

"No. There was no blood on the altar the night before either. Don's punch and Stanley's subsequent fall resulted in a small bump on the back of Stanley's head, nothing more," Harold said. "Stanley King was alive and well when Don left. Well enough to refuse his offer of help up and to curse him out, at least."

"Is that what Don told you?"

"Yes, ma'am."

What is with all this ma'am *stuff lately? Maybe it's time to start coloring my gray.*

"And you believe him?"

"Yes. His story corroborates the medical examiner's findings. There was a small goose egg on the back of Stanley's head, beneath the large bump and bloody gash caused by the burial urn."

"So we're back to square one."

"*We're* not back to anything, Pastor. Remember? You do the pastoring, I do the investigating."

Patricia sent me a warning look over her coffee cup, which I ignored. I was a priest on a mission.

"Okay, but what about my skeleton?"

178

"*Your* skeleton?"

"The one in my backyard. The one someone entered my yard in the middle of the night to check out, as I'm sure your deputy told you."

"Dylan said the grave wasn't disturbed, and it was most likely kids messing around."

"But who do you think it could be?"

"The kids?"

"No. My skeleton."

"I have no idea. We'll have to wait and see what the archaeologist says." Harold wiped his mouth with his napkin. "What I do know is, according to Doc Linden, those bones have been there for some time, and meanwhile, I'm knee-deep in the midst of an active murder investigation. Stanley's murder must be my focus."

"Are you saying you're not going to investigate my nameless skeleton?"

"No, I'm saying it's not at the top of my to-do list." Harold expelled another sigh. "There's nothing I can do about the skeleton until we get the archaeologist's report on the age of the bones. Since they're old, whatever happened is ancient history. Meanwhile, someone killed a member of my town, a member of my church. *Our* church. On our church grounds, no less. My job is to find out who that person is."

He's right. The sanctity of the small chapel and columbarium has been desecrated by a violent act. The most violent act of all. Even though I had met him only once and he'd left an unfavorable impression, Stanley King had been a member of Faith Chapel—a longtime member, and more importantly, one of God's children. One whose life had been violently snuffed out.

"Sorry, Chief," I said, suitably chastened. "You're right. Finding Stanley's killer takes precedence." Time to step up my efforts to try to figure out who murdered Stanley. Then in my spare time, I would do some sleuthing of my own on the skeleton in my yard.

*   *   *

Monday when I arrived at work, I found Riley's résumé slipped under the door. I made myself a cup of tea and sat down at my desk to review it. *Definitely not a run-of-the-mill résumé.* Riley had included screenshots of websites she had done for her friends and school, along with their URLs, so I could check out the websites myself. She also included a link to her own website, which showed an online portfolio of her graphics and artwork. As I looked through a one-sheet promoting the art department, my phone chirped with a text.

Hi Pastor Hope, it's Samantha King. You said to call if I needed anything. Is there any way you could come over?

I checked my calendar. Except for a meeting with Christopher at ten and a pastoral care visit to Albert Drummond later in the afternoon, I was free.

Me: *Sure. Is now a good time?*

Samantha: *Now would be perfect. Thank you so much!*

I poked my head into Christopher's office to tell him I was going to see Samantha but would be back in time for our meeting.

"Take all the time you need," he said. "Samantha is more important. We can always reschedule. Just give me a call and let me know."

"Or I could text you."

"You're determined to drag this old priest into the twenty-first century, aren't you?" He sighed. "Next you'll want me to take a selfish or whatever they call it."

"Nah. I'm not big on selfies either. We'll leave that to the Kardashians and the teenagers." I handed him Riley's résumé. "I would like you to take a look at this, though. I think I've found the perfect person to do the church bulletin and help us out with clerical work."

* * *

When I arrived at the King home, a red-eyed Samantha let me in.

"What's wrong? Are you okay?"

"No," she blubbed, leading me inside to chaos. Boxes, bags, artwork, and stacks of stuff littered the foyer.

"Since we're selling this monstrosity, Todd and I have to go through everything and decide what to do with it, and he wants to get rid of it all," she said, sniffling. "He helped me bring a bunch of stuff down from the attic, but he wants to toss everything in the garbage. I told him no, we need to sort through it all. There could be things we want that have special meaning—like Christmas ornaments or favorite childhood books or games—but he got mad and said as far as he's concerned, we could set a match to it all. Then he stormed out." Samantha burst into tears. "Todd and I never fight."

I hugged her. "It's okay. You two are under a lot of stress right now, lots of changes in your life. Emotions are running high. I'm sure Todd will cool down and be back soon."

"You think so?"

"Yes. He just needs some time. Your brother loves you."

"I know." She blew her nose and then looked around her. "But look at this mess. I'm so overwhelmed I don't even know where to start."

"That part's easy," I said, rolling up my sleeves. "I'm the queen of organization. We'll have this sorted in no time."

"Don't you have other things to do?"

"Not right now." I grabbed the nearest box of clothing and felt through it, making sure there was nothing breakable inside, then dumped the contents onto the floor and told Samantha about the three-piles philosophy: keep, discard, or donate, followed by the organizer's rule of keeping something only if it is loved, has been used in the past year, or holds great sentimental value.

She started sorting through the clothes, and I began pulling boxes to one side and stacking similar-sized ones with lids atop one another. As we worked, we talked. Samantha told me she was going back to school to get a teaching credential in special education. She had done some grade school substitute teaching, so we swapped stories from our respective teaching days.

Samantha slid a sidelong glance my way. "I'm sure you've heard some things about me. Like that I've been in rehab?"

"There's no shame in that. Good for you for acknowledging the problem and getting help."

"I wish my dad had felt that way. He kept saying I was like my mother and would wind up exactly like her too," she said bitterly.

"Tell me about your mother. What was she like? Do you remember much about her?"

Samantha's face softened, and her eyes took on a faraway look. "She had this beautiful red hair that went down to her waist.

She used to let me brush it for her. When the sun hit it, her hair looked like this shimmering waterfall of red and gold." Her mouth curved upward. "I remember her being a lot of fun too—before the drugs. She used to get down on the floor with Todd and me and play with us. Todd doesn't remember that, but then he barely remembers her at all. He was too little. She used to read us stories about castles and princesses and witches and dragons. Her favorite was Rapunzel. Not surprisingly."

Her mouth turned downward. "Uncle James said she felt like a prisoner here with no way to escape except drugs. Once or twice, she tried to leave—she was going to take us with her and run away from my father. Far, far away. Uncle James was helping her, but somehow or other Dad found out and stopped her. Told her she could never leave him. Then he banned her from seeing Uncle James. Wouldn't even allow him in the house. James tried to see her but couldn't. A month later she was dead."

"I'm so sorry. How old were you when that happened?"

"Six. Todd was four." Samantha brushed away tears. "The only way my mother could escape my father and this prison was to kill herself. Of course, Dad told everyone it was an accidental overdose. Couldn't let anyone know Stanley King's wife committed suicide," she said, her eyes flashing, "but I know she did." Samantha pulled out a heart-shaped silver locket from beneath her T-shirt. "Mom gave me this the week before she died—said she'd always be with me, no matter what." She opened the locket to reveal a lock of curly red hair on one side and a picture of a stunning young woman with a wide Julia Roberts smile on the other.

"She was beautiful. She looks so happy."

"That's how I try to remember her. Uncle James took that picture shortly after she had Todd. Before things started to go really bad." She looked at the picture through a sheen of tears.

"I think your mother would be very proud of you, Samantha. I know I would be if you were my daughter."

"Really?"

"Yes. You had an addiction and you sought help for it. Now look at you—you're going back to school so you can enter a profession that helps others. Jesus said, 'As you've done it unto the least of these, you've done it unto me.'"

"Thank you, Pastor Hope." She swiped at her eyes and closed the locket. "I guess we'd better get back to work, or we're never going to finish."

I walked over to an oversized box that looked like it contained everything but the backyard barbecue.

Samantha grimaced and said, "After an hour in the attic, Todd started grabbing stuff left and right and throwing it into the biggest boxes we had so we could be finished. My brother's not very patient."

"I can relate. I've had to learn that virtue over time." As I pulled the heavy box toward me, the side split and things began falling out. "Oops." I began picking stuff up off the floor, and Samantha hurried over to help. "Hey, what's this?" she said, holding up a bulky black-and-silver rectangular object with both hands.

"That, my dear, is what they call a boom box. It played these ancient things called cassettes in the seventies and eighties. That's how we listened to music."

Samantha gave me a blank look.

"Before CDs."

"Oh yeah, I remember. I had a CD with Disney songs on it when I was little." She set it off to one side.

"Way to make me feel old." I lifted up the boom box and looked at it. "Mine was a lot like this." Then I looked closer and pushed eject, popping out the cassette tape still inside. I saw *Romantic Love Songs* scrawled across the label in faded ink. "This is someone's mix tape. I haven't seen one of these in years. I wonder if this thing still works." I riffled through the box, found the cord, and plugged the boom box into a nearby outlet. Then I popped the tape back in and hit play. Elton John's "Your Song" filled the foyer.

"Ooh, I love this song!" I said, closing my eyes and singing along.

The sound of soft clapping moments later made my eyes fly open.

"Nice job, Pastor. I didn't know you were a singer," Samantha said, as Roberta Flack began "Killing Me Softly With His Song."

"As long as I can sing along with someone else, I'm good. This is a great tape. I wonder whose it was. I love seventies pop, although I wasn't allowed to listen to it as a kid."

"How come?"

"My parents thought pop and rock music was of the devil. The only music allowed in our house growing up was religious, classical, and the occasional country song—preferably country gospel." I pulled some empty picture frames and a broken alarm clock out of the box.

Samantha sent me a wry smile. "I guess I'm not the only one who had a strict childhood. Although I have to say, the only music my father ever banned from the house was rap."

"Are you a rap fan?"

"No, I prefer alternative rock and R and B."

"So whose cassette tape do you think this is? Your dad's?"

"I doubt it. Too sappy for him. Could have been my mom's, but it's kind of before her time. She liked Madonna and Michael Jackson. We used to dance to 'Billie Jean' together." Samantha smiled, remembering.

We continued going through items from the broken box as the music played in the background. I picked up a few dusty paperbacks and some plastic beads and asked Samantha if she wanted to keep them, but she told me to stick them in the discard pile. Then I pulled out a rolled-up piece of what looked like brown wrapping paper. I carefully unfurled the paper so as not to tear it. It turned out to be a smudged charcoal sketch of a beautiful woman with old-fashioned ringlets cascading over a bare left shoulder. The feathers in her dark hair, the sleeveless, fringed, tiny-waisted knee-length dress, and the black stockings she wore reminded me of the dance hall girls I had seen in the old Westerns my parents used to let us watch.

"Who's this?"

Samantha peered over my shoulder. "I have no idea. I've never seen it before. She's hot, though. Probably one of my dad's ancestors or something."

"Or maybe your mother's?"

"I guess. We could show it to Uncle James and ask him."

I peered closer at the drawing. The woman stood onstage in an old-fashioned theater, bestowing a mischievous gaze on the audience. Something about her drew me in.

Samantha started to put the drawing in the discard pile.

"If you don't want it, do you mind if I take it?"

"No problem. Todd would have tossed it anyway."

I rolled the drawing back up and set it near the door so I would not forget it. Then Samantha and I tackled several more boxes. We were deep into the ninth box when we heard the back door slam and Todd yell. "The prodigal has returned!" We could hear his footsteps tromping through the house as he approached. "Hey, Red, sorry about earlier—" He broke off when he saw me. "Pastor Hope, what are you doing here?"

"Helping me," Samantha said, glowering at him. "After you stormed out, I had a meltdown, and Pastor Hope came to my rescue."

Todd had the grace to look abashed. "Sorry, Sam. Sorry, Pastor. My temper sometimes gets the best of me. It's the red hair."

"Don't use that as an excuse," his sister said. "I have red hair too, and you don't see me flying off the handle and throwing a tantrum."

"You're right. Mea culpa, mea culpa." Todd held up a flat box wafting tantalizing aromas. "Can I make it up to you with pizza? Your favorite. Sausage and mushroom." He extended the pizza box to his sister.

My stomach growled. "If you don't accept his peace offering, Samantha, I will. Gladly."

"Okay, set it down on that box there. But don't think bribing me with pizza gives you a free pass from helping with this mess."

"Hey," a familiar male voice yelled from the direction of the kitchen, "where do you want this Dr. Pepper?"

"In here," Todd yelled back.

Moments later James Brandon walked through the doorway with a six-pack of soda, paper plates, and napkins in his hands. "Why Pastor Hope, nice to see you again."

"You too. You want to pass those paper plates over here, please? Samantha and I have worked up quite an appetite sorting through all this stuff."

"You got it." He handed me the plates. "I know better than to get in the way of a hungry woman."

"Smart man."

The only sounds for the next few minutes were the popping of soda cans, assorted "Mmm, goods," and the boom box continuing its string of seventies love songs.

James cocked his head to one side, listening. "Is that John Denver?"

"Who's John Denver?" Todd asked.

"He was really popular in the seventies."

"The seventies?" Todd said, grinning at me. "I didn't think you were that old, Pastor."

"I'm not, but I enjoy seventies pop music. John Denver was a singer-songwriter who played acoustic guitar and wrote folk-pop hits like 'Take Me Home, Country Roads,' 'Rocky Mountain High,' and 'Annie's Song,' which we're listening to now. I love his music."

"So did my mom," James said, an odd expression on his face.

"Oh, maybe it's her tape," Samantha said excitedly.

"What are you talking about?"

She jumped up to get the boom box and carried it over to her uncle. "We found this with a tape inside that someone made. We were trying to figure out whose it was."

James's eyebrows drew together as he hit the eject button and pulled out the tape. When he saw the handwriting on the label, he threw the tape across the room.

"What the hell?" said Todd.

Samantha and I stared at her uncle.

James's jaw clenched. "My mother—your grandmother, whom you never knew—made that tape for Lily and Stanley as a wedding gift. Right after she gave her legal consent for my underage sister to marry the man who destroyed her."

Chapter Seventeen

After James delivered that startling pronouncement, he stalked out the front door, saying, "I can't be here right now."

Samantha ran after him. "Uncle James, wait."

"Well, that explains a lot," her brother said.

"I'm sorry, Todd."

"For what?" He gave me a cynical smile. "Dear old Dad being a pervert? Or my druggy grandmother basically selling her underage daughter to a dirty old man?" He slapped the pizza box shut. "Or that my uncle never bothered to tell me?"

"I thought you didn't know your grandmother."

"I didn't, but when Samantha went into rehab, the great-and-powerful Stanley yelled at her that she was 'just like her mother and her druggy grandmother' and would probably end up the same way."

"I'm so sorry."

"Me too." He swiped the hair out of his eyes. "Thankfully, we're finally free of the King, and soon we'll be free of his castle too. Then at last we can both start living our own lives." Todd then began talking about his art, saying he planned to hold a show in a few months, once he had enough pieces finished.

Samantha returned with her uncle a few minutes later, and I left the three of them to work things out.

* * *

That afternoon I made a pastoral visit to Albert Drummond.

"Why Pastor, aren't you a lovely sight for these old eyes," Albert said when he answered the door. "Come on in. I'm afraid Bonnie's at the flower shop and Megan's at a school club meeting."

"That's okay. You're the one I came to see," I said, remembering to speak loudly enough so he could hear me. "I heard you were a bit under the weather. How are you?"

"Better than a poke in the eye with a sharp stick. Nothing wrong with me but a little cold." He sneezed and blew his nose. "I may be as old as the hills, but I'm still fit as a fiddle." He led me into a cozy living room, indicating I should sit on the floral sofa while he lowered himself into the leather recliner opposite.

"I'm afraid I owe you an apology, Pastor."

"For what?"

"I told you when we first met I knew where all the dead bodies were buried." His eyes twinkled. "Obviously I was wrong."

"You certainly were. I've heard of skeletons in the closet, but I've never had one in my backyard before."

A fit of coughing overtook him, and he grabbed a tissue from the end table beside him. Noticing his empty water glass, I hurried to the kitchen to fill it.

"Thank you." Albert took a long drink. His hands trembled as he set the glass down.

"What you need is a nice cup of hot tea."

"Don't go to any trouble."

"No trouble at all. I would love a cup of tea myself. Okay if I make us both one?"

He nodded. "The kettle's on the stove, and there's tea bags on the counter."

I filled the kettle with fresh water, found the box of lemon-ginger tea, and removed a PG Tips tea bag from my pocket stash. As I waited for the water to boil, I admired Bonnie's red-and-white kitchen. White quartz countertops held a red blender, red Kitchen-Aid, and red toaster, while an assortment of cookbooks were bookended by the figure of a ceramic rooster and a red crock holding spatulas and utensils. Red herb pots of basil, rosemary, and mint nestled beside the farmhouse sink, while white lace curtains fluttered in the breeze.

As I opened the fridge for milk, a plethora of family photos held in place by red rooster magnets caught my eye: Megan, her face smeared with chocolate, in a high chair at what was obviously her first birthday party. Megan gripping her mother's hand as she took her first steps. A ponytailed Megan in braces. Megan working at the flower shop and frowning at the camera. The final photo was a recent beaming picture of Don and Bonnie. Beneath the last picture, a calendar showed dentist appointments and Megan's school events. One entry caught my eye. Something penciled in had been erased. Donning my Trixie Belden hat, I looked closer and detected the faint imprint of initials and a time: *SK—FC, 4.* The date was the same day Stanley had been killed. Could the initials stand for Stanley King and Faith Chapel? If so, which member of this household had had an appointment with Stanley at four p.m. on the day he died?

The kettle whistled, interrupting my speculation. I made the tea, adding honey to Albert's ginger-lemon, and returned to the living room. "Albert, what time does Bonnie get off work?"

"Depends. Four thirty most days, but if she has a lot to do, she may stay until five thirty or six. Why?"

"I need to talk to her about the tea flowers and was thinking of dropping by when I leave." I took a sip of my tea and admired Megan's school photo hanging on the wall beside Albert. "Does Megan work at the flower shop every day after school?" I asked casually.

"No. Mondays, Wednesdays, and Fridays only. Tuesdays and Thursdays she has Spanish club."

So . . . Megan could have skipped out of Spanish club and gone over to Faith Chapel to meet Stanley. Then I thought back to my conversation with Riley in the cemetery and realized that that did not make sense. Stanley's coming on to Megan had repulsed her. She would want to stay as far away from him as possible. She certainly wouldn't meet him alone somewhere. No, it had to be someone else in the family.

As I set my mug down, a book on the coffee table caught my eye: *The Making of* The African Queen; *or, How I Went to Africa With Bogart, Bacall, and Huston and Almost Lost My Mind*, by Katharine Hepburn. I picked it up and began flipping through it, enjoying the rare behind-the-scenes photos from Africa. "I love *The African Queen*."

"It's my favorite," Albert said. "Bogart and Hepburn made a great team. She really gave Bogie what for."

I lifted my eyebrows in an impression of the great Kate as the psalm-singing missionary, making sure to speak loudly and clearly. "Nature, Mr. Allnut, is what we are put in this world to rise above."

Albert slapped his knee. "By golly, that's a good one. How do you know that, Pastor?"

"I'm an old movie buff, and my husband loved Bogie. We must have watched *The African Queen* at least a dozen times."

"Well, don't that beat all? It's a treat to find a young person who appreciates the classics. My daughter and granddaughter certainly don't. I've tried introducing Megan to favorites like *The Maltese Falcon* and *Treasure of the Sierra Madre*, but she refuses to watch black-and-white movies."

"Anytime you want to watch a black-and-white movie, you give me a call." Deepening my voice, I adopted an accent and an aggrieved tone. "'We don't need no stinkin' badges!'"

Albert laughed again. "Harry used to say that all the time."

"Harry Guthrie? The man who used to live in my house?"

"Yep. Harry was one of my oldest friends. We served in Korea together. I miss that old son-of-a-gun."

I switched investigative gears. If Albert had been friends with Harry in his younger days, he would be able to provide me a much more accurate take on him than Deputy Dylan and those who'd known him only in his older years. "Did you know Harry's wife too?"

"Betsy? Sure. We all went to school together. I was best man at their wedding." Albert got a pained expression on his face. "It like to killed Harry when Betsy ran off. He was out of town on a construction job, and when he got home, she was gone. Left him a Dear John saying she had fallen in love with someone else and was going to start a new life far away from, and I quote, 'this boring life and boring small town.' Broke Harry's heart."

"Wasn't that more than fifty years ago? How can you remember what the note said after all this time?"

"Because the poor schlub read it to me over and over again when he was drunk, and he was drunk every night for a solid year after Betsy left." Albert exhaled noisily. "I wish I'd tried harder to stop the wedding. Maybe Harry wouldn't have been so broken up if they hadn't been married."

"You tried to stop the wedding? Why?"

"Because Betsy was a selfish, impulsive woman in need of constant attention and adoration. I was worried Harry wouldn't be enough for her—that she would tire of him and move on, even though the poor guy adored her and showered her with compliments and trinkets. It still wasn't enough." Albert glowered. "She got mad when he would go out of town for work because then he wasn't fawning over her twenty-four seven, but Harry had to go where the work was. There wasn't enough construction work here to keep him busy. He had a mortgage and bills to pay. Bills his wife carelessly ran up. Betsy didn't work, so it was all up to him."

Hmmm. Could the financial pressure have been too much for Harry? Liliane and others had said Harry had a bad temper when he was young. Could it be he came home one night to one bill too many from Betsy's excesses and flew into a murderous rage, killing her?

Melodramatic much? Dial it down a notch, Sparky.

"Knowing Harry as well as you did," I said gently, "do you think there's any chance he might have killed Betsy?"

"Absolutely not." Albert's eyes blazed.

"Even in anger? I understand he had quite a temper."

"I don't care how angry Harry got, he'd never lay a finger on Betsy. She was everything to him. His whole world." Albert's hands shook. "I know folks are whispering, saying it might be Betsy in your backyard, but I'll bet my last dime it's not. It could be anyone from long before Harry and Betsy lived there—even someone from gold rush days. Lots of folks came through this area back then."

"That's true," I said in a soothing tone. "I know they're checking whether it might be Miwok remains."

"Well, there you go."

Seeking to distract Albert, I walked over to examine a family photo grouping on the opposite wall. "Is this you?" I asked, pointing to a black-and-white eight-by-ten of a handsome smiling man in uniform.

"Yep. That was taken right before I shipped out to Korea." He eased himself out of his recliner and came to stand beside me. His lips curved upward as he remembered. "Peggy and I were married a few hours earlier that day by a justice of the peace."

"No wonder you're smiling."

He inclined his head to a smaller black-and-white photo, where a young woman with wavy brown hair and a corsage pinned to her suit gazed adoringly up at Albert, who gazed adoringly back.

"She's lovely." I looked closer. "Reminds me of the daughter in *The Best Years of Our Lives*. What's her name again? She played Lou Gehrig's wife in *Pride of the Yankees*."

"Teresa Wright." Albert touched the photo. "Folks always told Peggy she looked like the actress, but I think my Peggy was even prettier."

"She's a beauty. You can tell Bonnie's her daughter."

"Bonnie looked a lot more like her mother when she was younger," he said, nodding to a high school photo of his daughter. Albert added that he and Peggy had wanted more children, but it didn't happen, much to his wife's regret. "After Bonnie was married and got pregnant, Peggy was over the moon at the prospect of having a grandchild," he said. Albert pointed to a photo of his wife holding Megan on the day she was born. "My Peggy passed away of cancer shortly after Megan's second birthday." He took out a handkerchief and blew his nose.

I squeezed his shoulder. "What happened to Bonnie's husband?"

He snorted. "That useless good-for-nothing abandoned his wife and child when Megan was only five. I knew he was trouble the moment I met him, but Bonnie had stars in her eyes and would not listen to a word against him. The only good thing I can say about their union was that it produced Megan. After her husband deserted them, Bonnie and Megan moved in with me and have lived with me ever since," he said. "Then Stanley came sniffing around about a year after the divorce. Bonnie was vulnerable, and he preyed on that. Talk about going from the frying pan into the fire."

Albert shook his head. "My daughter sure knows how to pick 'em. Stanley wined and dined her and swept her off her feet. Even took her and Megan to Disneyland. Completely hoodwinked Bonnie. Once he finally got what he wanted"—Albert's cheeks flushed—"sorry for being so indelicate, Pastor, but the truth is, once Stanley made my daughter the latest notch on his bedpost, he was out of there faster than a scalded cat." He made a fist and grinned. "He got his comeuppance though. You reap what you sow."

I looked at the frail aged man in front of me and recalled Susan saying the Korean War vet was not as weak as he looked. She also had said he would have decked Stanley if he ever heard about his coming on to Megan. Was it possible this nice old man who reminded me of Henry Fonda had overpowered Stanley and hit him over the head in the columbarium? *No*, I told myself. *That's ridiculous.* Stanley King was both younger and bigger than Albert. No way could Albert have gotten the jump on him. Could he?

"Albert, did you have many dealings with Stanley?"

"Not much. Although there was that time about a decade ago I punched the lowlife in the nose for how he treated Bonnie."

"You punched Stanley?"

"Yes, ma'am. Broke his nose, as a matter of fact," Albert said with satisfaction. "He kept his distance after that. No one messes with my family and gets away with it."

The theme from *The Godfather* hummed in my head, accompanied by visions of Sonny Corleone beating up his brother-in-law Carlo.

"Bonnie didn't date for a long time after Stanley," Albert continued, "but now she's seeing Don Forrester. Seems like a nice enough guy, although he reminds me of a used-car salesman with his constant smiling. He treats my daughter well, though, which is the important thing."

Albert tilted his head to one side and sent me an inquiring look. "What about you, Pastor?"

"What about me?"

"Are you seeing anyone?"

"No. Are you?"

He gave me a shocked look. "Oh no. My Peggy was my one and only."

"So you know how I feel. I had a wonderful marriage to a kind, loving man who also happened to be my best friend. I'm grateful for that. Many never know that kind of love."

Albert patted my hand, his rheumy eyes filled with compassion. "I understand. Believe me, I understand. There's a big difference between us, though. I'm old. You're still a young, good-looking woman with many years ahead of you. Do you want to live them alone?"

"I'm not alone. I have good friends, family, and God. And my dog, which as you know"—I grinned—"is God spelled backwards."

Albert agreed that there was nothing like a good dog. He had had some great canine companions over the years, he said, but a dog was not the same as a partner. A spouse. "Wouldn't you like to have a special someone again, Pastor?" he asked. "Someone to come home to at night? I know a great guy about your age I'd like to introduce you to. We play chess together. I think the two of you would really hit it off."

"Thanks, but I'm not in the market for romance. It's sweet of you to think of me, though."

*   *   *

It was *sweet*, I thought as I made my way to Main Street. Albert was a nice man trying to do a nice thing. I didn't fault him for that, but neither did I want anyone playing matchmaker for me. I had no desire to date. Not after being married to the best guy on the planet. Passing by Bob's Barber Shop, I noticed Bob Hastings giving someone a haircut. I smiled and waved. He glared at my priest's collar.

Next door, Bonnie's Blooms beckoned me in with its masses of beautiful flowers. Bonnie was busy talking to a customer, so I wandered through her shop, admiring the setup and basking in the floral perfume. White shelves attached to sage-green walls held vibrant flowerpots, assorted vases, and a mix of elegant and whimsical garden decorations. A large mosaic-framed quote by Oliver Wendell Holmes took pride of place on the top shelf: *The Amen of nature is always a flower.*

Weaving my way through colorful buckets of tulips, daffodils, roses, daisies, and calla lilies, I stopped before my favorite—peonies. I loved their delicate beauty so much that I had carried the ruffled pale-pink flowers in my wedding bouquet. Leaning forward, I inhaled the scent of the fragrant blooms and was instantly transported back to my wedding day and David's loving face smiling tenderly at me.

"Pastor Hope, how can I help you?" Bonnie said, her voice bringing me back to the David-less present. "Aren't those some gorgeous peonies?"

"Yes. I've always loved pink peonies."

"Would you like me to wrap up a bunch for you?"

"I'm not sure yet. Let me think about it. The main reason I stopped by was to thank you for your willingness to do the flowers for the tea. We really appreciate it."

"I'm happy to do so. An elegant afternoon tea for the women of Faith Chapel is a wonderful idea. I'll do whatever I can to help make it a special occasion."

"Thanks. I also wanted to let you know there is a good chance the tea might be a bit larger than we originally thought. I wasn't sure if you'd be able to accommodate that or not."

"How much larger?"

"Well, we don't know exactly yet." I sent her an apologetic smile. "It depends whether the vestry agrees to our opening it up to the whole town."

"The entire town?" Bonnie paled above her forest-green *Bonnie's Blooms* apron.

"Don't worry," I hastened to reassure her, "the parish hall holds sixty, but we're limiting it to the first fifty women who sign up. Again, this isn't a done deal yet—the vestry still needs to sign off on it." Then I realized. "Naturally, we wouldn't expect you to do the flowers at cost, since we may well be tripling the number of women now. I was just wondering if staff-wise you'd be able to manage flower arrangements for four or five more tables."

She tried, and failed, to suppress a sigh of relief. "Not a problem, Pastor Hope. That won't amount to more than a couple dozen roses, which isn't a big deal—roses come in bunches of twenty-five."

"You sure?"

"Positive."

I thanked her again for her generosity. "By the way, I had a nice visit with your father this afternoon. I enjoyed looking at all the family photos in your living room. You certainly take after your mom." I glanced around. "You have a great shop here. How long have you had it?"

"Ten years." Bonnie explained that she had bought the shop two years after her divorce. The original owner, whom she used to work for, had retired and sold the shop to her for a song. She then cleared out the shabby space, removing dated knickknacks and cutesy kitsch, gave the entire shop a fresh coat of paint, and added the shelves and decorative items. Even then, Bonnie said, she was in the red for the first couple of years, but thanks to her father's financial assistance, she had been able to keep the shop running.

"Now it's in the black and I've paid my father back," she said proudly.

"That must feel good."

"I can't tell you how much." She puffed out a sigh of relief, which fluttered her bangs.

"And Megan works here part-time? It must be fun to work with your daughter."

Bonnie grimaced. "*Fun* isn't exactly the right word. When Megan was younger, she loved coming to the flower shop and helping. When I hired her two years ago, she was thrilled to be earning her own money." She sighed. "These past few months, however, she's gotten so moody. All she does is grumble and complain. I have to keep her in the back so the customers aren't affected by her sullen attitude."

"Do you think it's the normal teenage stuff, or could something have happened?"

Bonnie's eyes filled. "Both." As the tears leaked down her face, she glanced up at the clock and moved to the front door, where she turned the sign to *Closed* and locked up. "May I speak to you confidentially, Pastor?"

"Of course. That's what I'm here for."

She ushered me to the back of the shop and led me to a small break table in the corner that held a microwave, coffeemaker, and a few mugs. "Would you like a cup of coffee?" she asked shakily.

"No, thanks." I nodded to one of the chairs. "Sit down and I'll make *you* some coffee."

"I'd rather have water." She indicated the water dispenser next to the sink. I rinsed out two mugs and filled them, then sat down opposite her.

Bonnie took a long drink and brushed the tears from her face. "This is so hard. I don't even know how to begin."

"Why don't we begin with prayer?"

She nodded gratefully.

Holding her hands in mine, I prayed for her, and then I prayed for Megan.

Bonnie's tears fell afresh. "I can't believe I let that pig Stanley in our lives," she said, repeating what Albert had told me about Stanley's wooing her a year after her divorce and how they'd dated for a while. "He won me over when he took the three of us down to Disneyland," she said. "Megan had wanted to go since she was three, but my ex kept making excuses why we couldn't: it was too expensive, she was too young, it was too long a drive, yada, yada. So when Stanley came along and made my baby's Disneyland dreams come true for her sixth birthday, I fell for it hook, line, and sinker." Bonnie's cheeks reddened, and she couldn't meet my eyes. "And then I fell into his bed. Less than a month later, he dumped me and moved on to his next conquest. I don't know how I could have been so stupid."

"Everyone makes mistakes," I said gently. "You were lonely and vulnerable and Stanley took advantage of that. Don't beat yourself up about it."

"What I beat myself up about is exposing my daughter to that creep." Bonnie took a deep breath and rushed the words out. "Recently, I learned Stanley hit on Megan. My sixteen-year-old daughter!" Her eyes flashed with pain and fury. She dashed away angry tears. "Can you believe it?"

"How did you find out?"

"I overheard Megan and Riley talking about it. They didn't know I'd come home at lunch to pick something up."

"When was this?"

"The day Stanley was killed."

Ah. It looked like she was the one who had penciled in the appointment with Stanley and then erased it. But just to be sure . . . "What did you do then?"

Bonnie lifted her chin. "I called Stanley and said I needed to talk to him privately. He said he had some church business with Father Christopher that afternoon but to meet him at four o'clock in the columbarium."

"What happened when you saw him?" I asked, holding my breath.

"I confronted him and told him to stay away from my daughter. And do you know what he did?" Her hazel eyes blazed. "He laughed and said, 'I think you're jealous that I find the young, delectable Megan more appealing than her middle-aged mother.' I slapped him and told him again to stay away from Megan, and then I ran out of there before he could see me crying." Her voice shook. "I was so upset I could hardly see straight. I went over to Don's office and told him what happened. He told me not to worry, he would take care of it. The next morning, you found Stanley dead in the columbarium."

Bonnie looked up at me with anguished eyes. "What if Don killed Stanley because of me?"

Chapter Eighteen

After reassuring Bonnie that I had it on good authority that Don had not killed Stanley, I suggested that she talk to both Don and Megan. "You need to let Megan know you're aware that Stanley came on to her and that she did nothing wrong—Stanley did. Reassure her that if anything like that ever happens again, she can come to you and you will deal with it together. Megan needs to know you'll always have her back."

"Of course I will," Bonnie said, affronted. "She's my daughter. My baby."

Tact and diplomacy, Hope. Tact and diplomacy. Grateful to be wearing my clerical collar, I said, "In your eyes, she'll always be your baby. However, Megan is a young woman on the cusp of adulthood. She needs to know you recognize she's growing up. By acknowledging that and not treating her like a little girl, you may be surprised at the reaction you get."

"You think so?"

I nodded.

Please, Megan, don't prove me wrong.

"And what about Don? What should I say to him?"

"Do you love him, Bonnie?"

Cher's line from *Moonstruck* picked that inopportune moment to pop into my head. *"Aw, Ma, I love him awful."*

"I do," she said.

"Then be honest with him. Tell him what you told me."

Bonnie gave me a bunch of pink peonies as a thank-you.

*   *   *

Walking back to Faith Chapel, I inhaled the pretty peonies as I enjoyed the sights and scents of spring all around me. Vivid azalea bushes hugged storefronts and fifty-foot apple trees offered a lacy pink canopy of fragrant blooms against a cerulean sky. Into this idyllic setting, thoughts of Stanley King intruded. My list of murder suspects was dwindling. After talking to both Bonnie and Albert, I felt confident that neither of them had killed Stanley. With Chief Beacham ruling out Don Forrester, whom did that leave? James Brandon. Todd King. Samantha King. Or some unknown thief. Although the last was seeming more remote by the minute, I hated the thought that either of the King children had committed patricide. Somehow I couldn't imagine Samantha murdering her father, and although Todd talked a good game about how much he hated "the King," deep down I didn't think he'd kill his father either.

That left James. The prospect of James being the murderer left me dismayed. He seemed like such a nice guy. It was clear that he loved his niece and nephew. If it turned out he had killed their father, Todd and Samantha's relationship with their uncle might be irretrievably broken. Unless . . . maybe they were all in on it together?

Stop it, Hope. Your love of Masterpiece Mystery *is coloring your judgment.*

Back at my office, I put the peonies in a vase on my desk so I could see them as I worked. Then I began preparing my notes for that night's vestry meeting.

Father Christopher knocked on my open door. "Got a minute?" he asked, his cherubic face absent its usual good humor.

"Sure."

Christopher sat down across from me and released a heavy sigh. He told me he had gone to the reading of Stanley's will at the request of Stanley's lawyer, and much to his surprise, Stanley King had left everything to Samantha, cutting out his son entirely.

"You're kidding. How did Todd respond to that?"

"Honestly? He seemed relieved. Said now he wasn't tied to his father in any way. Samantha was very upset, however, and said she'd split everything with Todd, but he told her he didn't want anything from the King."

"I can understand that, but knowing Samantha, I'm sure she'll figure out a way to share with her brother."

"I think so too." Christopher looked at me with an odd expression on his face. "Stanley also earmarked a sizable bequest to the church."

"Isn't that good news?"

"Depends on how you look at it. He specified the money must be used for a new, expansive parish hall which would also be used for community events."

Instantly I thought of our upcoming tea and the existing cramped hall and how we could include so many more if the venue were only larger. Oh well, we would just have to do another tea next year in the bigger—and better—hall. Maybe we could even get Virginia to cater it.

"There's a catch, though," Christopher said, with a frown, interrupting my tea imaginings. "The new building must be called King Hall."

*   *   *

At the vestry meeting that night, Patricia and I brought up the prospect of expanding our women's tea to a town-wide event.

"I think that's a great idea," Father Christopher said. "We're always trying to find ways to become more engaged with the community."

The rest of the vestry members agreed, except cradle-Episcopalian Marjorie, who did not like the idea of mixing with Baptists and Buddhists. She was overruled.

Next I said I had found a great candidate for our open clerical position as I passed around copies of Riley's résumé.

Marjorie peered down at the paper through her bifocals. "Riley Smith? You must be joking. Have you seen that horrible tattoo that covers her entire arm? What kind of image would that give of Faith Chapel? It's completely unsuitable, not to mention unprofessional."

A septuagenarian vestry member nodded in agreement.

"One thing it might do is draw younger people to church," Patricia said. "The bulk of our congregation is over sixty-five. If we don't want our church to die out with us, we need to be welcoming to youth."

"At what cost?" Marjorie bristled. "Are we going to have guitars and drums on the altar next? Shall we throw out our beautiful

Episcopal hymns in favor of insipid repetitive choruses? Or worse, that awful rap they try to pass off as music these days?"

"Actually," I said, "Riley told me one of the reasons she attends Faith Chapel is because she loves the music and the liturgy."

Marjorie looked taken aback, but not for long. "That may be all well and good, Pastor, but what you don't know, being new to Apple Springs, is that Riley Smith is a common thief." Her eyes gleamed with triumph. "We can't have a thief working at church."

I stifled my natural impulse to blurt out an impassioned defense of Riley, reminding myself that I wanted to try to make amends with Marjorie and that thus far all I had done was antagonize her further. As I looked at the indignant eighty-two-year-old in her peach polyester pantsuit, though, I saw that beneath her anger and spitefulness, Marjorie felt threatened and afraid, so I decided to cut her some slack.

"Marjorie," Father Christopher said gently, "it's true Riley shoplifted last year. She stole some cheap jewelry on a foolish dare from her friends. Everyone in town knows it. Even Hope. Riley told her. It was a stupid teenage mistake, and Riley knows and regrets it. However, it was a first offense and a minor one—as I recall, the item cost less than ten dollars—and she was not even charged. She apologized, returned the jewelry, made restitution to the store owner, and was released to her parents. She's learned her lesson. Riley was contrite and embarrassed. I don't think we need to worry about her ever doing anything like that again. She's a smart, honest young lady. Quite talented too."

"But Father," Marjorie protested, "what about the offering? Don't you think it might be a terrible temptation to her?"

"No, I don't. Riley, or whomever we end up hiring, will work part-time in the afternoons when either Hope or I am at the church. It's not even an issue."

"And that tattoo that covers her entire arm?" Marjorie said weakly.

Two other aging vestry members chimed in that tattoos were unprofessional for office work. It would be one thing if a tattooed person worked in a garage or some kind of music or artistic venue, they said, but *not* a church office.

Marjorie shot me a victorious look.

Patricia held up Riley's résumé. "Look at this girl's qualifications. Not only is she a computer whiz beyond everyone in this room, she is also a gifted graphic artist. Imagine how amazing she could make our bulletins and monthly newsletter look. She would certainly do a far better job than I have these past few months. I don't think we should automatically eliminate someone this qualified simply because she has a tattoo."

"I agree," Father Christopher said. "Tattoos are quite commonplace nowadays. People, especially the young, use them as a form of artistic expression."

The two septuagenarians harrumphed.

I thought about flashing my lower-back tattoo but didn't want to cause a heart attack.

"That may be true, Father," Marjorie said, "but the only tattooed people I've seen in our small town are Riley Smith and Tom Simmons over at the garage. Tom is a retired Marine who served his country with distinction. It makes sense for a military man to have patriotic tattoos, and it's not out of place on a mechanic. However, we are talking about an office worker in the church reception area. The person who will be the face of Faith Chapel to the public when they walk in. In that setting, a tattoo—particularly such a large one—is inappropriate and unprofessional."

I turned to the vestry's senior warden. "Patricia, when you were on the police force, did you know any officers with tattoos?"

"Plenty, but their ink had to be covered up when they were in uniform." Realization dawned, and she suppressed a smile when she addressed Marjorie and the other vestry members. "Tattoos anywhere on the head, face, or neck above the uniform collar were prohibited. Officers could have tattoos elsewhere on their body as long as they didn't show below the elbows and knees when they were in uniform."

Father Christopher suggested that the church take a page from the police playbook and establish its own dress code for employees. Faith Chapel would not prohibit tattoos, but its new dress code policy would state that tattoos could not be visible below knees and elbows or above the neck.

Everyone agreed, albeit some reluctantly. They also agreed that Christopher and I would interview Riley for the clerical position.

* * *

Arriving home at nine, I immediately took an impatient Bogie for a walk around the block. "Sorry, boy, you know how those vestry meetings can be." He gave me a look. Once we got home, I fed him extra lamb-and-rice kibbles to make amends. While he chowed down, I ate a Lean Cuisine lasagna. Then I washed my hands and pulled out the sketch I had found at the King house. Carefully unfurling it, I set it on the cleared kitchen table and anchored it on all four corners with books to hold it in place. Then I examined it closely in more detail.

Once again, the mysterious woman with the mischievous smile drew me in—much more so than the enigmatic *Mona Lisa* I'd seen in the Louvre with David. Who was this mystery woman? Someone from Stanley's family? Lily's? As a result of the unexpected drama over the seventies mix tape, I had forgotten to show the sketch to James Brandon to see if he could identify the woman in the picture. I made a mental note to call him and ask him to drop by. Then I could show him the sketch and see how he was doing at the same time. Although James was not one of my parishioners, his niece and nephew were, and I felt a certain responsibility for the fallout from the tape, since I was the one who had played it in the first place.

I looked at the drawing again. Perhaps the woman wasn't even a real person. Maybe some budding artist had seen her picture in a magazine or art book and copied it to practice his drawing skills. Or . . . maybe it was the initial sketch for some famous painting I didn't know. I snapped a picture of the drawing with my phone and sent it to my art-loving sister-in-law, asking if she recognized it. As a longtime member of the Fine Arts Museums of San Francisco, Virginia is always attending exhibits at the de Young and the Legion of Honor. If the sketch on my kitchen table was the precursor to a celebrated work of art I was unfamiliar with, she would likely be the one who could identify it.

Virginia texted back moments later. *Nope. Pretty woman from the mid-1800s by the look of it, but definitely not from any well-known artist I recognize. Did you check for the artist's signature? I couldn't see one in the photo, but it looks like there may be something in the bottom right corner?*

212

Duh. I looked at the drawing again and saw a dark smudge in the corner I hadn't noticed before. Were those letters in the smudge? I looked closer but couldn't make them out. Grabbing my readers, I bent my head low over the brown paper again, zeroing in on the smudge. This time I could just make out the faint letters *RC.*

You're brilliant! I texted back. *No signature, but the initials RC.*

Virginia: *The only RC I know is RC Cola. Remember Nancy Sinatra singing 'RC the one with the mad, mad taste! RC!'*

Me: *Before my time.*

Virginia: *Careful, Trixie.*

Me: *Bethann probably knows it though.*

Virginia: *Well maybe when she autographs my record she and I can do a duet of that '60s TV jingle.*

Me: *Maybe.*

My mind was not on the sixties jingle, however. I was still trying to figure out who RC was. Not a King relation, obviously.

Virginia: *BTW, where'd you get this sketch anyway?*

Me: *Long story. Tell you later. Gotta go. Skyping in a little while with Emily and Kelsey.*

Virginia: *OK. Give them love and kisses from Auntie Virginia.*

I examined the initials again. Wait a minute. RC? Could the letters possibly stand for Richard Chamberlain—not the hot *Thorn*

Birds priest, but Marjorie's ancestor? After all, the King home had been Marjorie's house before Stanley bought it. Was it possible the drawing had somehow gotten left behind in the attic when she moved? Maybe I should show the sketch to Marjorie and see if she recognized the woman.

Your best friend Marjorie, you mean?

Good point. Better to show it to James first and rule it out as one of his ancestors. If James didn't recognize the woman, then I'd show the picture to Marjorie and see if it was one of her relations. As meticulous as she was about her family history, she was bound to know.

Satisfied with my plan, I snuggled in with Bogie to watch *Casablanca,* setting my phone timer for my midnight Skype date with Emily and Kelsey in Germany. After Humphrey Bogart said to Claude Rains, "Louis, I think this is the beginning of a beautiful friendship," I turned off the TV, powered up my laptop, and launched Skype.

My granddaughter surprised me by greeting me in German: *Guten morgen, Oma. Wie gehts?* Then Kelsey showed off a hot-pink bandage on her knee, saying she didn't cry "very much" when she fell and hurt herself. She started chattering away in German, and Emily had to keep reminding her to speak English for Grammy. Emily and I caught up on the latest, and she asked me again when I was going to come visit.

"Hopefully later this year, once everything settles down." When I finally said good-night and turned off my laptop, Bogie insisted he had to go outside again.

"Okay, but you be quiet," I warned him. "People are sleeping." I snapped on his leash and took him out to the backyard, careful to stay away from the open grave site. Bogie whimpered and strained at the leash, trying to get at something in the ivy behind the porch. "No, boy, stay here," I whispered, afraid another rat might appear. "C'mon, do your business so we can go to bed."

A flicker of movement a few feet from Bogie caught my eye. I pulled on his leash and hissed, "Bogie, inside." Too late, I saw a flash of white, and an unmistakable scent filled the air. I yanked on the leash, and this time Bogie came running, bringing with him the distinctive smell of skunk. Once inside, I grabbed the deskunking kit David had taught me to make the first time Bogie got skunked a few years ago. I hurried to the bathroom with my now-whimpering dog and put him in the tub.

"Stay, Bogie, stay," I said in a soothing tone as I turned on the tap. "Good boy. Don't you worry, Mommy will have you fixed up soon."

I continued to offer reassuring words to Bogie as I pulled on rubber gloves and mixed the hydrogen peroxide, baking soda, and Dawn dishwashing liquid. After two applications of lather, rinse, repeat, the eau de skunk was a faint memory on my dog's coat. The same could not be said for my house. I poured vinegar into bowls and set them in all the rooms, and then I emailed Christopher to let him know I would be in late. It was two a.m. before I finally tumbled into bed.

Chapter Nineteen

Six hours later, Bogie awakened me with more frenzied barking. Was someone by the grave again? Bleary-eyed, I got up and glanced outside, but no one was in the backyard. I fell back into bed, but Bogie continued to bark. Beneath his barking, the faint chimes of the doorbell filtered through to my fuzzy brain. Stumbling down the hallway with Bogie on my heels, I opened the front door to discover Braveheart on my doorstep.

His shaggy eyebrows shot up. "Sorry for waking you," Deputy Dylan said. "I thought the clergy were early risers."

"Usually. Unless their dog has a run-in with a skunk that keeps them up to the wee hours."

"That would explain the vinegar smell." Dylan's eyes dropped to my legs. Belatedly I realized I was wearing only my night-shirt—an oversized T-shirt that skimmed my thighs. In addition, the inside of my mouth felt like two monster trucks had engaged in a race to the death on a dry, dusty road. I backed away so I wouldn't take the deputy out with my morning breath. "Give me a sec to get changed, and then you can tell me whatever it is you need to tell me."

I indicated that he should go to the living room as I continued to back away down the hallway so as not to flash him. *That's all I need. Priest flashes cop.* Once I reached my bedroom, I sprinted to the bath, where I brushed my teeth and finger-combed my bedhead hair. Then I changed into a fresh T-shirt and jeans and rejoined the deputy.

Dylan sat on the couch, absent-mindedly scratching Bogie's belly, his thoughts clearly on other things. I plopped down in the wingback opposite him.

"So what's up?"

His demeanor became brusque and businesslike. Dylan informed me that the forensic archaeologist had determined that the skeleton in my backyard was not Native American. He also said she would be coming over today to pack up the bones and take them to her lab.

"So I can finally have my yard back?"

"As soon as Doc Linden removes the skeleton. She said the bones are of a young woman around twenty to twenty-five." Dylan's jaw tightened. "Someone bashed her skull in."

"Oh no."

His curt tone continued. "She's not sure exactly how old the bones are yet—won't know for sure until she runs carbon-dating tests—but she estimates they could have been in the ground any-where from fifty to a hundred and fifty years."

"Really?" Then I realized why the deputy was being so brusque. Dylan was afraid the skeleton with the bashed-in head was his sur-rogate-grandfather Harry's wife. The wife who had supposedly left her husband and run off with a traveling salesman sixty years ago.

"I'm sorry," I said softly.

Dylan looked down at the floor. "The man I knew wouldn't kill his wife. He loved her."

"You don't know for sure it's Betsy Guthrie. Doc Linden said the bones could be up to a hundred and fifty years old."

His jaw worked. "Except the doc also said she found a tarnished locket with a broken chain in the grave. The locket had a worn inscription on the back: *B*—or maybe *R*—and *H. Always.* Dylan released a bitter laugh. "Harry really fooled everyone, didn't he? What's that saying? There's a sucker born every minute?" The deputy stood up abruptly, startling Bogie. He jammed his hat on his head. "Sorry I woke you, Pastor." He strode out the front door.

Bogie and I watched as Dylan got in his truck and slammed the door. Then he backed out of the driveway and peeled off.

Poor guy. Picking up the bowl of vinegar from the table beside me, I took it to the kitchen and poured it down the sink. Then I went through the rest of the house, collecting all the other bowls of vinegar and dumping them as well. Next I opened all the windows to air the place out. Bogie nudged me for his morning treat. I gave him his Milk-Bone and led him to the kitchen door to let him outside, but he would not budge.

"Poor baby. You don't want to run into that nasty skunk again, do you?" I patted his head. "I don't blame you. Although you know, those smelly critters only come out in the evening, right?"

He cocked his head and sent me an anxious look.

"Okay, buddy, after last night's debacle, I can understand your nervousness." I clipped on his leash and headed to the front door. "Let's go for a quick run." Bogie gave an excited yip and almost took me out with his tail propeller.

When we returned, I took a quick shower, put the kettle on, and toasted an English muffin. Then I settled in with my PG Tips, muffin, and prayer book. As I said my morning prayers, I included Deputy Dylan in them.

By that afternoon, the news of the young woman in my yard with a bashed-in skull was all over town. After connecting with Christopher and doing some paperwork in my office, I stopped by Suzie's for a late lunch. Susan was running ragged around the full diner as everyone discussed the latest bombshell.

Dorothy and Patricia beckoned me to join them. As I slid into the booth beside Patricia, I said, "Well, I guess this has pushed Stanley's murder out of everyone's minds."

"Not everyone's," Patricia said. "It's still at the forefront of the police investigation. Folks just like having something new and juicy to talk about."

The bell over the front door jangled, and Liliane Turner fluttered in, wearing a purple caftan shot through with gold threads. Upon seeing us, she rushed over and squeezed in next to Dorothy. "What did I tell you?" she asked with a triumphant smile.

"What?" Dorothy asked innocently.

"Didn't you hear?" Liliane's face was flushed with excitement. "The bones in Pastor Hope's backyard are of a murdered young woman in her early twenties!"

"You don't say."

"Ah most certainly do." Then Liliane saw Dorothy trying to suppress a smile. "Oh, you're teasing. I should have known y'all would already know." She focused her denim-blue eyes on me. "What *you* probably don't know, Pastor, is that poor Betsy was only twenty-one when she disappeared." Liliane expelled a dramatic sigh. "And ah hear an old locket was found in the grave as well. Harry gave Betsy a silver locket in high school. That *proves* it's Betsy!"

"Not necessarily," Dorothy said. "Plenty of people have lockets, including me." She pressed the heart-shaped gold locket resting against her red silk blouse. "I keep my Randy's photo on one side and my wedding photo on the other."

Patricia said she had a locket as well—a Mother's Day gift from her kids. She wasn't wearing it because the clasp had broken and she hadn't had a chance to get it fixed yet.

Liliane did not let those pieces of logic deter her, however. She babbled on, her theatrical southern accent coming and going as she gestured dramatically with her hands. Tuning her out, I thought of Dylan's disillusionment, which made me wonder how this latest information would hit Albert Drummond, Harry Guthrie's war buddy and longtime friend. I resolved to pay another visit to Albert.

"Ah don't care what anyone says." Liliane's impassioned voice punctured my pastoral musings. "I'll bet my bottom dollar that's poor Betsy Guthrie in that grave, and you can't tell me any different." She sent us a knowing smile.

"Well, aren't you precious?" Bethann Jackson said, stepping out from the booth behind us, Wendell at her side. "Liliane, ah do declare, you're grinnin' like a possum eatin' a sweet potato. Be careful it don't go down the wrong way, now." Bethann, clad in a pink-and-purple flower-power dress, matching bow, and her ubiquitous white boots, sent Liliane a syrupy smile. The former leader of the Blondelles then nodded to the rest of us. "Pastor. Nice to see you again. You too, Patricia. Dorothy. Ah'm really lookin' forward to that nice ladies' tea y'all are having. Let me know if you need any help now, hear?"

As Bethann walked away, her arm linked in Wendell's, Liliane muttered under her breath, "I doubt we'll be having Twinkies at the tea."

* * *

The next day *The Apple Springs Bulletin* blared the headline "Murdered Woman's Bones Found in Harry Guthrie's Yard!" The lead article repeated the archaeologist's findings along with everything else known about the skeleton so far, ending with the sentence, "Could this be Betsy Guthrie?"

Nice to see objective journalism is alive and well in small towns.

Albert Drummond phoned me, beside himself. "It's not true, Pastor," he said in a quavery voice. "I know that's not Betsy. Harry wouldn't have touched a hair on her head. His good name is being dragged through the mud. Can't you do something? They are decimating a man's reputation, and he's not here to defend himself. It's not right."

No, it wasn't right. I promised Albert I would see what I could do. I knew my backyard skeleton was a low priority for the police, and I understood why, but that didn't mean I couldn't do a little sleuthing of my own to find out more. The question was, where to begin?

How about where it all began, my inner Trixie suggested.

Huh?

Outside.

There was nothing there now except an empty grave. Doc Linden had removed the skeleton the day before and taken it to the lab.

Yes, but maybe inspiration will strike when you return to the scene of the crime. Besides, you need to fill in the hole anyway before someone falls in it, right? Like your next-door neighbor Maddie, for instance?

Good point. Since I wasn't working until later, I pulled on my faded UCLA T-shirt and grubbiest pair of jeans and went to the backyard, a hesitant Bogie on my heels. "It's okay, boy. The bad skunk is gone." Bogie skirted the area where he'd been sprayed, however, and stuck close to my side, lying down beside me as I squatted on my haunches in front of the now-empty grave.

Looking into the six-foot-long, four-foot-deep cavity in the ground, I tried to imagine who the murdered young woman might have been. The obvious answer was Harry Guthrie's wife, Betsy. What if I looked beyond the obvious, however, and examined the facts logically and unemotionally, like Sherlock Holmes, for instance?

Sherlock Holmes would have already solved this mystery, my inner naysayer snarked. *Especially the one played by that yummy Benedict Cumberbatch. You have to admit, you don't have his brilliance or deductive reasoning skills.*

True. However, I could take the facts I had, line them up, and go from there.

Fact one: The skeleton was a young woman between the ages of twenty and twenty-five.

Fact two: The young woman had lived between fifty and a hundred and fifty years ago.

Fact three: The young woman had been in love with someone who gave her a locket with their initials and the word *Always* engraved on it.

Fact four: Those initials were apparently *B* or *R* and *H*.

Fact five: The young woman had been murdered by someone who bashed her skull in.

Putting all those facts together, it was simply a matter of looking for a young woman whose first name began with the initial *B*, *R*, or *H* and who had gone missing during that hundred-year time frame. Piece of cake. Needle in a haystack. I picked up the shovel and began filling in the hole. As I did, I ran through potential *B* names in my head: *Barbara, Beatrice, Betty, Belle, Belinda, Bonnie, Bailee.* I scratched the last one—too contemporary. Then I started on the *R*s: *Rachel, Ruth, Rebecca, Ramona, Regina, Rose, Rosemary, Rosalie* . . . As I tamped down the final shovelfuls of dirt, I came up with several old-fashioned *H* names: *Hannah, Hattie, Hilda, Hester, Hermione, Hildegarde, Hortense* . . .

When I finished, I went inside, scarfed down a peanut-butter-and-banana sandwich, and opened my laptop, where I typed into a Word doc all the women's names I'd come up with. Then I did a Google search of missing women within a sixty-mile radius of Apple Springs during the relevant hundred-year period. Instantly a couple dozen stories of missing women popped up. As I skimmed the headlines, however, I discovered that the stories all related to the same older woman with dementia who had gone missing from a nearby community last year. Luckily, she had been found. I narrowed my search by adding in the twentysomething age range. No help. The same current stories reappeared. *Maybe if I typed in a specific year?* I took a wild guess and typed in *1900*. Nada. 1905? Nothing. 1920? Same. This wasn't getting me anywhere.

What about The Apple Springs Bulletin? *Maybe it's online.*

It was, but only for the past decade.

Then I realized I had neglected to come up with men's names. Someone had to have given my mystery woman the romantic locket; therefore, one of the initials inscribed on the back belonged to a man. I exhaled a sigh and did another Google search, this time looking for old-fashioned men's names beginning with the letter *B*, *H*, or *R*. I added the following names to my list: *Barclay, Barney, Bartholomew, Benjamin, Bertram, Bradford, Balthazar.* Then I typed in the *Hs*: *Harold, Henry, Howard, Herbert, Herman, Hiram, Homer.* I ended with the *Rs*: *Randolph, Raymond, Reuben, Richard, Robert, Roger, Russell.*

My phone chirped with a text from Virginia.

Virginia: *Wazzup, Trixie?*

I filled her in on my futile search for the identity of the murdered woman in my backyard.

Virginia: *Can't you narrow down the parameters? A hundred years is a long time.*

Me: *I know. I may have to wait until I get a more specific timeframe from the archaeologist.*

Virginia: *Sounds like a plan, man.* ☺ *What about the Stanley murder? Anything new there?*

Me: *Nope. Same old, same old.*

Virginia: *Keep me posted.*

At choir that night, the room was buzzing with the rumor that Harry Guthrie had killed his wife, Betsy.

"Harry always was a jealous guy," Rosemary said to an enthralled audience during break. "My mother went to high school with him, and she said if any boy even dared to talk to Betsy, Harry would beat him up."

"Oh my goodness," murmured her pal, second-soprano Helen. "Really?"

"Sounds like one of those controlling types," Ed the lone bass said.

"I've known a few of those," said alto Judy, sending me a knowing glance. "Nothing makes me run for the hills faster."

Rosemary turned to me. "Pastor Hope, it must be awful for you, living in the same house where poor Betsy was murdered." She shuddered. "I know I certainly couldn't do it."

"Me either," soprano Helen said.

Before I could respond, Elizabeth called us back to rehearsal, which was probably a good thing.

Chapter Twenty

S unday I preached my first sermon at Faith Chapel. I would
be lying if I said I wasn't nervous. Already I wasn't batting
a thousand with some members of the congregation—Marjorie,
Bob Hastings, and a couple of Bob's old-guard cronies—and what
I had to say might just push them over the edge.

I had a fun, feel-good sermon I'd already delivered to great
success at St. Luke's last year that I figured would be a slam-dunk
with the congregation—even Marjorie—and I was sorely tempted
to use it. After all, who doesn't want to hit a home run their first
time up to bat? It would even work well with the scripture texts
appointed for this Sunday. Yet with everything that had happened
since I'd arrived in Apple Springs, and particularly with all the
rumors and speculation swirling through town, I felt compelled
to deliver a different sermon altogether.

Saturday I stayed up half the night studying, praying, and
refining my homily. By the time Sunday morning arrived, I was
exhausted, but peaceful. Although my words would likely ruffle
some feathers, I knew they were the ones that needed saying. This
was confirmed Sunday morning when we sang the ancient Irish

hymn "Be Thou My Vision," which reminded me to heed not riches or man's empty praise but to keep God my vision above all.

Ascending the pulpit, I looked out at the small congregation and saw the expectant smiling faces of the Beachams, Dorothy and her son Randy, Todd and Samantha King, Bonnie and Megan Cunningham, Albert Drummond, Riley Smith, the choir, and a dozen or so other church members.

Marjorie and Lottie sat together in Marjorie's customary second pew on the left. Lottie gave me a tentative smile, while Marjorie looked skeptical. I did not see Bob Hastings, but then I hadn't expected to. Nor had I expected to see such non–Faith Chapel–goers as Liliane Turner, Don Forrester, and James Brandon. All three were there, however, sitting next to their Faith Chapel friends. James, sandwiched between Todd and Samantha, sent me a lopsided grin.

Riley Smith, who had sailed through her job interview and hadn't gotten offended when told she would have to cover her sleeve tattoo at work, gave me a wide smile and a thumbs-up.

Then I began to preach. Referencing Proverbs 12:18, *Rash words are like sword thrusts, but the tongue of the wise brings healing*, I talked about the power of the tongue and how easy it is to make a rush to judgment before having all the facts, and how damaging both can be. I made sure not to look at Liliane or Rosemary as I preached. Instead, I shared a difficult mean-girl anecdote from my college days: I was trying so hard to fit in and be part of the cool crowd that my gossip hurt someone I cared about and caused them great emotional pain. Thankfully, the hurt in my friend's eyes pierced me like the proverbial sword, and in that moment I realized that nothing was worth causing that kind of pain to someone—particularly someone I loved.

"Let us try to look upon others through the eyes of Jesus," I preached, "rather than through our own limited, sometimes judgmental, perspective. Jesus said the greatest commandment is to 'love the Lord our God with all our hearts, minds, and souls, and to love our neighbors as ourselves.' Let us leave this morning following his commandment."

After we processed out and waited to receive the congregation, Christopher hugged me and said in a stage whisper, "Great job! You knocked it out of the park."

Others echoed his sentiment, starting with vestry senior warden Patricia. Behind her, Harold sent me a thumbs-up.

"Nicely done," Elizabeth Davis said, shaking my hand with her slender piano hand. "Although we missed you in choir, your voice was more needed in the pulpit."

Riley Smith approached. "Pastor Hope, your sermon rocked!" She gave me a big hug.

"Sure did," said Megan Cunningham, just behind her. Megan stood beside her mother, a smile lighting up her teen face in place of her usual sullen expression. "Women rule."

While enjoying a drama-free chat with Riley, Megan, and Bonnie, I noticed Liliane Turner slip out the side door.

Don Forrester linked his arm with Bonnie and flashed his blinding-white teeth at me. "Well, Pastor, this morning was a couple of firsts for me. First time in an Episcopal church service, and first time hearing a woman preacher."

"Welcome. I hope I didn't scald your ears too much."

"Not at all. It was a good sermon—I like a preacher who tells it like it is." He pretended to mop his forehead. "But you

Episcopalians sure like to give a guy his morning workout. Baptists don't pop up and down so much."

"We call that pew aerobics."

He guffawed.

Albert Drummond followed Don, taking both my hands in his. "Thank you, Pastor," he said in a husky tone, his eyes bright. "You made my day. Harry's too, I'll wager." His lips curved upward. "I hope you don't mind my saying this, but you preach as good as you look."

"I'll second that," James said, coming up behind Albert with a smiling Todd and Samantha. I was happy to see that the family members seemed to have patched up their differences.

"James!" Albert clapped his hand on James's shoulder in delight. "Pastor Hope, have you met my friend James Brandon? He's my chess buddy."

* * *

That afternoon we held a dry run of the women's tea at my house to test the recipes and presentation. Patricia, Dorothy, and Lottie all promised to bring their specialties, with Lottie and Patricia each baking a different kind of scone as well. Susan had to work but sent a sampling of her fruit tarts home with me.

As I made Virginia's ham and apricot cream cheese sandwiches, I mused over the morning. I was relieved and pleased at how well the sermon had gone and hoped it might make people think before they spoke. Then my thoughts turned to Albert and his friend James. Even though I had no interest in dating, I had to admit Albert had good matchmaking taste.

I invited my next-door neighbors Nikki and Maddie to join us for the tea dress rehearsal, since I had promised Maddie a tea party when we first met. Recalling her request for cookies that sparkled, I picked up a roll of sugar-cookie dough from the market and baked a batch, adding pink sugar crystals to the top. Nikki had cautioned me that her finicky daughter did not like fish, so in place of Patricia's salmon-salad, I made a PB&J sandwich without crusts for Maddie in the shape of a heart.

The tea committee arrived together in Patricia's car. We all oohed and aahed over the three-tiered Old Country Roses cake stand Dorothy brought to display the food courses on. Patricia then showed us a photo on her phone of the classic white three-tiered fluted tray she'd snagged at Pottery Barn for the tea. "I loved it so much, I bought two," she said. "And check it out"— she swiped her phone to the next photo—"Dorothy, Lottie and I found an old tarnished silver-plated tea stand at an antique store in Sutter Creek." She swiped her phone again to reveal the formerly blackened stand in all its gleaming glory.

"Wow!" everyone chorused.

"All it needed was a good polishing," Dorothy said. "Add a paper-lace doily to each level and it's perfect."

Susan then showed us a photo of the three-tiered clear glass serving tower she'd gotten from Target, and I contributed my two porcelain cake stands—one pink-and-green floral, one blue-and-white—I'd snagged from a Walnut Creek thrift shop years ago.

We arranged the cucumber, ham, and salmon-salad sand-wiches on the two bottom layers of mine and Dorothy's floral china stands, added the scones to the middle layer, and topped off both tiered towers with Dorothy's lemon squares, Lottie's petite brownies, and Susan's fruit tarts. I placed Maddie's sparkly sugar cookies on a separate floral plate with a paper doily. Then we covered all the food with plastic wrap as we waited for the water to boil and our next-door guests to arrive.

Meanwhile, I led the committee into the dining room to show them where we would be eating and to have them choose their favorite teacup. Not a fan of everything having to be matchy-matchy, over the years I had collected an assortment of English bone china to mix and match. Atop the lace-covered table gleamed a floral mixture of Royal Doulton, Royal Albert, Royal Worcester, Spode, and Wedgwood offset by a bouquet of pink, red, and yellow roses nestled in my thrift-store rose-patterned teapot, the lid of which had broken in my move.

"Hope, this is beautiful," Dorothy breathed. "I feel like I'm back in England again."

"So lovely," Patricia said, admiring each place setting.

"Well, I may not be a cook, but I'm good with presentation."

The doorbell rang as the teakettle whistled. Patricia and Lottie followed me to the kitchen while Dorothy answered the door. When we returned to the dining room with pots of steaming Earl Grey and my ubiquitous PG Tips, we found Maddie and her mother seated at the table in their Sunday best. Maddie looked adorable in a pink-and-white gingham dress dotted with tulips and daisies. A pink rhinestone tiara sparkled against her dark curls.

"My goodness, I didn't realize we were entertaining royalty today," I said. "Welcome, Princess Maddie."

"I'm not a princess," my young neighbor said imperiously. "I am the Queen."

"Oh, I beg your pardon, Your Majesty," I said, giving a slight curtsy. "Would you care for sugar in your tea?" I passed the bowl of sugar cubes and silver tongs to Nikki, who set them down beside her daughter.

Maddie peered into the china container. "Ooh, the sugar has frosting flowers on it," she squealed.

"Nothing's too good for the Queen."

We all began noshing on the dainty tea sandwiches, chatting away, although Dorothy seemed unusually quiet. Everyone liked her classic cucumber and Patricia's salmon-salad, but the hit of the day was the ham and apricot cream cheese. When it came time for the scone course, Dorothy showed us the proper English way to eat a scone—sliced in half horizontally, then spread first with jam or lemon curd and topped with Devonshire cream. "In Devon they put the cream on first and top it with jam," she said, "but I prefer it the Cornish way with cream on top." Her voice lacked its usual enthusiasm, however, and recalling her troubled look at the funeral reception, I decided to talk to her privately once everyone left.

Two hours later Nikki took a sleepy Maddie home while the rest of us debriefed. Everyone agreed the desserts were perfect.

"Your lemon squares melted in my mouth, Dorothy," I said. "Yum. So delicious." I turned to Lottie. "Those were definitely the best brownies I've ever had. You have to give me the recipe."

Patricia raised an eyebrow. "I thought you didn't cook?"

"I don't. This is baking. And chocolate. That's a whole different story."

As we cleared the table and the women packed up their things, I asked Dorothy if she could stay a while. She begged off, saying she was exhausted and desperately in need of a nap. Noticing her leaning heavily on her cane reminded me that the sweetheart of Faith Chapel was eighty-one years old. Our talk would have to wait for another day.

Wondering if another eightysomething also took Sunday afternoon naps, I called Marjorie after my tea guests departed and asked if I could pop by for a quick visit. She demurred at first, saying she was in the middle of something, but when I told her it was important, she grudgingly agreed and asked me to give her an hour.

While I waited, I pulled out the charcoal sketch of the ringleted woman and examined it again. When I had shown it to James Brandon, he had admired the woman's beauty but had not recognized her and said she didn't resemble any of his grandparents.

More convinced than ever that the artist's initials stood for Richard Chamberlain and that the drawing had remained in the attic, overlooked, when his great-granddaughter moved out, I felt a frisson of excitement about showing the sketch to Marjorie. Not only would I at last learn the identity of the unknown woman, but returning the sketch to its rightful owner might also lessen Marjorie's antipathy toward me and allow us to start fresh.

Forty-five minutes later, I knocked on the front door of Marjorie Chamberlain's Victorian in time to see Lottie scurry out the back gate. I waved, but Lottie was in too much of a hurry to see me. Marjorie answered the door moments later clad in a blue-and-white cotton caftan, which made the head of the altar guild look softer and less formidable than she did in her ubiquitous pantsuits.

I extended a peace offering of daffodils from my garden, which brought a surprised smile to Marjorie's lined face. She ushered me inside.

"Lottie didn't need to leave," I said as I followed her down the hall and into a formal living room that bore a striking resemblance to the King living room. "She could have stayed."

"Lottie?"

"Yes. I saw her leaving out back when I arrived."

"I think it's time for glasses, Pastor," Marjorie said in a frosty tone. "That wasn't Lottie. That was my housekeeper." She sat down stiffly on a high-backed rose-colored sofa that looked as though it harkened back to Victorian times. Marjorie placed the vase of daffodils on the mahogany pie crust table beside her.

Let it go, Hope. The last thing you want to do is start this conversation with an argument.

"Thank you for seeing me on such short notice." I sat down in the matching love seat across from Marjorie. "I've wanted to talk to you for a while, but with all that's been going on, I haven't had a chance." I leaned forward and looked her in the eye. "I owe you an apology for the way I handled this whole ladies' tea. I didn't mean to be ungracious when you offered to take the helm for me. You obviously have much more experience than I do organizing a tea."

Marjorie's icy demeanor began to thaw. She relaxed back into the couch, a satisfied smile playing across her lips.

I lifted my shoulders in a shrug. "It's just . . . being the new associate pastor, I saw the tea as a way of getting to know all the women of Faith Chapel. I guess you could say I was trying to prove myself. To be honest, it's not easy being the first woman priest at a church. You always have to prove yourself—especially to the men. Men like Stanley."

Marjorie's eyes flickered. I got the sense she was waiting to see what I said next.

This is it, Hope. Bring it home, baby.

"By taking charge of the tea, however, I didn't mean to shut you out. I would really love to have you come to the tea, Marjorie. We all would. You are an integral part of not only Faith Chapel but also Apple Springs. The tea won't be the same without you," I said. "In fact, I wanted to ask if you would please consider being a table hostess. I understand you have some gorgeous heirloom silver and family china. Each table hostess is bringing her own china, silverware, and water goblets, and we'll be awarding a prize for the most beautifully decorated table." Glancing around the finely furnished room, I took in the lush Oriental carpets, antiques, original oil paintings, and classic blue-and-white porcelain vases. "Just seeing your lovely home, I have a feeling your table would be a top contender, if not the actual winner."

Suck up much?

Marjorie preened. "Well, my great-great-grandmother's Limoges, which she imported from France, has been in our family since the 1800s. I'll venture no one else in town has china with such a provenance."

"I certainly don't." I grinned at my—hopefully, former—nemesis. "Most of my china is thrift store or garage sale finds, although I do have a Spode teacup I brought back from England on my honeymoon."

Her thin lips slid over her teeth in what looked like a grimace but was actually a smile. "I have some Spode also—the

Blue Room collection." Marjorie regarded me with a thoughtful expression. "For the tea, I could bring the beautiful Waterford goblets my grandfather brought back from Ireland years ago," she said proudly.

Score. I did an inner fist bump. *You made peace with Marjorie and got your final table hostess as well.*

"That sounds perfect. Gorgeous, in fact. I can't wait to see your table in all its splendor." I reached down into my tote that bore Audrey Hepburn's iconic *Breakfast at Tiffany's* visage. "And now, I have a surprise I think you're going to like." I removed the rolled-up piece of brown paper with eager anticipation.

Marjorie sent me a curious look. "What's that?"

"You'll see." Carrying the charcoal sketch over to her, I sat down next to Marjorie as I gently unfurled the old drawing and set it on the coffee table before us. "We found this in Stanley King's attic—*your* former attic, actually." I anchored the four sides of the delicate paper with crystal coasters to hold it in place. "I think this drawing was done by your great-grandfather Richard Chamberlain—see the initials in the corner? Is this lovely lady one of your ancestors? Your great-grandmother, perhaps?"

Beside me, Marjorie went rigid. She reached out and yanked the sketch from the table. Then she tore it in half and threw it at me. Flecks of the fragile brown paper dotted my clergy vest. Marjorie shot to her feet shaking, her eyes shooting daggers. "How dare you suggest my great-grandmother was some cheap dance hall floozy?" Her chest heaved with outrage, and she pointed to the door. "Get out of my house and take that piece of trash with you!"

So, I guess this means you're not going to be a table hostess?

Chapter
Twenty-One

I arrived at the diner just as Susan turned the sign to *Closed.* Unlocking the door, she ushered me in.

"What's wrong? You look like you just lost your best friend."

"Definitely *not* my best friend. I may have lost one of our parishioners, though." Sliding into the first booth, I laid my head on my arms.

I had really stepped in it now. What if Marjorie left Faith Chapel because of me?

"I think someone needs a cup of tea."

"Only if you put brandy in it. Or better yet, tequila."

"Tequila in tea? Sounds not only disgusting but also a waste of good tequila. I'll go start your tea water."

"I don't want any tea," I mumbled.

"Now I know something is seriously wrong." I heard Susan slip into the booth across from me. "Want to tell me what happened?"

I lifted my head. "I have no idea. One minute I was at Marjorie's having a nice conversation and putting all that antagonism behind us, and the next minute she went all Anthony Perkins in *Psycho* on me."

"Why? What did you do?"

Pulling the torn sketch out of my Audrey tote, I set the now-tattered pieces on the table. "All I did was show her this and ask if it might be her great-grandmother, and she flipped out."

Susan stood up abruptly, returning moments later with a tape dispenser. She carefully taped the crumbling two halves of paper together. Then she looked at the drawing. "Well, whoever she is, she's a hottie. What made you think she was Marjorie's great-grandma?"

I explained about the drawing being found in Stanley's attic and how the woman wasn't from either Stanley or Lily King's family, so I thought it might be Marjorie's ancestor, seeing as how Chamberlains had lived in the house for more than a century before Stanley took ownership. Pointing to the faint initials in the corner, I said, "I thought *RC* might stand for Richard Chamberlain."

"Seems logical." Susan peered closer at the sketch. "Hey, that theater looks familiar. Particularly the balcony. I think it might be the one in Nevada City."

"Where's Nevada City?"

"About an hour and a half north of here." She sent me a sly grin. "You want to take a field trip?"

"How soon can we leave?" I jumped up.

"Hang on there, Sloopy; I have a date with Mike tonight. The theater will still be there tomorrow."

"But I won't," I pouted. "My schedule's packed for the next three days." We agreed to scope out the theater on Thursday, my day off, after the diner's lunch rush.

Once I arrived home that evening, I called Christopher to inform him of the odd Marjorie debacle and to say I was concerned that, because of whatever I had done wrong, she might not darken our church doorstep again.

Father Christopher chuckled. "Don't worry. Marjorie will never leave Faith Chapel."

Relieved, I called Virginia and filled her in as well. As we chatted, I cashed in one of my best-friend chips and asked my sister-in-law to be my final tea-table hostess.

*   *   *

Monday morning, lost in thought and still musing over Marjorie's strange behavior, I took Bogie on his walk. All at once, a terrible wailing assaulted my ears. Looking up, I almost ran into Dylan in sweats jogging past as he belted out the worst rendition of Journey's "Don't Stop Believin'" I'd ever heard.

Bogie's ears splayed back and he sent me a pitiful look, which I translated to mean, *Please make it stop, Mom.*

The deputy grinned and pulled out his earbuds. "Pastor Hope." He knelt down and scratched Bogie behind the ears. "Hi there, fella. Remember me?"

Bogie's tail wagged now that the awful noise had ceased.

"Someone's in a good mood today."

"I got some good news. Doc Linden called the station this morning and said the female skeleton in your backyard is more than a hundred years old, probably closer to a hundred and fifty years."

"Not Betsy Guthrie, then."

"Definitely not Betsy." A huge smile split his craggy face.

"That is good news. Albert Drummond will be happy to hear that."

"Yep. And now people can stop dragging Harry's name through the mud."

I nodded. "I don't suppose this means you and the chief will try to figure out who the woman was?"

"Not anytime in the near future. There's no urgency in discovering her identity—not while we're in the midst of an active murder investigation."

"Of course."

That did not mean I couldn't continue my own investigation, though. Now that I had a tighter historical time frame to work with, it should make my search a little easier. The first place I planned to look was the local paper. Since *The Apple Springs Bulletin* had been online for only the past decade, they were bound to have archival copies of past issues at the newspaper office, and I knew those issues went back more than a hundred years—as trumpeted by the banner under the masthead, which said, "Bringing You the News Since 1860."

Look at you. Investigating not one, but two women of mystery, and trying to figure out Stanley's killer as well. You should hang up your clerical collar and hang out a detective shingle instead.

Not a chance. I love my job. Although I have to admit, it is fun playing Trixie Belden on the side.

* * *

During our weekly staff meeting, I brought Father Christopher and Elizabeth up to date on the community tea. "We'll have a full house Saturday with fifty women. Everything's on track and going well. Harold's got all his male servers in place." I inclined my head to Christopher. "Thank you, Father, for volunteering."

"I'm only coming for the scones with jam and cream," he joked.

"The cream!" I pulled out my phone and began tapping a note on my to-do list. "I almost forgot. I have to drive to Sacramento Friday to pick up the jars of Devonshire cream from Whole Foods." At seven bucks a pop and with one jar serving only four people, the cream did not come cheap. Dorothy had said that for a true English tea experience, however, clotted or Devonshire cream was essential. Not wanting to strain the church's limited finances, I'd opted to donate the cream myself.

"I can pick up the cream on my way home from work and bring it to the church Friday night." Elizabeth offered. "Whole Foods is near my work, and that will save you a trip to Sacramento."

"You're an angel."

Christopher then asked about any vacation plans for the year so that Riley could add them to the office calendar. Elizabeth had no plans, and I said I hoped to visit my family in Germany for a couple of weeks in the fall but hadn't firmed up dates yet.

Father Christopher announced that he would be taking nine days off in mid-July to see friends in Southern California and to visit the Getty, the Broad, and a few other museums. "Now that you're here for backup, Hope, I'm looking forward to some time off to visit with my friends. We haven't seen each other in quite a while." The seventy-five-year-old priest practically bounced in his seat with excitement. "We also got tickets to see Luca Giordano in *La Traviata*."

"Ooh, can you squeeze me in your suitcase? I've always wanted to hear him sing in person." I sighed. "One of these days." I turned to Faith Chapel's best singer and choir director. "Elizabeth, have you ever seen him perform?"

She nodded, her usually listless hazel eyes sparkling. "I had the once-in-a-lifetime experience of seeing Luca Giordano in *La Bohème* in San Francisco." Elizabeth's face took on an unexpected radiance. "It was incredible. A highlight of my life."

A memory nagged at the edge of my consciousness. Someone else in Apple Springs had also seen the famed tenor in *La Bohéme*. Who was it?

Then I remembered.

*   *   *

Thursday after the lunch crowd at the diner dissipated, Susan and I headed to Nevada City in her old pickup. Our aim was to discover whether the theater in that Gold Country town was the same one featured in the now-tattered charcoal sketch of the unknown woman. I had called ahead and explained to the woman who answered the phone at the theater what we wanted. She said she would meet us at the historic building at four.

As we drove into the picture-postcard nineteenth-century town nestled in the Sierra foothills and dotted with beautiful Victorians, I knew I would have to come back again when I had more time to take in the quaint town's myriad charms. Today, though, I was on a mission.

Arriving at the red-brick theater with oversized black shutters, we introduced ourselves to Kim, the gray-ponytailed woman who served as a docent for some of the museums in town. She proudly informed us that both Mark Twain and Lillie Langtry—the Jersey Lily—had performed at the venerable theater, and that the 1865 building was a registered historical landmark. Kim led us inside and onto the stage so we could get a view of the entire theater.

Susan crowed, "I thought so! This is definitely the place. Check out the balcony."

I removed the taped sketch from my bag, unrolling it carefully so as not to tear it even more, and set it on a nearby wooden podium. I looked at the sketch again, then out into the empty audience seating and up to the balcony. "You're right. She stood on this very stage." My breath quickened. At last we were getting somewhere.

A curious Kim peered over my shoulder. "Why that's Ruby Garnette."

"What?" I yelled.

Startled by my outburst, she took a step back.

"I'm sorry," I said in a normal tone. "We've just been trying to learn her identity ever since we found this drawing, and nobody's recognized her. Who did you say she was again?"

"Ruby Garnette. At least that was her stage name. Many of the entertainers back then gave themselves fancy stage names. Ruby was a popular singer and dancer from the post–gold rush era. All the men loved her. In fact"—Kim glanced at my clerical collar before continuing—"if you'll pardon my saying so, Pastor, rumor has it she was also a 'soiled dove.'"

"Soiled dove?"

"That's what they called ladies of the evening in the Old West."

Susan snorted. "No wonder Marjorie got her knickers in such a twist when you asked if it was her great-grandmother."

No wonder, indeed. Although, how would Marjorie have known the woman in the picture was a soiled dove, so to speak?

"Do you know when Ruby performed here?" I asked.

"During the early days of the theater—1866 and 1867, if I remember correctly," local history buff Kim said.

"What happened to her after that?"

"She left the area to make it big in San Francisco."

Susan and I both pulled out our phones at the same time. I tapped in *Ruby Garnette* and *San Francisco* in Google but came up empty. Then I added in *singer, dancer, mid-1800s,* and *soiled dove.* A bunch of black-and-white pictures of naked, nameless women from more than a century ago filled my screen. I quickly *X*'d out.

"Susan?"

"Nada. There's no record of a Ruby Garnette ever performing in San Francisco."

My sigh spoke volumes.

"I'm sorry I don't have any more information for you," Kim said.

"No need to apologize. What you gave us is pure gold," I said. "Now at last we know who our mystery woman is. Was. That means everything. Thank you so much."

She flushed with pleasure. "Would you like to see the painting that your sketch became?"

"The painting?" Susan and I exchanged astonished glances.

"Sure. That's how I recognized Ruby right away. I used to pass by her painting every day. For years there was a gallery of stars from the early days of the theater hanging in the lobby." She led us backstage. "That is, until a couple decades ago, when they were replaced with more current actors."

I could hardly contain my excitement. Not only did we at last have a name for our mystery woman, but we were finally going to see her in the flesh, so to speak.

We followed Kim into a cluttered storeroom overflowing with props and theatrical bits and bobs. "Now let me see . . . I know it's around here somewhere." She rummaged through some wooden crates. "Ah, here it is." She pulled out a small oil painting in a gilt frame, blew the dust off it, and turned it around to face us.

"Wowza." Susan said.

The charcoal sketch had not done her justice. In color, Ruby Garnette was drop-dead gorgeous. Her emerald-green gown set off her creamy skin and matched her vivid Emma Stone eyes beneath gleaming chestnut-brown ringlets. As I looked closer at the painting, I sucked in my breath. The antique charcoal drawing I had been staring at for days had smudges in places, rendering some of the details indistinguishable. The oil painting, however, was in pristine condition, with each detail standing out in stark relief.

Including the silver locket around Ruby's neck.

Chapter
Twenty-Two

"*R* is for Ruby," I whispered.

"What was that?" Kim asked.

"Nothing."

Could it really be? What were the odds? I snapped a few close-ups of the painting with my phone, then glanced at my watch. "Sorry, we need to get going."

After thanking Kim for her help and promising to come back again to see a play at the theater, I hustled Susan outside.

"What's up, Buttercup? Why the rush?"

"I think Ruby Garnette and the skeleton from my backyard may be one and the same."

"What?"

As we drove back to Apple Springs, I reminded Susan that the archaeologist estimated the skeleton to be around a hundred and fifty years old.

"That doesn't prove anything."

"No, but it is one piece of the puzzle." I scrolled through my phone contacts until I found Doc Linden's number. Then I texted her a close-up photo of the locket from the painting and asked her if it matched the tarnished locket she had found in the grave.

"According to our new friend Kim," I said, "Ruby Garnette left Nevada City around 1867 to make it big in San Francisco, yet after that, there's no information on her. She just disappeared."

"Easy enough to do in a big city. People fall through the cracks all the time. It could also be that maybe she wasn't a good enough performer for the City by the Bay," Susan said. "Back then, San Francisco was like the New York of the West, and as such, able to attract big-name talent. Ruby Garnette was not a big name. Success on a Nevada City stage doesn't equate to success in San Francisco."

"True," I said reluctantly.

"She also could have gotten married and become Ruby Smith or Jones, or maybe even McGillicuddy."

"Way to rain on my parade. Are you always such a wet blanket?"

"That's what Mike says. I prefer to think of myself as pragmatic."

My phone chirped with a text. Doc Linden sent me side-by-side photos of the locket from the grave and the one in the painting. She had cleaned up the tarnished oval locket, and although it was worn and battered, it was identical to the one around Ruby's neck, down to the tiny ruby in the center.

Goose bumps erupted on my arms, and I let out a gasp.

"What is it?"

"Fasten your seat belt, Ms. Pragmatic. It's going to be a bumpy night." I texted Doc Linden back and asked why she hadn't said there was a tiny ruby on the locket found in the grave.

Dr. Linden: *An archaeologist doesn't reveal all her secrets at once. Gotta keep 'em guessing. So tell me, who is the woman in the painting?*

That I knew. What I did not know yet was why Ruby Garnette's body had been buried in my backyard. Nor did I know who had murdered the singer and dancer who looked so vibrant and full of life in her painting. Or who the man was who had loved her and given her the locket engraved *Always.*

Me: *A priest doesn't reveal all her secrets at once either. One last question: when you cleaned the locket, did the initials show up any clearer? Was it a B and an R, or an R and an H?*

Dr. Linden: *Neither. Two R's.*

And I knew.

* * *

As much as my inner Trixie Belden wanted to immediately follow up on Ruby and the man who loved her, my pastoral duties came first. Friday was all about preparation for my Faith Chapel debut event—the community women's tea on Saturday. Gulp. Several women in town had stopped me during my daily walks the past week to say how excited they were about Saturday and how much they were looking forward to a genuine English tea with all the trimmings.

"It will be just like *Downton Abbey,*" one of them trilled.

No pressure.

List girl that I am, I created lists for every aspect of the tea:

•   Menu

- Decorations
- Who was making which menu item and when
- Order of food prep for Saturday
- Table hostess names and requisite hostess items for each table
- Seating assignments by table
- Male servers
- Schedule for Friday and Saturday
- Items I needed to set up and decorate my table of eight

In addition to the requisite china, flatware, and water goblets, I would be setting my table with vintage linens I had picked up at estate sales. I had a beautiful white table runner embroidered with pale-pink roses and edged with cutwork that would nicely complement the pink tablecloth from Patricia. Silver-plated teacup napkin rings I'd found on Etsy would encircle my embroidered napkins, and a jam caddy with three cut-glass bowls would hold my jam, lemon curd, and Devonshire cream. I had opted to keep my table decorations simple. (Not kosher for the priest in charge to win the Best Decorated Table contest.) In addition to Bonnie's floral centerpiece, I was simply adding a trio of antique tea tins and a small porcelain plaque featuring a C. S. Lewis quote: *You can never get a cup of tea large enough or a book long enough to suit me.*

Riley Smith, who had fast become an indispensable member of the Faith Chapel staff, had offered to paint a floral scene for the parish hall. She knocked on my office door Friday, with Megan in tow and carrying something beneath her arm. "Pastor Hope, can we show you something?"

"Sure. Come in." I glanced at the wall clock, which showed a few minutes after one. "Wait, don't you have school today?"

"It's a minimum day, so we got off early." Riley and Megan then proceeded to unfurl a large fabric painting of an English cottage garden anchored by a thatched-roof cottage and bursting with vibrant hollyhocks, delphiniums, sweet peas, peonies, and roses. Masses and masses of roses.

"Wow. Just wow. That's incredible, Riley! I feel as if I'm back in England."

"Really?" She sent me a shy smile.

"Yes. This is the crowning touch. The women will love this." I hugged her. "The best thing we ever did was hire you."

Riley beamed. Then she reached down and picked up a white poster board. "I thought maybe this would be nice for everyone to see when they first walk in." She added quickly, "You don't have to use it if you don't want to, though." Riley turned the board around to reveal the full tea menu written in an Olde English calligraphy script and offset by trailing vines and pink-and-yellow roses.

"Not use it? Are you kidding? It's perfect. You rock!" Led Zeppelin's "Stairway to Heaven" blasted from my cell. "Sorry. Hang on a sec." I turned down the volume and answered the phone. "Hey, favorite sister-in-law. You on your way?"

A croak sounded in my ear.

"Virginia?"

"I'm sicker than a dog," she rasped weakly. "Been puking my guts out for the past hour and I'm achy all over."

"Oh no." My heart sank.

"I thought I'd be better soon and could still come, but it's not happening. I'm so sorry to bail on you like this."

Not as sorry as I am. Instantly I regretted my lack of compassion for my sick sister-in-law.

"It's okay, we'll be fine. You just take care of yourself, okay? And get thee to a doctor stat." Ending the call, I sent a plaintive glance heavenward. "Where am I going to find a table hostess at the eleventh hour?"

"Pastor Hope?" Megan said. "Can more than one person host a table? How about my mom, Riley, and me together? We're all coming to the tea anyway."

Thank you, Jesus.

"Hadn't you better check with your mom first? She may be too busy doing all the flower arrangements to host a table as well."

"No prob." Megan's black-manicured fingers flew over her phone. "Riley and I can do most of it—we'll just use Mom's things. She's got lots of cool dishes and stuff."

After getting Bonnie's buy-in and expressing my profuse thanks, I handed Megan the table hostess sheet listing all the items the trio would need. Then I checked my watch and my Friday schedule. At two, Liliane and Lottie were on task to bake brownies and half the scones over at Lottie's, while Dorothy, Patricia, and I would make lemon squares and the other half of the scones at my house. Following that, the tea committee would all meet at the parish hall at five to begin setting up the tables, and Bonnie would deliver the flower arrangements.

I had asked Dorothy to come half an hour before Patricia so she could show me how to prep the cucumbers for the sandwiches. We would make all three kinds of sandwiches at church in the morning to keep them fresh, but the fillings would be prepared ahead of time.

As we sat on my kitchen barstools slicing the cucumbers, Dorothy and I chatted. She talked about growing up with her twin sister in Kansas, while I told her about my Wisconsin child-hood. During a lull in the conversation, I asked, "Are you okay, Dorothy? Ever since Stanley's funeral, I've sensed something's been troubling you." I looked into the beloved face of Faith Chapel's sweetheart, and my heart fluttered. "Please tell me you're not sick."

"Oh no, I'm fine. A little tired, that's all. I often take a daily nap about this time." A ghost of a smile flickered across her face. "You'll understand once you hit seventy."

"I'm already a big fan of naps. I take a twenty-minute power nap once or twice a week, and it always recharges me." I smiled at her and said gently, "If there's something wrong, Dorothy, I'd like to help. That's what I'm here for, you know."

Her warm brown eyes met mine, and in them I saw confusion and distress. "I know, Pastor, but after your sermon, I don't want to rush to judgment or say anything that might hurt someone. I don't want to gossip." She pinched the bridge of her nose beneath her bifocals. "Something has been weighing heavy on my mind, though."

"I'm here to listen," I said, touching her hand. "Anything you say to me is confidential and won't leave this kitchen." Trying to put her at ease, I joked, "Although if you tell me you offed Stanley, I'd have to counsel you to show true repentance by turning your-self in to Harold."

Dorothy dropped her snowy head into her hands and burst into tears. "I didn't kill Stanley," she said in a muffled voice, "but I think I know who did." Her shoulders shook. "I—I saw someone leaving the columbarium area the night we now know Stanley King died."

Relieved, I hugged her and patted her back. "Are you talking about Don Forrester? It's okay. The police have already talked to Don and cleared him." I handed her a tissue.

She blew her nose. "Not Don Forrester." Anguished tears spilled down her cheeks. "It was that sweet Samantha King."

My stomach clenched. *Samantha?* "Tell me what you saw."

Dorothy swiped at her tears. "That Thursday night I'd gone to the rectory to get a book from Father Christopher. I arrived a few minutes past six, and Father invited me in. We chatted for maybe ten or fifteen minutes, and then I left. As I was driving away, I saw Samantha running from behind the church in the area of the columbarium. She was sobbing her heart out and clutching her cheek."

Not Samantha. Please. Anyone but Samantha. That poor kid has been through enough already, and she's finally on the cusp of a new beginning.

"That doesn't mean she killed her father," I said, trying to convince myself as well as Dorothy. "There could be a perfectly reasonable explanation for what you saw. Maybe she had just had an argument with someone. A boyfriend, perhaps?"

"I didn't know Samantha had a boyfriend," Dorothy said, sniffling.

"I don't know whether she does or not—she hasn't said anything to me, but then why would she? Maybe she's in a new relationship and they just don't want everyone knowing yet, what with her dad dying and all."

She sent me a hopeful look. "Do you think so?"

"Could be, or it could be some other problem altogether."

"That's what I thought after I saw her that night. Then when I heard those choir women at Stanley's funeral say they thought

Samantha killed her father for the inheritance, I began to wonder." Dorothy looked at me, embarrassed. "I know. I shouldn't listen to gossip, but when it went around town that Stanley left everything to his daughter in his will, I worried it might be true."

"Tell you what. I'll go see Samantha once we get through the tea and offer a listening ear—if she wants it."

"Thank you, Pastor. I feel much better now," Dorothy said, blowing her nose again. "Now let's finish up the cucumbers so we can get cracking on those lemon squares."

As I sliced the final cucumber, I recalled Samantha's words in the diner after her father's death: "What are we going to do? I don't know what to do. What if someone finds out?" And my stomach turned.

Chapter
Twenty-Three

Saturday morning at seven forty-five, I hurried over to the church with my lists and the ham slices and cream cheese spread to get a head start on the preparations for the eleven-thirty tea. The tables had all been set up and decorated last night, with the exception of last-minute-addition Megan, Bonnie, and Riley's, which was half done. They had left early to search out more decorations and promised to be in first thing this morning to finish their table.

I ran through the final prep in my head as I walked toward the parish hall. *Sandwich fixings? Check.* Patricia had made up her delicious salmon salad last night and stuck it in the church refrigerator, ready for spreading onto buttermilk bread this morning. Dorothy had stored the cream cheese, butter, and dill mixture for the cucumber sandwiches in a plastic container in the fridge, next to the container of cucumbers sprinkled with water to keep them from drying out overnight, and I had the final sandwich ingredients in my hands. I planned three assembly-line stations with two sandwich makers apiece.

Scones and cream? Check. Elizabeth had delivered the Devonshire cream from Whole Foods last night as promised, and Patricia and Liliane would be bringing the two kinds of scones.

Desserts? Check. Dorothy's famous lemon squares were in the fridge, while Lottie's brownies sat covered on the counter. Susan's miniature fruit tarts would arrive with her this morning.

Tea? Check. In addition to my beloved PG Tips (which we were calling English Breakfast for a more elegant cachet), we were also serving classic Earl Grey, and a peach herbal for those who needed decaf—or as I thought of them, the decaffeinators.

Flowers? Check. Bonnie had placed her gorgeous flower arrangements on each table last night. The profusion of yellow, coral, cream, lavender, and two-shades-of-pink cabbage roses in china teapots elicited exclamations of delight from the prep workers. The main centerpiece took pride of place on the food table—a stunning arrangement of roses, lavender, delphiniums, and my favorite, pink peonies.

Entering the kitchen, I froze. The loaves of bread we'd left sitting neatly on the counter were ripped open and dumped onto the floor. Patricia's bowl of salmon spread, the plastic wrap removed, lay tipped over on the counter, the contents spilled out, leaving a faint scent of fish gone bad. I turned and surveyed the rest of the room in a daze. Next to the ruined salmon salad stood the expensive jars of Devonshire cream, opened. *Wait, is that mold?* I stepped closer and peered inside. *Not mold. Black pepper.* Someone had put pepper into each bottle of cream, rendering it inedible.

The cucumbers Dorothy and I had sliced yesterday were dumped into the sink. The two pans of Lottie's petite brownies that had been sitting on the counter last night were down to one pan now. *Oh no, what about the lemon squares?* I rushed to the fridge, where I was relieved to find both pans intact. Small consolation. Now I knew what the police term *malicious mischief* meant. Vandals had broken in and destroyed things. But why? Had anything been stolen? I looked around to check. The only thing missing was one pan of Lottie's brownies. *Apparently, the thief is a chocoholic, but how did he—or she—get in?* I looked for broken glass from a window, but there was none. *Did someone not close the door tightly when we left last night? Who was the last to leave?*

A shriek sent me rushing from the kitchen into the parish hall.

Megan, Riley, and Patricia stared openmouthed at the tables. "What happened to my mom's flowers?" Megan said, her hand to her mouth. My eyes tracked her horrified gaze to see that all the roses on every table—save the food table centerpiece—had been snipped off, leaving a bunch of naked stems in each teapot.

"Oh no! Not here too."

Former cop Patricia sent me a sharp glance. "What do you mean, *too?*"

I told them about the food destruction. A scowling Patricia headed to the kitchen, but Riley and Megan remained rooted to the spot. "Who would do such a horrible thing?" Megan wailed.

Trailing my vestry senior warden, I heard Patricia's gasp, followed by an expletive.

"I know. I'm so sorry about your salmon salad."

Patricia pulled out her phone.

"What are you doing?"

"Calling Harold."

I laid my hand on her arm. "Please don't." I showed Patricia the rest of the damage, ending with the missing pan of brownies.

Then I directed her to the locked and unbroken windows. "The kitchen door was locked when I arrived."

"So was the parish hall door. I unlocked it." Patricia opened the outside kitchen door and examined the lock. "No scratches or indications that someone jimmied the lock." She closed the door and narrowed her eyes. "This wasn't a break-in. Whoever did this had a key."

That's what I was afraid of.

We exchanged glances. Patricia put her phone away.

Someone from Faith Chapel had deliberately sabotaged the tea.

A tearful Megan and Riley entered the kitchen, followed by Susan, carrying a tray of her mini fruit tarts. "What the hell?" Susan said, upon seeing the ruined food. "Sorry. Heck." She set the tarts down at the farthest end of the counter away from the spoiled fish.

Riley then informed us that the sugar bowls on every table contained salt, not sugar. When she set down her bag of decorations, she'd inadvertently knocked over the sugar bowl on their table. In the process of cleaning up the spilled granules, she had licked a stray granule off her finger and tasted salt. She then checked all the other tables and found salt as well.

Why did I suddenly feel like Lot's wife?

At that moment, the back kitchen door flew open to admit Dorothy, Lottie, and Liliane bearing bags of scones. "Good morning, everyone," Dorothy sang out. "Isn't this a lovely day for a tea?"

Silence.

"Why all the glum looks?" Then she saw. "Oh my goodness!" Dorothy dropped her bag of scones and sat down heavily on a stool, gripping her cane.

"What happened?" Liliane asked, her eyes widening at the carnage.

Lottie cried, "Everything's ruined! We'll have to cancel the tea."

"Oh no, we're not canceling anything," I said. "We all worked too hard on this."

"But the salmon salad can't be used," Dorothy said. "We're not going to have enough sandwiches now." Then she noticed the opened jars of spoiled cream on the counter. "Not the cream!" Her eyes glistened with unshed tears, and her mouth quivered. "We can't have an English tea without Devonshire cream."

Looking around at the dejected group, I said, "Hang on a minute. Let me think."

Lord, how I wish Virginia were here—she's always good in a crisis, particularly a food one.

"*Snap out of it!*" Cher's *Moonstruck* voice sounded in my head.

Wait a minute: food crisis and Virginia. I had helped my sister-in-law cater events in the past, and there were occasionally food hiccups and sometimes full-on crises. Virginia never let it throw her, though. She always had a plan B. We needed a plan B. I thought for a few moments, then pulled out my phone and did a quick Google search. *Got it.*

"Okay, everyone, here's what we're going to do."

I sent Megan and Riley to the market to pick up more bread and the other items I needed. Susan told the teens that if the market came up short on anything, they should go to the diner and Mike would make up the food difference. Then I directed Lottie to dump all the salt from the sugar bowls and replace it with sugar.

259

After she finished that, she could fill the jam and lemon curd dishes. Before I could ask, Patricia dumped the ruined cream and salmon salad into the trash, along with the spoiled cucumbers. She took the trash to the dumpster. Susan wiped the counters down, and Liliane opened the windows to air out the kitchen. I tasked Dorothy with placing all the scones on the tea trays.

Then I called Bonnie.

"Megan already told me," she said, crying. "I can't believe it. Who would do something like this?"

"I know. I am so sorry this happened to your beautiful flowers. Thankfully, they left your amazing centerpiece alone." Then, since time was of the essence, I asked if she could come a little early and bring seven single roses or carnations that I could place on each table in bud vases. "And Bonnie?"

"Yes, Pastor?"

"Let's keep this between us. You know how fast word travels. No need to upset our guests and spoil their afternoon."

"You got it."

Once Megan and Riley returned from the store, I gathered everyone around and said, "What happened here stays here. No one else needs to know about this. For some reason, someone, or someones, wanted to disrupt this community event, but we're not going to let them. Are we?"

"No," Riley said.

"What was that?"

"No!" the rest of the group chorused.

"Well, all righty then." I wanted to close with an inspiring *Downton Abbey* quote, but the only one that came to mind was Maggie Smith asking, "What is a week*end*?" I decided to go with an old sports-movie quote instead. Punching the air, I said, "Now let's go out there and win one for the Gipper!"

Megan and Riley gave me blank looks.

The over-seventies smiled, and Susan burst out laughing. "Okay, Knute Rockne. Or is that Ronald Reagan?"

Then I gave everyone their marching orders. While Susan quickly sliced the replacement cucumbers, I began whipping the mock Devonshire cream—the recipe for which I had found on my phone—and the others started assembling sandwiches.

Half an hour later, with everyone's help, the sandwiches were finished and the mock cream—not as thick as the real stuff— rested in individual serving bowls in the fridge, waiting to be placed on tables at the last possible moment. Dorothy cut her lemon squares while Susan placed her mini fruit tarts on the top of each tiered tray and Lottie and Patricia topped the petite brownies with whipped cream and a cherry.

I left the kitchen to go put the individual flowers in the bud vases. When I reentered the hall, I blinked at what I saw. Bonnie, Megan, and Riley were just finishing lush new floral arrangements in the denuded teapots. Instead of a mass of cabbage roses, each teapot now held clusters of pink-and-white mini carnations, three complementary roses, greenery, and one ruffled pink peony in the center. The snipped off cabbage-rose heads nestled against the base of each teapot, offering a fragrant foundation.

"Wh . . . how . . . how did you do that?" I asked.

"Where there's a will, there's a way," Megan said. "Right, Mom?"

"Right," Bonnie said, hugging her smiling daughter, while Riley grinned.

"Thank you so much. Everything looks beautiful." I glanced at my watch. Twenty minutes until show time. I puffed out a sigh of relief. Everything was running like clockwork. Harold, Christopher, and the rest of the male servers would be arriving at any moment.

"Hope," Patricia called from the kitchen. "Can you come here, please?"

"What's up?" I asked as I returned to the food hub.

"We're short on the third dessert. There's not enough brownies for each table."

Lottie looked downcast.

I groaned. I had forgotten all about the missing pan of brownies. Too late to send anyone to the store to buy cookies. I looked around the expectant group. What could we use to fill in for the absent petite dessert? My Walkers shortbread would be perfect, but I didn't have time to go home and get it. Besides, there were only three left in the package.

Pulling out my phone, I punched in a number. "Bethann, can you do me a huge favor?"

*   *   *

The tea was a rousing success.

"Oh my goodness," said an elderly woman from First Baptist. "Look at those beautiful floral arrangements with the gorgeous peony in the center."

"And all the fabulous table decorations," her younger friend said. "I've never seen anything like this. I feel as if I'm in England or Scotland."

As predicted, Riley's painting of the English cottage garden on fabric was a huge hit. "It's so beautiful," several tea guests exclaimed. "Exquisite," one woman breathed. The latter sought out Riley to say she'd commission her to paint something similar for her home.

After welcoming everyone and offering a blessing, I announced that we had encountered some unexpected technical difficulties and had had to make some last-minute adjustments to the menu. "I can tell you, though, that I've been nibbling in the kitchen all morning," I said, "and everything is absolutely delicious, so please dig in."

The women raved over the food, inhaling the ham sandwiches and saying they liked the touch of childhood whimsy in the heart-shaped PB&J sandwiches and the bite-sized Twinkies sliced horizontally and then vertically in half to resemble a cream puff of sorts. The scones were the biggest hit, however.

"So decadent."

"I know. Who would have thought to put jam and cream on a scone? Yum!"

Baptists broke bread with Catholics, Episcopalians chatted with charismatics, Buddhists sipped tea with Presbyterians, and nondenominationalists swapped recipes with New Agers and nonchurchgoers. As Father Christopher refilled the teacups at my table, he murmured in my ear, "Great job, Hope. Another home run."

The trio of Riley, Megan, and Bonnie won the prize for Best Decorated Table for their fun and creative reimagining of the Mad Hatter's Tea Party. I presented them with a gift basket of assorted teas and chocolates. "You'll have to fight over the See's Candy."

*   *   *

Afterward during cleanup, Lottie avoided me. I took her outside, away from everyone, and said, "Do you have something you'd like to tell me?"

Lottie broke down weeping. "I'm so sorry, Pastor Hope. I didn't want to do it, but Marjorie and I have been friends for a long time. I owe her a lot. She was so angry, and she has a way of making people do what she wants." She squared her shoulders and looked me in the eye. "That is no excuse, however. What I did was awful and unforgivable."

"Nothing's unforgivable, Lottie," I said softly.

Another outbreak of weeping followed.

"It could have been worse. All the food could have been ruined, leaving me with no alternative than to cancel the tea, but it wasn't. Just a few items. I think perhaps you had something to do with that, yes?"

Lottie nodded. Then she told me everything.

* * *

Fifteen minutes later, after securing Lottie's promise not to talk to Marjorie, I knocked on the cradle Episcopalian's door, a plate of leftovers in hand.

"Lottie, I've been trying to reach you," Marjorie said, flinging open the door. "Oh, it's you."

"May I come in?" I extended the plate to her. "I brought goodies from the tea—everything was delicious. I'm sorry you missed it. It was quite an event."

Marjorie's nostrils flared, and she turned her back on me. "I have nothing to say to you."

"But I have something to say to you. We can do this inside or out here on the porch, where your neighbors can see and hear. It's up to you."

She huffed and retreated into the house. *At least she didn't slam the door in my face.*

"Marjorie," I said as I followed her into the living room. "It was never my intent to steal the tea away from you. I understand you were hurt and angry—that was why I came here and apologized and tried to make amends. But then I showed you the sketch of Ruby Garnette, and that was that."

Marjorie whirled around at the sound of Ruby's name.

Was that fear I saw on her face?

"Where did you hear that name?" she stammered.

"From a Nevada City docent. There's a beautiful oil portrait of Ruby in the theater there," I said, "painted by your great-grandfather Richard Chamberlain. He loved her, didn't he?"

"No! She was nothing but a dance hall hussy." Marjorie spat the words out. "A soiled dove who shared her body with any man who had two shiny nickels to rub together."

"What happened?" I said gently. "Did she cheat on your grandfather and he found out and killed her?"

"No. Supposedly she 'fell in love' and became a one-man woman." Marjorie snorted. "Grandpa Richard was completely besotted. She really snookered him. Thought she could hitch a ride on the gravy train of the Chamberlain money for the rest of her life."

"They got married?"

"A Chamberlain and some harlot named *Ruby Garnette?*" Her voice dripped with disdain. "Not likely. His mother, my grandmother Cordelia, would never allow that to happen." Marjorie's eyes took on a haunted look. "And she didn't."

I stared at her, realization dawning. "Your great-great-grandmother killed Ruby, didn't she?"

Marjorie sat down hard on her Victorian sofa and released a weary sigh. "Now that you know our dirty laundry, I suppose you're going to start blackmailing me too, just like Stanley did."

The pieces fell into place. *Extortion.* "That's why you sold your house to Stanley. He found out about Ruby."

She nodded. "Years ago at Chamberlain House during one of my Christmas Eve open houses, Stanley was snooping around, unbeknownst to me. He found a leather-bound journal that had belonged to my great-grandfather." Marjorie passed a shaking hand over her face. "Two weeks later Stanley paid me a private visit, journal in hand. He announced that Cordelia Chamberlain, my grandfather's mother, had murdered a dance hall floozy to prevent her from marrying her son." Marjorie's eyes narrowed. "I'll never forget the contemptuous look on that vile man's face or the way he talked to me. Stanley said he wondered what that information would do to the respected Chamberlain name and reputation if it was made public."

And the family name and reputation means more to you than anything, I thought. *You would go to any length to protect it, including sabotaging a tea. It wasn't just jealousy—you were trying to distract me, since I was asking questions about the woman in the sketch. I was getting too close.*

She drew herself up with a haughty sniff. "I told Stanley he was lying, but then he showed me the journal." Dejection replaced her haughtiness. "And then I read my grandfather's account of the night he brought Ruby Garnette home." Marjorie fixed her gaze on me. "Not to Chamberlain House—it wasn't built yet. The original family home was where you live now."

I nodded, acknowledging the connection.

"Richard wrote that he brought Ruby over to introduce her to his mother and to inform her of their engagement," she said quietly. "He said Ruby had dressed carefully for the occasion, eschewing her normal dance hall wardrobe in favor of a demure, high-necked velvet gown and looking every inch the lady with her hair swept up and wearing the locket he had given her."

Marjorie clasped and unclasped her hands. "Ruby said she was nervous about meeting Cordelia—that she would never accept her—but Richard naïvely assured her that his mother loved him and wanted him to be happy. Once she saw how happy Ruby made him, Cordelia was bound to give them her blessing. The meeting was initially awkward, and the conversation stilted, he wrote, but then his mother became her usual gracious self to Ruby, and he was elated." A nervous tic pulsed behind Marjorie's eye. "The evening was chilly, and Cordelia asked Richard to fetch her shawl from her bedroom. He wrote that he mouthed 'I love you' to Ruby as he left the room." Marjorie's voice fell flat. "When my grandfather returned minutes later, he found Ruby dead on the floor, his mother standing over her, a bloody fireplace poker in hand."

Chapter
Twenty-Four

"Is your curiosity satisfied now?" Marjorie said bitterly. "What price do I have to pay for your silence?" Her fingers tightened on the armrest. "Stanley King took my home away from me and held my ugly family secret over my head for years." She leaned forward, eyes glittering. "Do you know what that does to a person?"

My stomach lurched. *Give them a strong motivation for murder?*

Marjorie might be over eighty, but she is a formidable woman from strong pioneer stock, my inner Trixie reminded me. *She could easily have bashed Stanley in the head. Murder is in her genes, after all.* I glanced at the angry woman across from me and felt a stab of fear, especially when I noticed the antique fireplace poker within easy reach.

Hope, you did not think this through.

I began to pray.

"Well?" Marjorie said. "What do I have to do to ensure your silence?"

Please don't kill me.

Then to my surprise, Marjorie began to weep. "I can't go through this again," she sobbed. "I'm an old woman. When Stanley died, I was so relieved, thinking my secret had died with him. I didn't have to live in fear of that horrible man exposing my family skeletons to the world any longer." Tears gushed down her lined cheeks. "But then you came along and started showing that sketch to everyone, and I knew it was just a matter of time before you discovered the truth." She sent me a pleading look. "Please don't tell anyone."

"I'm not going to tell anyone, Marjorie." I sat down next to my weeping parishioner and took her hand in mine. "You have my word."

Marjorie leaned into me and cried like a baby. I held her and prayed.

When her sobs finally subsided, I said. "Why don't we have a nice cup of tea? I happen to have some tasty scones."

After Marjorie's crying jag ended and we were drinking our tea and scarfing down scones, she offered up another first. An apology. *A grudging one, but still.* I accepted it, but said she also needed to apologize to the women who had all worked so hard on the tea. Marjorie pulled out her checkbook and said she would reimburse them for the damages and donate a sizable amount to Faith Chapel's events fund.

"You can't buy your way out of this, Marjorie." I tilted my head and sent her a gentle look to soften the reproach. "Those women worked their butts off and spent countless hours planning, preparing, baking, and giving their all to make this special event an expression of God's love from our church to the community."

269

She lowered her head, but not before I saw a flicker of shame cross the lined face of the descendant of one of Faith Chapel's founding families. Marjorie gave a slight nod. "I guess this is my penance," she said in a small voice, adding that once she apologized to the women, everyone in Apple Springs would know what she did.

"No, they won't," I said, holding up my hand in a three-fingered salute. "Priest's honor."

* * *

By the time I finally got home, I was in desperate need of more than a power nap. Thankfully, Nikki had texted me earlier saying she and Maddie had fed and walked Bogie. Removing my clerical collar, I flopped on the bed and groaned. "What a day."

Bogie licked my hand. I patted the bed, and he jumped up and lay down beside me. Within moments, I slept the sleep of the dead, Bogie snoring beside me.

* * *

The next morning after church, everyone was gushing about the tea.

"Pastor Hope, that was amazing!" Samantha said. "I've never been to a tea before. Everything was scrumptious, and so pretty."

"Very elegant," said Elizabeth Davis.

"It was Dorothy's idea in the first place. I've never done an English tea before. I had no clue how to make cucumber sandwiches or even scones." I sent a fond glance to my favorite parishioner. "Dorothy is the queen of scones."

Several women clustered around Dorothy, asking for her scone recipe.

"Y'all did a great job," Bethann said, her arm linked with Wendell's. She was wearing the same vintage pink pillbox hat perched atop her blonde beehive that she had worn to the tea yesterday. "Ah 'specially liked those cute li'l peanut-butter-and-jelly sandwiches in the shape of a heart." She winked at me. "A course the tiny Twinkies were mah personal favorite."

Father Christopher nodded sagely. "You can never go wrong with Twinkies. Naturally, Dorothy's famous lemon squares were delicious, as always. So were the fruit tarts and the one-too-many brownies I sampled." He patted his potbelly.

As I stood chatting with Patricia and Bonnie, an uncertain Marjorie approached with Lottie, who looked less timid than usual.

"I'm sorry I missed the tea yesterday," Marjorie said. "I hear everything was wonderful." She lifted her chin and looked at me straight on. "I hope we'll have another one soon, Pastor. I'll bring my curried-chicken salad." Then she turned to Megan and Riley and congratulated them on winning Best Decorated Table.

Patricia stared after her as she walked away. "Will wonders never cease."

*   *   *

Instead of my usual Sunday lunch at Suzie's, today I had a lunch date with Samantha King at her house. After Marjorie's big reveal yesterday, I had texted Samantha to see if she needed any more help organizing and packing. I offered to pack the books in the library, which would allow me to surreptitiously search for Richard Chamberlain's antique journal and return it to Marjorie.

Samantha texted back, however, that Todd had already finished packing up most of the books yesterday. Only a couple now remained on the shelves.

Great. Now I'll have to go through all the packed boxes to find the journal. What excuse could I give Samantha as my reason for doing so? I suppressed a sigh. *The whole not-being-able-to-lie thing sure complicates things.*

You could always just come right out and ask Samantha about it. Chances are Stanley would not have left the blackmail journal in the library anyway. He probably kept it under lock and key somewhere.

That was exactly what he had done.

Samantha handed me the cracked brown leather journal, held closed by a worn strip of rawhide and covered in scratches. "Here you go. I found this in Dad's desk after he passed. I saw the name *R. Chamberlain* inside and realized it must belong to Marjorie's family. I meant to give it to her weeks ago, but in all the craziness of the funeral, selling the house, and packing everything up, I forgot."

"Thanks. I'm sure Marjorie will be happy to get this. Did you happen to read it?" I asked casually.

"I flipped through the first few pages. Nothing exciting—just lists of groceries. Stuff was cheap in those days. Like a pound of sugar? Nine cents. Quart of beans? Eight cents. Pound of lard?" Samantha wrinkled her nose. "Thirteen cents. And a pound of coffee? A whopping twenty-three cents."

"Clearly they didn't have Starbucks back then." I slipped the journal into my tote bag.

"Yeah, my vanilla latte would have broken the bank." She grinned.

We sat down in the living room, bare now except for a leather couch and two chairs, and chatted as we waited for lunch. When I first arrived, Samantha had said she hoped I didn't mind, but Todd and her uncle James would be joining us for lunch. They had gone to pick up pizza from Margheritaville and would be back any minute.

"Not a problem. As long as they're not wasting away there," I said.

Samantha gave me a blank look.

I sang a snatch of the classic Jimmy Buffett song.

She lifted her shoulders in a shrug. "Sorry. I've never heard that before."

"Ouch. Way to make me feel old. We definitely don't want to play any seventies mix tapes."

She laughed.

I thought back to my Dorothy conversation. "Samantha . . . do you have a boyfriend?"

"I wish." She gave me a rueful smile. "Not a lot of choices for someone my age in Apple Springs. That's one of the reasons I'm looking forward to moving to the City."

"You're moving to San Francisco?"

A door slammed from the back of the house. "Food's here," Todd yelled. He and his uncle joined us.

James, who was wearing jeans and a white button-down and carrying a six-pack of Dr. Pepper, sent me a lopsided smile. "We have to stop meeting like this, Pastor. What will people say?"

I stroked my dog collar reflectively. "They'll say that James Brandon sure must have a lot of things to confess."

Todd chortled.

As we ate, the King siblings told me about Marjorie buying her house back and her plans to move in by the end of the month.

"This is a pretty big house for one person." I said.

"She's going to have a roommate." Samantha took a swig of her Dr. Pepper. "Her friend Lottie."

The image of Cary Grant's two maiden aunts in *Arsenic and Old Lace* popped into my head. When I visited Marjorie and Lottie here, I would be sure not to have any elderberry wine.

Then Todd and Samantha shared their big news, their eyes sparkling with excitement. The next day they were going to San Francisco with their Realtor uncle to start looking for a house to buy.

"Maybe we'll get a high-rise condo. Something sleek and modern downtown that would be a real chick magnet." Todd gave his sister an exaggerated wink.

"Uncle James, we're definitely going to need a place with separate entrances," Samantha said. "I think a painted lady in Pacific Heights would be nice."

"Let's see now," James said, "that's sleek and modern downtown, and old and classic at least twenty blocks away. I can definitely guarantee separate entrances."

We all laughed. Then the doorbell rang.

Samantha jumped up, still chuckling. "I'll get it."

She returned moments later, white-faced and followed by Harold Beacham and Dylan MacGregor, both in uniform and looking grim.

Harold acknowledged my presence with a brief nod before focusing his full attention on Todd and Samantha. "We have some news about your father's murder."

274

Samantha trembled and shot a frightened look at her brother, who moved next to her and put his arm around her.

"Stanley's missing Rolex was found in a Sacramento pawnshop," Harold said. "The owner said a young, red-haired woman sold it to him."

I sucked in my breath.

The chief looked straight at Samantha. "That woman was you."

"I—I guess I should have worn a disguise," a chalk-white Samantha said as her eyes filled. "But I wasn't thinking clearly. I didn't have access to any cash. My father controlled my finances completely, and I have no money of my own. I needed my own money!" she said desperately.

"We also found your prints in the columbarium and on the murder weapon," Harold said quietly, his aged brown eyes full of sadness as he gazed at the young woman before him. "Samantha King, I'm arresting you on suspicion of the murder of Stanley King."

Samantha swayed against Todd, and James leapt to his feet.

"Stop it," Todd said. "Leave her alone."

"Todd, no," Samantha said, tears pouring down her face. "I'm so sorry," she sobbed. "You took the Rolex so it would look like a robbery, but then I went and ruined everything by going and selling it. Why didn't I wait? I just saw that stupid shiny expensive watch of his that he was always flashing around, and I lost it. I didn't want to look at it anymore; I didn't even want it in the house—it symbolized everything about him I hated—I wanted to get rid of it and get some of my own money at last."

"It's okay, Red." He gently wiped her tears. "We knew this might happen." Todd turned to Harold and Dylan. "Samantha didn't do it—I did. I killed my father."

Chapter
Twenty-Five

As the police took her brother away, a sobbing Samantha tried to follow. James hugged her and assured her he would go to the station and call the family lawyer on the way. He sent me a beseeching look over his niece's head before releasing her.

Nodding at James, I led Samantha over to the couch, where she continued to weep.

"It's all my fault," she cried, as great shuddering sobs racked her body. "It's all my fault."

I held her and made soothing noises as I sent up prayers. Then Samantha revealed all.

She and Todd had met their father in the columbarium, where he sometimes went to spend time with Lily. "Or at least that's what he told everyone. It looked good to play the loving husband paying his respects to his dead wife. Respect. Ha," she said bitterly. Samantha had taken Todd along for moral support when she broke the news to Stanley that she was moving out and going back to school. As expected, her father, who'd had a few drinks, lost it and started yelling at her and saying mean, hurtful things.

"That's when I hit him—slapped him in the face," Samantha said. "He slapped me back and yelled that I wasn't going anywhere. That he *owned* me." She began to shake, the tears dripping onto the carpet. "Todd told him to leave me alone, and Dad said Todd wasn't man enough to make him. Then he grabbed me by the hair and yanked my head back, hurting me. That's when Todd hit him with the urn and told me to get out of there."

Samantha looked at me with anguished eyes. "My brother killed our father trying to protect me, and now his life is over, all because of me." She sobbed anew.

*   *   *

The news of Todd killing his father spread through town like a certain leader's tweets. As I walked Bogie Sunday night, several people, including Liliane, stopped me to cluck and press me for information. The same thing happened today on my walk to work. I decided to skip tea and Susan's blueberry muffins at the diner to escape others wanting all the juicy details. Instead, I opted for a cup of PG Tips and a granola bar at my desk for breakfast.

As I sipped my tea and thought about Todd and Samantha, my heart ached. Only yesterday they had been bubbling over with excitement about house hunting in San Francisco. I bent my head and included them in my morning prayers. Once Father Christopher got in, we planned to discuss the best ways to help the siblings, spiritually and practically. When I'd called Christopher last night to tell him Todd had killed Stanley and that I was at the house comforting Samantha, he'd been shocked but had told me he'd go right over to the jail to visit Todd.

"Pastor Hope? Could I talk to you?"

I looked up to see our choir director standing in the doorway, an odd expression on her face.

"Of course, Elizabeth. Come in."

"Actually, could we go to the small chapel and talk there instead?"

"Sure." We made small talk as we walked down the shade-dappled stone walkway, past the camellias and vivid fuchsia azaleas. Beside me, Elizabeth hummed with a nervous tension.

As we sat down in the chapel crypt facing the stained-glass windows, Elizabeth fixed her eyes on the cross. After a moment, she bowed her head and prayed. I joined her. When Elizabeth lifted her head, she crossed herself and said softly, "This is where it all happened." Then she turned to me with a resolute gaze. "Pastor, I need to confess. I killed Stanley. Suffocated the SOB. After we're done here, I'm going to the police station to turn myself in, but I wanted to talk to you first and make my confession. When I heard this morning that that poor innocent boy had been arrested, I came straight here.

"Stanley and I had been lovers until recently," Elizabeth said. Then she proceeded to tell me in a calm, detached voice how her entire life had been one bad relationship after another—a distant, uninterested father, an abusive high school boyfriend, a marriage she vowed would be forever but instead ended in an unwanted divorce on her part after years of her husband's unfaithfulness. A divorce that left her shattered and teetering on the financial edge.

"My sole solace was music," she said. "Still fragile from the divorce, I took the choir director position at Faith Chapel. There I met Stanley, a self-professed music lover, who wooed me and

278

swept me off my feet with under-the-radar dinners and concerts. We both agreed we wanted to keep our relationship private, away from town gossip," Elizabeth said, adding that Stanley even took her to San Francisco to see her favorite tenor in her favorite opera, *La Bohème*. "It wasn't long before I fell head over heels.

"Then Stanley started to change," she said. "He canceled plans and began acting distant. I didn't understand what was happening. He turned cruel and dismissive. Then one day a couple months ago, he told me it was over; he had met someone else. Someone younger. Prettier," she said sadly. "I told him I loved him and reminded him of what we meant to each other, but he just looked right through me as if I didn't exist and walked out."

Elizabeth nodded her head to the door on our right and said that on the night Stanley died, she'd been in the music closet searching for a particular piece of music when she heard angry voices in the columbarium. She recognized Stanley's voice immediately—"he'd had one too many drinks, as usual"—and then she heard Don Forrester tell Stanley to stay away from Bonnie and her teenage daughter or he would file a police complaint.

"Stanley then made a lewd and disgusting comment about Megan," Elizabeth said, "and a moment later I heard a loud crash, followed by Stanley cursing Don. I opened the door to the columbarium and Don was gone, but Stanley was on the ground, rubbing his head," she said. "When he saw me, he snarled, 'What the hell are you looking at?' and I said, 'A pedophile, apparently.'" Elizabeth shuddered and closed her eyes. She added in a whisper that I had to lean forward to hear, "Then he licked his lips and said, 'Nothing better than sweet young meat.'"

My insides churned.

"I felt sick to my stomach," she said. "I couldn't believe I'd fallen for such a vile, loathsome pig."

After Stanley's repellent comment, Elizabeth said they heard Todd and Samantha approaching. "Stanley jerked his head at me to return to the closet," she said. "There I overheard an ugly family fight when Samantha told her father she was moving out." Elizabeth looked at me through eyes deadened by years of disillusionment. "Stanley said some awful things to his children, including telling Samantha he *owned* her. Then I heard what sounded like a struggle, followed by a loud thud and Todd telling Samantha to get out of there. After that, there was silence. I waited a couple minutes and then cautiously opened the door. Both the kids were gone, and Stanley was lying on the floor, quite still, his head in a pool of blood. I thought he was dead. I was relieved he was dead," she said. "Then he couldn't hurt anyone anymore. Then I heard a faint sound. I bent down and realized the sound was Stanley still breathing. I knew if he lived, he would continue to use and abuse other women as well as prey on innocent teenage girls. He'd also make Todd and Samantha's lives a living hell."

Elizabeth looked straight at me. "So I put my hand over his nose and mouth and held it there until he stopped breathing."

* * *

A month later, things had returned to normal in Apple Springs. Papers once again covered Christopher's office, only now they were confined to neat stacks on his desk, thanks to Riley. Susan was baking delicious peach pies and bragging about how she would beat me the next time we played Silver Screen Trivial Pursuit (after I skunked her seven times in a row). Harold and Patricia were enjoying an Alaskan cruise with their kids and grandkids, although Harold had worried how the town would manage in his absence. Deputy Dylan was busy keeping law and order—so far he had logged two parking tickets, one jaywalking citation, and no murders—which made him happy. Marjorie and Lottie were holding court at Chamberlain House and bickering like an old married couple over what food to serve at the next vestry dinner.

Riley graduated from high school with honors and celebrated by getting another tattoo—*Carpe Diem* on her left ankle. Bethann and Wendell Jackson renewed their wedding vows at Faith Chapel and celebrated with a huge backyard reception where they served Spam sandwiches, pigs in a blanket, and more Twinkies than I had ever seen together in one place. James Brandon's real-estate business was booming—having found a great place in Russian Hill for Todd and Samantha near the San Francisco Art Institute and sold Marjorie's former Victorian to my sister-in-law Virginia.

As for me?

Albert Drummond is teaching me how to play chess, Susan is teaching me how to bake pies, and Albert and I watch old black-and-white movies together regularly, with occasionally James and sometimes Dorothy joining us. I continue to sing in choir (we're looking for a new choir director), get together monthly with the Downton Divas for our *Downton Abbey* fix, and preach every other week. Twice a week I make a pastoral visit to a calm and at-peace Elizabeth Davis at the Sacramento jail, where she serenely awaits sentencing. Virginia and I go on daily power walks—happily, I haven't stumbled onto any more dead bodies—and I enjoy chillin' out with Bogie in the backyard, where I take great care of my new garnet-colored rosebush named Ruby Ruby.

Pastor Hope's
Movie Guide

I'm a movie geek, so everyone always asks, "What's your favorite old movie?"—a question that is impossible to answer. I thought maybe I could narrow it down to my top five, but that's also impossible, so I played that old game "If you were trapped on a desert island, what movies would you take?" (Assuming that said isle has electricity, the necessary electronic viewing devices, hot buttered popcorn, and Junior Mints.) I chose old friends, movies that always bring me comfort, joy, and hope—and sometimes much-needed laughter.

Top 11 Desert Island Old-Movie Picks
(in no particular order)

1. *The African Queen.* You'll never find a more mismatched couple than the scruffy, gin-swilling riverboat captain played by Humphrey Bogart and the prim, "psalm-singing skinny old maid" played by Katharine Hepburn. Forced together on a perilous journey at the start of World War I on Bogie's broken-down boat, they encounter many obstacles ("Leeches.

Filthy little devils"), unite against a common enemy, fall in love, fight against evil, and triumph in the end. **Favorite line**: "Nature, Mr. Allnut, is what we are put in this world to rise above."

2. ***The Best Years of Our Lives.*** In this inspiring forties classic, Fredric March, Dana Andrews, and Harold Russell play three returning veterans of World War II who have trouble readjusting to life back home. Myrna Loy (the elegant Nora Charles from *The Thin Man* series) and Teresa Wright (who played the wife of Lou Gehrig in another inspiring favorite, *Pride of the Yankees*) play the women who love them. Harold Russell, a WWII vet who lost both hands in a training accident and wore prosthetic hooks, had never acted before. He won a Supporting Actor Oscar for his sensitive portrayal of disabled small-town boy Homer. In one scene between Homer and his faithful fiancée Wilma, the wounded Homer—in a noble attempt to release the girl he loves from their prior engagement—shows his fiancée what life with him would be like now. He removes his prosthetic "hands" as he is getting ready for bed, and says, "This is when I know I'm helpless . . . as dependent as a baby . . ." Wilma hugs him and replies, "I love you and I'm never going to leave you . . . never." Then she tucks him in and kisses him good-night. Leaves me ugly-crying every time.

3. ***What's Up, Doc?*** After sobbing over *The Best Years of Our Lives*, I am in serious need of comic relief. Barbra Streisand, Ryan O'Neal, Madeline Kahn—in her screen debut—and this seventies comedy from Peter Bogdanovich that's an homage to *Bringing Up Baby*, the quintessential screwball comedy,

always delivers. (I watched both *Bringing Up Baby* and *What's Up, Doc?* recently, and although Cary Grant is far superior to Ryan O'Neal, I must confess to laughing more at *What's Up, Doc?* than the thirties classic.)

4. *Casablanca.* "Of all the gin joints, in all the towns, in all the world, she walks into mine." This is one of the greatest movies of all time, with some of the most-quoted lines in film history: "Round up the usual suspects . . . I think this is the beginning of a beautiful friendship . . . It doesn't take much to see that the problems of three little people don't amount to a hill of beans in this crazy world . . . We'll always have Paris . . . Here's looking at you, kid." (For the record, "Play it again, Sam," is never said.) Humphrey Bogart, the epitome of unruffled coolness, plays Rick, the cynical café owner, while the luminous Ingrid Bergman is Ilsa, the love of his life married to Victor Laszlo (Paul Henreid), the hero of the French Resistance. This star-crossed love story with its themes of nobility, honor, and sacrifice is timeless, even after seventy-five years. **Favorite scene:** When Victor Laszlo leads the entire nightclub in singing the patriotic "La Marseillaise" to drown out the Nazis.

5. *Meet Me in St. Louis.* I watch this nostalgic favorite every Christmas. Starring a radiant Judy Garland and the delightful Margaret O'Brien as young tomboy Tootie, this 1944 gem contains such classic songs as "The Boy Next Door," "The Trolley Song," and the beautiful and heartbreaking "Have Yourself a Merry Little Christmas" sung by a wistful Judy, resplendent in red velvet. **Trivia:** Director Vincente Minnelli and Judy fell in love during the making of the movie and later married. They went on to make several movies together and produced a

daughter, Liza Minnelli, who grew up to win the Best Actress Oscar for her star-making turn in *Cabaret*, another excellent, albeit very different, musical.

6. ***Singin' in the Rain.*** Best. Movie. Musical. Ever. Gene Kelly, Donald O'Connor, and an energetic, seventeen-year-old Debbie Reynolds. Yep, seventeen. I didn't realize she was that young when the movie began filming. (Gene was forty.) Great songs like "Good Morning," "You Were Meant for Me," and Donald O'Connor's showstopping "Make 'Em Laugh," one of the best, and funniest, musical sequences on film. And of course, the title song with the irrepressible Gene Kelly and that umbrella exuberantly splashing and dancin' in the rain. Pure movie magic. **Behind-the-scenes trivia:** After Debbie Reynolds passed away, I read several articles that said her relentless practicing of the "Good Morning" number wound up bursting capillaries in her feet. As a result, Debbie couldn't walk, and she had to be carried off the set by the crew due to her poor swollen and painful feet.

7. ***The Great Escape.*** Based on the largest prison escape attempt—through underground tunnels—from a German POW camp during World War II, this 1963 war classic stars Steve McQueen, James Garner, Richard Attenborough, David McCallum, and a young Charles Bronson. Some of the cast members were actual POWs during World War II—including Donald Pleasence, who played "The Forger." **Backstage gossip:** During filming, Charles Bronson—who found fame in *The Magnificent Seven*, *The Dirty Dozen*, and the seventies' *Death Wish* movies—fell for David McCallum's actress wife, Jill Ireland, and joked that he was going to steal her away from

him. After McCallum and Ireland divorced in 1967, Bronson married her.

8. ***Born Yesterday.*** An overlooked gem, this modern-day Pygmalion story from 1950 (brought to screen after its successful long-term Broadway run) stars the flawless and irrepressible Judy Holliday as the hilarious "dumb blonde" Billie Dawn, mobster's moll to the blustering millionaire and former junk dealer Harry Brock, played by Broderick Crawford. The corrupt Harry, who's come to Washington, DC, to buy politicians and push through his latest shady deal, hires journalist Paul Verrall (William Holden) to tutor brassy Billie in proper etiquette while they're in the nation's capital—and gets more than he bargained for. **Note:** Judy beat out both Bette Davis in *All About Eve* and Gloria Swanson in *Sunset Boulevard* to win the Oscar for Best Actress for this funny film that never grows old.

9. ***The Inn of the Sixth Happiness.*** In this film, based on a true story, the always-inspiring Ingrid Bergman plays Gladys Aylward, a humble, working-class Englishwoman who longed to be a missionary in China all her life but was unqualified and rejected due to her lack of education. Gladys goes to China anyway, where she winds up working for an elderly missionary and eventually becomes a "foot inspector," traveling throughout the countryside to enforce the government's new law against foot binding. When Japan invades China, the uneducated Gladys heroically leads a hundred orphaned children through the mountains to safety.

10. ***Roman Holiday.*** What can I say about the movie that introduced the gamine, gorgeous, and inimitable Audrey Hepburn to the world in 1953? I love it! What's not to love? Rome,

Audrey, and Gregory Peck. Be still my heart. **Trivia:** Audrey won the Best Actress Oscar, beating out Deborah Kerr, who was the odds-on favorite to win for her steamy turn in *From Here to Eternity.*

11. ***Lars and the Real Girl.*** Okay, so this doesn't qualify as an "old" movie, since it came out in 2007, but I included it because I love its weird quirkiness and message of love and acceptance. An awkward, shy, reclusive guy (played by heart-throb Ryan Gosling, who shot to fame in *The Notebook* and was so good in *La La Land*) grew up detached from human contact and doesn't know how to interact with people. He buys a sex doll from the internet but doesn't use it for sex—he has a chaste, meaningful relationship with his wheelchair-bound missionary "girlfriend" Bianca. Many missed this small indie gem when it was released, so I don't want to say too much and spoil the story, but its poignant message is one we all need to hear. Two ecclesiastical thumbs way up.

Faith Chapel Tea Recipes
Cucumber Sandwiches

It's best to use English cucumbers, as there is no need to peel this variety, plus the skins add extra color to the sandwiches.

English cucumber
Butter, softened
*Cream cheese, softened
Dill or basil (depending on your preference)
Soft white or light wheat bread

Cut cucumber into slices about ¼ inch thick and spread them out between two paper towels to absorb the extra moisture. You'll need about four slices per sandwich. In a small bowl and using a fork, mix one part butter and two parts cream cheese together until smooth. Mix in dill (or basil) to your taste preference. This is the "glue" that holds the sandwich together, so spread a thin layer of cream cheese mixture on each slice. Build the sandwiches, cut the crusts off the bread, and cut the sandwiches into four squares. This sandwich works best in squares, since tiny cucumber pieces tend to spill out of if you cut the sandwiches into triangles.

*Some people prefer butter only on their cucumber sandwiches, but we like cream cheese for an added dollop of flavor.

Note: Place a damp cloth or paper towel over the sandwiches so they don't dry out before serving.

Ham and Apricot Cream Cheese Sandwiches

Thanks to David Daigh for this recipe that we've adapted slightly.

Medium-thick slices of ham (not shaved or too thin)
Cream cheese (brick style; do not use whipped)
Apricot preserves
Buttermilk bread (or Hawaiian rolls, if you prefer your
    sandwiches sweeter)

Mix equal parts cream cheese and apricot preserves together. This is the "glue" that holds the sandwich together, so spread a thin layer of cream cheese mixture on each slice. Add a slice of ham. Build the sandwiches, cut the crusts from the bread, cut the sandwiches into four triangles, and serve.

Classic English scones

Thanks to my longtime English friend Patricia Smith from Poole, in lovely Dorset, for her recipe.

1 cup self-rising flour
1 teaspoon baking powder
4 tablespoons butter
2 tablespoons superfine granulated sugar
5 tablespoons milk
1 egg

Preheat oven to 400 degrees. Sift flour and baking powder. Cut in the butter. Add sugar. Add milk and egg. Stir until just mixed. Roll to ½ inch thick and cut out rounds. Brush with milk. Bake for 12 minutes or until golden brown.

Serve with strawberry jam and Devonshire (or clotted) cream (usually found at Whole Foods, Cost Plus, or other specialty grocery stores.) Jam first, then cream? Or cream, then jam? Depends on where you are. Even the Brits don't agree on this one.

Lemon Squares

Thanks to Rachel Young for sharing her grandmother's family recipe.

Crust:

Sift together 2 cups flour and ½ cup powdered sugar.

Cut in 1 cup butter (add a touch of lemon zest).

Press into a 9 × 13–inch pan and bake at 350 degrees for 20–25 minutes, or until light brown.

Lemon filling:

Beat together:

    2 cups sugar

    4 eggs

    ⅓ cup lemon juice

    Dash lemon zest

Sift together:

    ¼ cup flour

    ½ teaspoon baking powder

Add flour mixture to egg mixture.

Pour lemon filling over the crust.

Bake at 350 degrees for 25 minutes (or longer, until light brown). Sprinkle with powdered sugar. Cut into squares when cool.

Triple Chocolate Brownies

Best. Brownies. Ever.

3 ounces unsweetened baking chocolate
6 tablespoons (salted) butter
4 teaspoons unsweetened cocoa powder
2 eggs
¼ teaspoon salt
1½ cups sugar
1 tablespoon vanilla extract (yes, tablespoon)
¾ cup sifted flour
1 cup semisweet chocolate chips

You'll want a double boiler and stand mixer for this one. Since there is no leavening, we're using air to create the special texture of these brownies.

Prepare the double boiler. Break up the chocolate into little bits. Cut up the butter (if it's still cold). Melt the chocolate, butter, and cocoa powder in the double boiler, stirring frequently until smooth. Set aside to cool. Preheat oven to 375 degrees and grease/flour an 8 × 8–inch baking pan.

Move to the mixer. Beat eggs and salt. Slowly add the sugar, then the vanilla. Continue to beat forever (actually about 6 to 8 minutes.)

If the chocolate mixture is still warm, you can speed up the cooling by setting the bowl in cold water. Just don't let it get too cold and turn solid again.

Sift the flour. Yes, this is important. We're adding more air and breaking up any small clumps. If you don't have a sifter, use a fine-mesh strainer. That works just fine.

When all the parts are ready, use a rubber spatula to gently fold the cooled chocolate mixture into the eggs and sugar until just incorporated. Then gently fold in the flour, again until just incorporated. Fold in the chocolate chips, then pour the batter into the baking pan. Bake for about 20 minutes and check for doneness. If the batter springs back when you gently press on it, it's done. Sorry, but the inserted knife or toothpick test won't work because of the chocolate chips. Better to underbake than overbake.

Let the brownies cool completely before you cut them, or they'll crumble. (That's not necessarily a bad thing.)

Acknowledgments

When I began writing my first mystery novel, one of the minor characters made it quite clear that she was not to be relegated to the back pew. She was a major character who deserved her own story. Thus, I took the plunge and started writing two cozy mysteries simultaneously. After I shared the opening chapters with my agent, he LOVED the story starring the female Episcopal priest/accidental sleuth. "*That's* the story you need to tell," he said. And so I did. Thanks, Chip. You were right. I owe you.

Thanks also to my editor, Faith Black Ross, for loving Hope's story as well and for making it better. Added thanks to Melissa Rechter, Madeline Rathle, and the rest of the great team at Crooked Lane.

I may be an Episcopalian, but I'm not a member of the clergy and don't have the inside scoop on being a priest. Luckily, I happen to know a few Episcopal priests who generously allowed me to pick their clerical brains. Deepest gratitude to the Reverend Mary Claugus, the Reverend George Foxworth, and the Very Reverend Canon Mary Hauck. Extra thanks to Mary Hauck, my first rector, who met with me several times, answered my repeated questions, and graciously read the first draft—along with her husband, Paul—to ensure I'd gotten things right with Pastor Hope and Faith Chapel. Any errors are my own. Thanks also to former police officer the Reverend Michael Kerrick for answering my law enforcement questions about probable cause, detention, and jail time.

Props to my old reporter pal, Patty Reyes, and her husband, Rob Humphrey, for providing the myriad G.I. Joe details and answering all my Joe questions. Who knew?

Thank you to writer friends Cindy Coloma, Cathy Elliott, Dave Meurer, Jenny Lundquist, Holly Lorincz, and Eileen Rendahl, who read the initial first few chapters and provided feedback. Special thanks to Gayle Roper and Erica Ruth Neubauer, who generously read my book with a critical eye while busy writing their own.

Also, thanks to early readers and cheerleaders Cheryl Harris, Marian Hitchings, and Katie Souva.

Heartfelt thanks to my dear friends Dave and Dale Meurer for letting me steal away to their lovely home on a writing retreat—and for their gracious hospitality.

Everlasting gratitude to Kim Orendor for always being there—I couldn't have done this without you, Kimmie.

And as always, to Michael, for everything.